The Demon's Minions Attack

The Demon's Minions Attack

Evangelina, Warrior Angel

Russell Marrone

RESOURCE *Publications* · Eugene, Oregon

THE DEMON'S MINIONS ATTACK

Evangelina, Warrior Angel

Resource Publications
An Imprint of Wipf and Stock Publishers
199 W. 8th Ave., Suite 3
Eugene, OR 97401

www.wipfandstock.com

PAPERBACK ISBN: 979-8-3852-4650-2
HARDCOVER ISBN: 979-8-3852-4651-9
EBOOK ISBN: 979-8-3852-4652-6

05/09/25

To my amazing wife,
who always delights in every twist of a good murder case.
Your love and unwavering support has helped in this endeavor.

CONTENTS

Contents

Chapter 1

THE BUMPKIN REPORT

OR Envio the Imp, this was a joyous day, the best of his life. This was the day he awoke, prepared to execute his mission to bring his master, the Emperor Lucifer, a special message—one he had been waiting on for ten years. The imp spruced up for the trip, grinding his teeth and claws into sharp weapons; polishing his mighty, bat-like wings; honing his small antlers to a fine point and finally filing the spikes on his powerful, ultrathin tail needed to propel him through the tunnels. Posing into the mirror, he congratulated himself on the impression he was certain to make on Lucifer. *I may be tiny and bony, but I am mighty.*

He set out, his thoughts filled with grandiose ideas of what this journey would bring him. After all, it would be *he,* a lowly imp in the chain of command of demons, to deliver the happy news none of Lucifer's hundreds of minions were able to accomplish. This opportunity would surely elevate his humble standing in the imp community.

Reaching the entry to the gates of Hell, he paused. While his heart pounded in happy anticipation, his innate fear of Lucifer's unpredictable rage made his head spin. *I hope he's in a good mood. I don't want to end up as dinner for the three-headed hound, Cerberus.*

He stooped over the entrance to the tunnel to test the temperature. Finding it tolerable, he made the leap. As he descended lower and deeper into the maze of tubes and passageways, the temperature soared hotter and hotter. His already deep red, leathery skin parched darker from the slow fire now searing his batlike wings, turning them nearly useless. The acrid stench of sulfur rose proportionally with the rising heat and burned his nostrils. Sweat poured from his brow as he continued his mission. The deeper he travelled the redder the lava tunnel burned.

Finally reaching the lowest level of Hell, he bumped into a demon strolling through the lava tube reading *Book of the Dead*.

"Excuse me, but do you know where Lucifer is right now?" he asked.

"Who wants to know?"

"I am Envio, imp of the woodland and faithful subject of Lucifer. I have important news for the Emperor."

"Well, well, I am Ammit, the Egyptian soul eater," said the demon. "Have you checked his meeting room?"

"Ah, good idea! Is it left or right at the next intersection?"

"Go left and then right at the first right. It's about halfway down," said Ammit, burping up a soul. Her tongue shot out and wrapped around it, capturing its fleeing essence. She then slurped the screaming mortal soul back into her mouth. "Excuse me. I must find my Gas-X."

Envio stifled a laugh as the bizarre, crocodile-headed creature with a body of a hippo and the front paws of a lion waddled down the tube before turning and continuing down the glowing corridor.

"Ooh, aah . . . ooh, aah . . . " Envio screamed out, his toes and long spiked tail popping him up and down across the burning floor in rhythm to his cries.

Beyond the embers, he spotted his destination and raced closer and closer to finally stand in the sitting area of the Emperor's meeting room, its floor tempered by cooling ice.

In preparation for the meeting, he rehearsed his opening statement. "Good evening, Sire. I'm Envio, your faithful imp, dedicated to serving you." Happy with his opening he reminded himself the Emperor of Hell liked things short and concise. He didn't want to anger His Majesty with a long-drawn-out presentation. *Just get in, give my new information, and get out with my head still intact.* While his heart pounded in anticipation to meet his master, his brain reminded him of Lucifer's unpredictable rage. *Please, please, please, may he be in a good mood. I'm too boney to be dog chow.*

Envio drew a deep breath and raised a trembling claw to knock on the bejeweled, heavy wooden door. After a seemingly long wait, his original vigor dimmed.

The heavy door groaned open and Envio recognized Kobal, Lucifer's funnyman, also known as the demon of laughter. Kobal was called to Lucifer's side on days when he needed his spirit lightened. Bowing to Envio, he ushered the imp into the highly ornamented conference room and announced, "Envio, lowly imp of the earth, prankster of the forest, servant to minor demons, and MIGHTY TASTY ON A PLATE . . . "

"On with it!" ordered Lucifer.

"Yes, Sire. DINNER IS SERVED!" boomed Kobal. An evil smirk crossed his face and landed on Envio.

Envio's eyes widened and he stumbled back, clinging to the wall behind, shaking his head "No." Seizing Envio's arm, Kobal spit out a malicious laugh and dragged the little imp to face Lucifer.

"Would you like a little salt and pepper, Sire?"

One look at the crooked grin on Lucifer's face threw Envio into frenzied panic, sending him to his knees. Lucifer stroked his beard and licked his lips.

"No, this is a mistake. I'm not here to be your dinner, Sire. I bring you news," pleaded Envio.

Lucifer began to laugh in chorus with Kobal. The imp looked back and forth between the two with wild eyes awash in tears. Exposing his sharp fangs, he positioned himself to do battle if necessary.

Lilith stepped from behind Lucifer's chair. "Enough fun, boys. Let the imp speak." Her voice of reason gave Envio hope.

"Thank you, Kobal. I needed a little bit of dark humor. You may go."

Kobal exited the sitting room leaving Envio on his knees, but not before letting out a hearty laugh and casting one last jab. "You'd better wipe those salty tears, little guy. Don't be a crybaby."

Envio obeyed and dried his tears, embarrassed by his frenetic behavior, certainly not the first impression he hoped to convey as a stalwart worker for his Emperor.

"Rise, imp. What news do you bring me?"

Wobbly from his brush with death, the imp faced Lucifer. He smoothed his attire and stood with head bowed. Clearing his wheezy throat, he raised himself tall, as tall as his three-foot body would allow, and began.

"Oh, great and powerful Emperor of Hell, you had sent me, your simple imp, and all your followers into deep forests to spy on the people living on the earth. I bring you my efforts. I bring you good news."

"Well, stop blabbering and spit it out!"

"Your Majesty, I have located the Glory Child, God's gift to the world."

"You WHAT? Are you sure? If you are mistaken and this is another mischievous prank imps like to play, I will eat you alive, piece by teeny, tiny piece."

"I am certain, Your Majesty."

"How? How did a dinky scamp like you track down a child my demons have been searching for? It's been many years and yet none of my armies have been able to unearth the family. They moved out of their home and went into hiding so quickly."

"I've known for years your desire to kidnap God's Glory Child. When your demon army gave up the fight, I took it upon myself to enter the search. First, I granted a real estate agent a favor and in return he searched the tax records. The agent found them when the family bought a house, Your Majesty." Envio unrolled a scroll containing a map with the address and location of the home of the Puro family and handed it with pride to Lucifer.

"I see. Creative. Resourceful," said Lucifer. "Lilith, make this imp a guest of honor at my State of Hell speech next week. Meanwhile, Envio, go to the banquet hall and enjoy the feast my scullions will prepare for you for your efforts. When you have had your fill, head to the Quaker Burial Ground to assist the demon lord I send. Do not tarry!"

"Oh, thank you Your Majesty, thank you. As you wish, Master."

As Envio backed away toward the chamber door, bowing vigorously from his torso, he misjudged the distance and banged into the wall, falling to the floor. He jumped quickly to see who had noticed. Unfortunately, the room sat snickering. After much ado, he turned to exit. But his miniature frame could hardly muscle the strength to reach the knob without jumping up, leveraging his versatile tail, and catching the handle with two hands to swing to and fro. Eventually he managed to leave, but not before he heard one demon joke . . . something about needing a new court jester. In the hallway he thought, what *an idiot I am.*

"Should I schedule Envio for a short speech next week?" asked Lilith.

"Are you kidding? That bumpkin? As I like to say, 'HOT HELL, NO."

"As you wish, Sire."

Lucifer relaxed in his regal chair and stared at the scroll, analyzing the best way to address this new situation. In previous schemes he sent Princes of Hell and powerful demons into battle to do his dirty work, to capture and hold the Glory Child captive—all to taunt God.

None were successful. He remained agonized over the precocious Jonathan Puro and God's plans for him to enhance God's glory on Earth. Rumor has it the boy has the intellect to change the face of all humanity. Lucifer lamented over losing long and ferocious battles to a novice guardian angel named Evangelina and her earthly protégé, Nori, sent to protect the boy. He resigned from the notion of kidnapping him, at least temporarily. He no longer had faith that his cadre of stalwart demons were capable of holding the child hostage. Plus, he'd lost stature among his minions. But now, after this visit from that little imp, Envio, he felt invigorated.

Many millenniums previous, he signed an agreement with God to promise that neither he, nor his minions, would kill a human. God promised retaliation of the worst kind would be visited upon him if he broke the bargain. So, for him, killing the boy was out of the question.

"No, I need someone creative." Lucifer slouched into his chair and closed his eyes but left his mind open to resolve the "Glory Boy" issue.

It had been a long, agitated hour mulling over the situation, before his heavy lids snapped spontaneously upward as an inspirational thought began to flower. Maybe, just maybe, neither I nor my usual minions will be the ones to dispatch the boy, thereby angering God and breaking my contract with him. Lucifer popped up and screamed "Brilliant! I am brilliant."

"I'll give this to my friend, Archduke Andras, the Assassin." Lucifer understood this demon's talents were not restricted to assassinations, however. Andras also has the talent to access earthlings' minds and incite them to perform horrible, dirty deeds, including murder, using their own instruments against their own. Human on human. "Could I entice Andras to apply this ability to agitate humans to kill Jonathan? That would be a curveball to circumvent my contract with God. After all, neither I nor Andras would be the slayer of Jonathan Puro, the Glory child. And best yet, it would sidestep that infernal angel, Evangelina."

Raising tall off his throne, he bellowed for Lilith sitting on the opposite side of the room, planning for his upcoming State of Hell speech.

"Lilith, call in Archduke Andras."

"He's in the Philippines. It might take him some time to get here."

"I don't care. Get him here, pronto quick. I have an assignment for him. Tell him to hone his sword."

"As you wish, Your Majesty."

No angel, no matter how clever or powerful, would stand in my way this time. As the Emperor of the underworld, I will never concede. I will prevail.

Chapter 2

Nori and the Doggie Dilemma

Nori's Narrative

I T HAD BEEN NEARLY ten years since the brazen kidnapping of two-year old Jonathan Puro. The story of the kidnapping circulated around the world. Once the abductors had the child in their vehicle, they found they needed someone to care for him while they drove to the gates of Hell. That someone was Nori, a petite Asian woman—an escapee from a guarded military encampment. Through her wit and fearless tenacity, she risked her life, along with her young daughter's, to enter the United States and become an American citizen. It was this same courageous bravery that outwitted the kidnappers Beelzebub and the minor demon Blisdon, ordered by Lucifer, the devil himself, to capture and hold the child Jonathan Puro captive—a child, ordained at birth by God to be the Glory Child—a once in a millennium gift to mortals. A gift that would globally address the cycle of poverty.

To all, she became a hero in the eyes of the nation. The world would never know of the two underworld demons from the deep.

What the world never knew and would never know is that Nori did not work alone during those treacherous days. Nori stood side by side warrior angel Evangelina, Jonathan's guardian angel, and even a reformed Blisdon in the fight to protect the two-year-old from the sinister Beelzebub, aka Bub, in the Montana cavern.

Daily life had been calm and quiet since that life-saving battle. Nori thought of Blisdon often. Having been exiled from Hell for helping mortals, he was allowed to live somewhere on Earth, but banished to a nomad's existence, dodging bounty hunters daily. While she had not seen or talked with him for all those years, every month, like clockwork, she received an envelope of cash from him delivered to her post office box. From its postmark she knew he roamed somewhere in the Detroit Metro area, but the postmark changed every month.

Evie aka Evangelina, the warrior angel, and Nori remained close in their commitment to protect the child, never taking for granted Lucifer's silence.

In the end, the Puro's brought Nori into their family as a full-bodied, beloved member. They would never learn, however, that their son was handpicked by God to be the Golden Child; that he was destined to one day perform a miracle that eases human suffering.

Nori sat at the oak table sipping her green tea, watching the clock. She had fifteen minutes before leaving to pick Jonathan up from school. The aroma of two fresh baked breads filled the kitchen as they sat on the kitchen counter next to a jar of peanut butter and red raspberry jam. She concentrated on the kitchen clock and watched the minutes tick by until it was time to prepare Jonathan's afterschool open-faced snack to have ready and waiting for him—a ritual since he started school. She finished her tea, went for the dog leash hanging by the door and called for Emma, Jonathan's dog. The toy Schnitsu, her tail wagging, knew the drill and heeled, making it convenient for Nori to attach her leash. The half Schnauzer, half Shih Tzu barked in excited anticipation as they hurried out the door together into the warm sunshine. They made the trek so often to the school, that Emma easily led the way, pulling at her leash and, despite she was a senior dog and the distance from home to school sometimes left her panting, she never slowed.

As they traipsed along the sidewalk under the canopy of blooming trees, a chorus of birds filled the air with their songs. Tulips and crocuses adorned the flower beds along the way. The sweet smell of fresh air mixed with the fragrant aroma of the blooming buds created an atmosphere of earthly delight.

Turning the corner, they saw the school and heard the dismissal bell ring. A roar of voices shattered the quiet as a stream of young students bolted through the front door. Nori scoured the crowd to find Jonathan standing on the top step of the entrance, backpack slung over one shoulder, surveying the mass in search of Nori. As their eyes met, Jonathan beamed and waved. Happy to see his Emma, he scrambled down the steps to meet them at the sidewalk.

"Emmie, hi girl. How's my puppy doing?" Jonathan bent to scratch her underside and pat her head. When he stood to face Nori eye to eye, he realized he was taller than his lovable, munchkin caretaker and held back the urge to kiss her atop her head.

"Hi, Nori."

"You getting so big. You grow faster than bamboo. You hungry?"

"I could eat a horse."

"No horse, but fresh bread for your PB&J. What's envelope in your hand?

"My counselor gave it to me to give to Mom and Dad."

"You been bad boy?"

"No. I don't know what it's for."

"You do all your schoolwork?"

"Always. Got As on all my tests today."

"Hmm. Well, we go home and fix your sandwich."

The two began their casual walk home. "Your turn," said Nori, handing Jonathan Emma's leash. That he let the dog sniff every tree along the way, annoyed Nori.

"He sniff and wee-wee on trees, then lick your face. Not clean. You get sick."

Jonathan laughed and scoffed at another one of her theories. "Nori, it's in the doggie manual that sniffing dogs are happy dogs."

"Bah."

As they turned the corner Nori spied ahead an unleashed, super-charged dog galloping toward them, its hackles raised. She knew this was going to be trouble and reacted without hesitation. Searching the ground, she snatched a fallen branch from the lawn and planted herself in front of Jonathan. The Rottweiler's muscled legs were driving him threateningly close.

"Take Emma," Nori commanded. "Start to move back toward school. I handle this. You go."

"But Nori, I can't leave you alone against this dog."

"You do as I say. Now go!"

Emma spotted the angry canine and began barking wildly in Jonathan's arms, struggling to get at the charging beast. As Jonathan retreated, Nori prepared herself for war. She had dealt with aggressive dogs before in the camps. It wasn't unusual for packs of hungry dogs to invade the camps looking for food or anything they could eat. She folded her arms still holding the thick branch and turned toward the approaching dog. Once she saw the dog wore a collar, she knew he was a pet—not a homeless, starving attack dog. This was to her advantage.

Nori stood unwavering, knowing exactly what she had to do: *Protect the boy.* The dog, his hackles bristling, came to a stop and growled ferociously, baring his teeth up at her. But Nori faced down the snarling dog and refused to move. Losing interest in the Asian woman, he spotted Jonathan retreating with Emma. They appealed to him as easier prey. When the aggressive beast moved to bypass her in favor of the boy and his dog, Nori sprang into action.

As he maneuvered to sweep by her, she nabbed him by his collar. With the branch firmly entrenched in her hand, she rammed it under the collar and twisted it with all the might of her skinny arms. The collar tightened around the dog's throat, and he struggled to breathe. But Nori maintained control against the battling Rottweiler. Finally, he went limp from lack of oxygen and collapsed on the sidewalk, unconscious.

In the distance, a distressed young jogger waving half a leash in his hand ran toward a gathering crowd cheering the old lady doing battle. He bolted to the group, fighting for air and holding his side as sweat poured from his brow.

"Thank you, thank you for capturing Bruno. He broke from his leash when he saw a cat. I am so sorry. I've been chasing him for blocks. I hope he didn't hurt you."

"No. Me fine. Dog be okay in few minutes."

Bruno slowly regained consciousness. Fully embarrassed, the young man seized the weakened dog by his collar, scolding and dragging him in front of an audience of applauding bystanders watching the two hobble back along the sidewalk from where they came. Nori and Jonathan watched the pair turn the corner out of sight.

Nori turned to Jonathan and hugged him tight. "That enough excitement for today," she said. "We no need to tell Momma about dog. She no need worry."

"I agree. If she found out about this, she'd make me wear armor to school. But wow, you're as tough as nails, Nori."

"Not so tough as smart. In old country if you not smart, dog take your dinner. You learn to be smarter than dog or you and your children starve."

Jonathan, intrigued by Nori's actions, slowed his steps and looked at his Nori. She'd taken on a new stature in his eyes.

"You certainly taught that dog a lesson. And the people cheered you. How cool."

"Yeah, Nori tough lady. Like I say, my people in the prison encampments had to fight dogs and rats, too, for food."

"You never talk about those times. And I've never thought to ask."

"Nori spend many hungry days in old country. We never got much to eat, but we would make do. Learned to make dinner out of one fish and rice for family. Cheap sushi."

"That's all you had to eat?"

"Sometime no fish."

"Wow. Lucky you escaped."

"Thankful for blessings every day. This great country. Bounty everywhere. If only all world had what we have."

Jonathan considered her words. "Everyone should have food to eat every day. No child should starve."

"Many little ones die in old country. Starve to death. So sad."

"How can we have so much and the rest of the world have so little?"

"It why people die trying to get to America. A better life. A better chance to live."

"That has to change."

"We send food to poor countries, but there's never enough."

Nori's narrative brought him to silence. As they moved along, her words roamed his mind like a poker stick, prodding him to take notice. The images she created talked to him and expected answers. He simultaneously felt sadness and excitement urging him to act. But how?

The two reached the Puro home and ambled up the drive to the smell of fresh baked bread wafting on the breeze through the kitchen window. Jonathan picked up his pace and whizzed through the door, bypassing the PB&J alongside a tall glass of milk on the table.

"Where you go? Snacks on table. Fresh bread just for you."

"Oh, yeah, sorry," he said and returned to wolf down the sandwich and guzzle the milk. "Oh, here, give my folks this envelop from school," he said tossing it on the table. "Gotta go. I have some thinking to do . . . "

"Huh? Thinking? Why you no go outside to think? Beautiful day! Find friends to play and think with until dinner."

"Oh, Nori, you nag like Mom. I've told you too many times, I don't enjoy the kids from school. Please, please, take my side on these talks." Nori could hear him mumbling as he left the room: "Everyone, let me be."

Hearing the conditions of Nori's early life sent Jonathan immediately to his room, to his computer. He was curious about her description of her diet in the old country. How could she have survived on just fish and rice? *Was she exaggerating like Dad did when he talked about growing up in Detroit?*

He searched the internet and found some entries about the cuisine from her country. Kimchi (fermented cabbage), rice dishes, porridge, and silver needle noodles with sides of grilled meat were listed. *That doesn't seem so bad*, he thought, *Nori's telling me a tall tale.*

An entry about an actual young girl from Nori's country talking about their food on video caught his eye. Clicking the entry, it opened to a teenage Asian girl. He clicked the start arrow and what she said gave new meaning to the term "humanity."

She spoke the nasty truth about the conditions from which she escaped. The girl spoke of working on a collective farm, just as Nori had. She spoke of the brutal conditions they toiled under and the treatment they received.

When she spoke of food and eating, it shocked him. The young Asian teen said that after months of hard work, the harvest would come. After all their backbreaking work, the government would come in and take more than the majority of their labor and leave very little for them.

The people of her community would have to conserve as much as they could for the winter. Meals were quite lean, and they supplemented it with rats, insects and an occasional fish someone had caught. When winter came, they dipped into their reserves, but that never lasted for the whole winter.

Late winter was a terrible time. With no food left and nothing growing it was a terrible time. Filling their bellies with water and sawdust was their only option. The sick were the first to die. Next, the elderly and the small children would pass. It was always such a terrible time.

When the video ended, Jonathan sat back in his chair, wide-eyed and mouth open. *I didn't know,* he thought, *I just didn't know.* He continued his search and found each year 822 million people were malnourished and nine million people starve to death every year. Of those nine million deaths, over three million and growing are young children. Taken aback by the staggering numbers, Jonathan stood up from his desk, shook his head and said, "This can't go on. NO. It won't go on because I'm going to fix it."

Once finished, he typed in: "World Hunger," took a deep breath and smiled broadly. This was his eureka moment.

Chapter 3

PARENTAL CONCERNS

"HELLO, I'M HOME," SHOUTED Mary, dropping her bookbag at the door to follow the delicious smells streaming from the kitchen.

"Is that fresh bread I smell?"

"Made two loaves today."

"What's in the oven?"

"You forget? Today it's fresh bread, and everyone's favorite, Mac and cheese and Chinese cabbage slaw."

"Oh, my God, I'm starved. It smells so good. When will it be ready?"

"Oh . . . maybe thirty minutes. Be done before Joe get home. How was your day?"

"Trying, but rewarding," she said, her eyes landing on the hand-written envelope addressed to the Parents of Jonathan Puro laying on the counter. "What's this?" she said, uneasily turning it over and over before opening it.

"You afraid, Mary?"

"I suppose I am. It seems too personal. Ya know, the handwritten envelop and all."

She searched the all-purpose drawer for the letter opener, and cleanly sliced an opening on the top. "Here goes." She delicately withdrew the letter inside.

Dear Parents of Jonathan Puro,

After conferring with Principal George Whiting, Jonathan's teachers, and reviewing his M-STEP scores, we have come to a consensus, along with the administration, that his appropriate placement next year should be in the ninth grade at Farmington High School. Please contact me to discuss this matter at your earliest convenience.

Counselor, Bill Persons

"Smart boy," said Nori, stirring the miso soup.

"Yes, I know, but he's only eleven years old."

"He twelve soon."

"Still, he's young . . . too young to be thrown in with fourteen-year-olds . . . and older."

"He smart boy and bored with school. Not good for brain. Needs challenge."

"I know, but he's not ready. Socially."

"You talk with Joe. You two decide."

"You're right. We need to discuss this and decide together."

Minutes after Mary left the room, the back door swung open and she heard Joe's boots hit the landing.

He entered the kitchen and issued Nori a swift kiss on the cheek. "What's my favorite chef got cookin'? It smells wonderful."

"Everybody's favorite Mac 'n Cheese," she said, placing the thick-sliced bread in a breadbasket on the table.

"Great, I'll wash my hands."

"Be quick. Everybody hungry."

After setting all the food on the table, she called down the hallway to the bedrooms: "Dinner time! Come! Dinner time!"

Rushing footsteps scrambled through the kitchen door, each shooting for their usual seat, their eyes devouring Nori's beloved Mac 'n Cheese. Once seated, they locked hands and speedily recited their dinner prayer, followed by a hurried "Amen." With that, the family plunged in, more interested in filling their plates than conversation. Nori chuckled watching her boy shovel the mound of food down his throat, with barely a few bites. He then wiped his mouth and stood slowly backing out the kitchen. "May I be excused?"

"What's the problem, son? What's goin' on?" asked Joe.

"There's a documentary on the National Geographic channel on fifteen challenges facing the globe."

"U-huh, I see," he said, but thought *What the hell?* "Sounds good. But what you say that after the show we play some catch in the backyard?"

"I guess. But I'd prefer not to? I've got a cough." He coughed unconvincingly.

"The fresh air will do you good. I'll come getcha in an hour or so."

Obviously he didn't hear me. Jonathan darted out the kitchen, forcing a loud sneeze for reinforcement, and backed to his room to become lost in the documentary just starting. In the hours after school, he had already earmarked an endless list of articles to read regarding how the human body processes food, the effects of malnutrition, how the digestive system works, ways to create nutrient rich foods. In just a few hours his vessel of information grew, along with the understanding he had so much to learn. All this invigorated him with newfound enthusiasm. The one obstacle in his way was the time wasted at school. He was hoping a sniffle and cough were enough to keep him home for a few undisturbed days. He needed time to read and research everything he could get his hands on about biology, chemistry and nutrition—the ingredients essential to sustain a healthy life all compacted into one product, lowly priced and mass produced. Perhaps a patty. In the back of his mind, he reminded himself of the challenges of efficient food production and distribution, especially to impoverished areas.

With Jonathan out of the room, Mary pulled up the school letter and handed it to Joe.

"What's this?" As he read, he smiled. "That's my boy!"

"Wait a minute, Joe, he's only eleven years old. How is he going to coexist in a school where he is the youngest, smartest kid?"

"You just said it. He's a smart kid. He'll adapt."

"What if he doesn't? What if they bully him or worse, corrupt him?"

"And, like I said, he's smart. He knows right from wrong. I'm sure he'll be able to handle anything they throw at him."

"I only hope what they're throwing isn't rocks."

"We'll throw him into some karate classes. He'll learn to duck and kick," Joe said, sopping the leftover sauce with a piece of fresh bread.

"I don't know. He's still my baby. It's so hard to let him go."

"Don't let *your* insecurities hold him back. He's a good kid and deserves the best opportunities we can give him."

"I want what's best for him, but I worry. Let me think about it."

We have time. Go to the meeting with an open mind. See what they have to say."

"You're not coming?" said Mary, her forehead curled down with concern.

"We start mandatory overtime next week and I'm required to be there."

"Can't you . . . ?"

"Sorry, but no. I vote we don't hold Jonathan back and we move him to high school."

"This is so hard, Joe."

"Unfortunately, Mary, kids don't come with operating manuals."

"It would be so much easier. Well, let's talk later. I got papers to grade, tonight." Handing Nori her plate, she paused. "Joe, do you promise the decision will be mutual?"

"Absolutely . . . but, Mary, we can't leave Jonathan out of our discussions." Her sober expression as she left the room told Joe nothing and he called out, "Remember, keep an open mind."

"The same goes for you . . . I can tell yours is made up. So much for mutual."

With Mary out of the room, Nori stopped fussing with the dishes and turned a serious face to Mr. Joe. Never one to interfere in family matters, she did feel compelled to say something in this case.

"What is it, Nori?"

Out of the range of being heard, she whispered, "Mr. Joe, when I get boy after school today, he tell me he love math and science but he say they teaching what he already know. He very smart. Very, very intelligent. Tell him the good and bad about new change. Let him help you decide. But include him."

"Thanks, Nori. I'll talk with him tonight."

Joe rapped softly on Jonathan's door and waited for a response. After a second knock and no answer, he entered without invitation to find Jonathan propped on a pillow, staring at the TV, a mess of papers spread loosely across his bed.

Joe stood looking at his son refusing to face him. "Look, son, if you have a problem, you can talk to me. That's why I'm here."

As if brought up from a haze, Jonathan faced his dad. "Did you say something? I'm sorry, I'm preoccupied" As if a light bulb turned on, he uttered " . . . oh, oh, I know, you're here to ask me to play catch."

"I just thought we agreed to throw the ball around after dinner."

"I think I said I'm not interested. But you obviously weren't listening as usual." He reached for a tissue and sniffled into it, along with a minor cough. "I don't feel well. Besides, when did you decide you could enter my room without knocking? Do I need to post a sign?"

"What's wrong? Tell me. Why did you retreat to your room?" Instinct told Joe to not scold his son for his newly belligerent attitude. Was he having girl problems, *he hoped*? Maybe it's puberty and the changes that come with it. Could he be gay? "You know my dad died before I turned ten. I never had a father figure. There was no one to talk to me about girls, puberty. I want to be there for you. Are you being bullied? We can fix that . . . maybe your mom is right. She blames me for your lack of interest in sports 'cuz I never asked you to play ball . . . "

"Dad, stop that. Stop! You're a great dad. If you have to know, it's about a project I have an urgent need to work on." Eager to share his project, desperate for someone to confer with, Jonathan studied his dad before speaking again.

Joe stared and waited for more. Jonathan saw confusion, almost desperation etched into his father's face.

"Okay, Dad, here goes (cough, sneeze). But it's between us. Not for anyone else—you understand?"

The two stood eyeball to eyeball, as if in a standoff. In spite of his son's admonition, Joe's need to hear his son's secret took precedence over his loyalty to his wife. He accepted the ultimatum and agreed.

Jonathan blurted out: "I dream of making a difference in the lives of people who are less fortunate. I've been working on a plan to put an end to hunger across the world by the time I'm fifteen, maybe before."

Utter silence prevailed for a good thirty seconds while Jonathan waited for his father's reaction . . . and possible support, or at least understanding.

My son's delusional. Or is he truly a precocious young boy with a brilliant mind?

Joe's involuntary response startled them both when he burst into laughter, a laugh from the gut. One he could not stop, until he looked at Jonathan's stoic face showing disappointment in having confided in him.

"Jonathan, listen to me, son. I recognize you have a remarkable intellect, far beyond your years, but researchers around the world have spent years probing to resolve this problem. And you expect to accomplish this in two or three years?"

Surprised, Jonathan didn't speak out to defend himself, he ended by saying, "Look, I don't pretend to know anything about what it would take for you to accomplish your dream; my concern is that you're setting your expectations too high . . . setting yourself up for disappointment."

Jonathan's only disappointment was that his father was scoffing at him, not taking the time to engage him in a serious discussion. "Well, Pops, remember, the only thing I'm asking from you is that you keep my secret as your secret." With that he opened the bedroom door and nodded for him to exit, but not before asking, "Dad, have you ever talked to Nori about her early years in Asia."

"Some. Come to think of it, she generally avoids those conversations. Why do you ask?"

"Just wondering. Maybe you should."

"Oh, and Jon, about the sniffing, sneezing, and coughing . . . I suppose you should take tomorrow off. I'll tell your mother. But, by my estimation you have symptomatology suggestive of a fake cold."

"Huh?"

"You're a bad actor."

Slumped in the lazy boy lounger, Joe wrestled with his son's disclosure. Generally a decisive man, he agreed with himself to address his problems head-on. *No. My son is not crazy. Yes, he's brilliant, who knows, perhaps a genius. Naïve? Probably.* The practical side of Joe examined Jonathan's goal. *He'd need to know everything about the digestive system. How could he learn biology, chemistry, nutrition, and malnutrition in just two or three years? And then how would the food be distributed? And what about patents, copyrights, and so many other legalities that will cost a fortune?* He again asked himself about his son's inflated ego. And then his sanity. Finally, he let out a sigh; he'd made a decision to stand by his boy's wishes. Now he could get enough sleep to work the long hours expected from him at his job.

Knowing he had permission to sleep in, he spent hours through the night flicking from website to website, referencing and cross-referencing and charting as much data as his brain could hold. Around 6 a.m., Jonathan drifted off. It was nearly 11 a.m. when Emma stood at the side of his bed, whining and barking that she needed to be taken out. "Oh, girl, it's almost noon. I'm so sorry." Bending down to her, struggling to be lifted, his eyes landed on a package in the corner.

It wasn't a package per se. It was a stack of books. All from the library. Not just books but marked magazines as well. He fell beside "Malnutrition and Nutrient Deficiency," "The Enzyme Factor," *My First Book About the Ocean*. He ran through books on the anatomy, the brain. Articles regarding famous dieticians and herbalists and "Creating A Prototype." He came across a note in his father's writing:

> *Dear Jonboy,*
> *Don't thank me, just get working.*

Chapter 4

DECISIONS, DECISIONS . . .

THAT EVENING, PROPPED ON pillows against the headboard of his bed, under a dimly lit reading lamp, Jonathan poured over an article on his tablet about photosynthesis. So focused, he disregarded a soft knock at his bedroom door. Mary cracked the door and squinted in to see her son awake and reading. She cleared her throat, hoping to distract him, but he didn't react. Resigned, she slipped into the room and switched on the overhead light and planted herself at the foot of his bed.

"Whatcha, ya reading, sweetie?"

"Oh . . . ah, Mom. What?"

"Whatcha reading?"

"Oh, just an article about photosynthesis."

"And what did you learn?"

"Lots. Did you know seaweed is one of the most nutritious and healthiest plants you can eat and there's a type of seaweed called 'Nori'?"

"Nori? Huh, whadda coincidence. Does Nori know about it?"

"Not yet."

Mary moved the magazines and books scattered on the bed to allow room for her to sit on the edge, close to her son.

"Hey . . . don't touch . . . sheesh." He set about reorganizing the materials around him, mumbling something about respect.

As Nori generally cleaned his room, Mary had little reason to spend time there. Now, looking about, she faced a map of memories right in front of her. So much of his childhood on display. Memories forgotten. Science paraphernalia, books, magazines and assortments of things he had built since a toddler. His dinosaur diorama sat by his window and the model of the solar system hung from the ceiling. The rocket he built sat on the table next to his bed. One wall was dedicated to a shelf of trophies and a billboard of medals.

Recognizing the harsh way he spoke to his mother and her sad quietness, he felt regret. "Mom, I saw a commercial on a science documentary and it said there were millions of children suffering from malnutrition in the world. I saw pictures of little kids, even babies with skinny arms and balloon shaped bellies brought from starvation. Thousands are dying. I want to help them."

"Dear, you're just a little boy and it's a big problem. Maybe you could do your part through a school club."

"You don't get it, do you Mom?"

"I'm trying to understand you . . . your obsessive interest in science. Your constant talk about what you will do in the future. But never about today and the life you could be living today. I'm always thinking about who you *are*. Your thoughts are about who you *will* be."

"When I read my books and how I might make this a better world, I am happy. It *is* what I am today. But you know what brings me down?"

She didn't respond, afraid of the answer.

"You. Sometimes I sit in my room, so sad I disappoint you, knowing I can't be the kind of kid you want me to be. Those thoughts hurt me."

Long silent seconds passed, each afraid of offending the other with their next words.

Finally Mary spoke. She promised Joe they would have this discussion as a threesome, but she pressed on.

"I read the letter from your school counselor."

"Oh, the letter I brought home."

"This is a discussion that should include your dad. But right now is a good time. The letter said your teachers, the counselor, and Principal Whiting are considering promoting you directly to high school. You'd skip middle school."

"Skip middle school? Really?"

"Yes, really."

"Finally I'm being taken seriously. No more simple-minded, teeny tot heads."

"Whoa! You have a gift. Accept it with humility, not with contempt for others who are less fortunate."

"But Mom, the teachers teach stuff over and over and the kids still don't get it."

"I don't care. You may be smart, but not mature. Besides, I think you exaggerate. Many may have talents you're not aware of."

Their discussion veered off topic. "Now, what do you seriously think about entering high school in the fall?"

"Y-E-S! I can't wait!"

"Hang on there. It's not settled. Your father and I are going to decide what *we* feel is best for you. You know there is a lot to consider."

"Like what, Mom?"

"Will the work be too hard for you?"

"Mom," whined Jonathan, "you're joking, right?"

"All right, will you be safe there? There are some really big boys there, football types, ready to pick on the 11-year-old smarty pants too puffed up with himself."

"Mom, I know better. If I can't outsmart a bully, then I'm stupid."

"What if they tease you? Make fun of you? Try to intimidate you? Tempt you to do wrong things?"

"I may be eleven, Mom, I've already been through those things in elementary school. They're just bigger in high school. C'mon Mom, I really want to go."

"Bottom line for me, though, is because you've chosen to isolate yourself from others, you'll be too inexperienced to deal with everyday problems out there in real world. Are you mature enough to mingle with the big boys? Well, I'm going to think about it. I'm meeting with your counselor on Monday."

"Please, Mom. Please!"

"I'll talk with Dad one more time and then your counselor."

"I'm going to high school. Yes!"

"We shall see."

Mary leaned over and placed a kiss on Jonathan's forehead. With a mother's tenderness she rubbed his cheek and smiled.

"Bedtime, sweetie."

"But Mom . . . "

"No buts. It's late."

The two cleaned off the bed for him and he hopped under the covers, pulled them to his chin, and closed his eyes. Standing in the doorway, Mary paused to reflect on her ultimate decision. *He's too young.* She closed the door and sighed. Her thoughts revisited her son's room and his amassed collection of awards. *The room is talking to me, telling me something too big for me to understand.* She found herself against the hall wall, sobbing as she remembered her son's words: *You* Mom. *I disappoint you. I'm not who you want as a child. I may not show it, but it hurts me, knowing I can't be like other boys. Those thoughts hurt me.*

Mary found Joe sprawled out on the couch with his pants comfortably unhitched, watching the baseball game. She sat down to cuddle and deflect his attention away from the game by saying:

"I jumped the gun, Joe. I spoke with Jonathan, and he's excited about going to high school next fall."

"And?"

"I still don't know."

"What's not to know? We have a gifted boy who's outgrown what they can teach him. We can't stand in his way. It's our job to give him all the opportunities we can. Did he talk to you about his future goal?" With the secret delivery of his care package to Jonathan, he realized he sanctioned his son's future goal without Mary's approval. He was going against his promise to Mary to remain open. Did his son reveal to Mary his tacit intentions to support him?

"Same stuff about feeding the world?"

Joe reflected on the promise he'd made his son. A promise is a promise. To him, however, betrayal is betrayal. By not confiding in Mary on his talk with Jonathan could be considered a breach of trust. Until Jonathan reveals his complete plans to Mary or she agrees to send him on, Joe would feel a sense of duplicity.

"I tell you what," Joe continued, "at the first sign of trouble, we will merely transfer him back to eighth grade."

"He'd be so unhappy and blame me. But Joe, I need to confess something. In his room tonight, looking over his entire world for his last ten years, it struck me that I took his love of science for granted. I've never seen who he is, only what I want him to be. He as much told me that."

"We're all imperfect, but this I know, Mary, you're a perfect mom."

"It's set then, I'll go alone on Monday and talk to his counselor. He will have to convince me this is the right move."

"Okay. Know whatever you decide, I have your back. But for the record, I say he goes.

It had been a nearly a week since the episode with the Rottweiler, and Nori was noticing subtle changes in her charge. He spent longer hours in his room, avoiding her and their everyday after school chitchat about his day, TV shows, and the like. Conversations at dinner were brief as his thoughts appeared elsewhere; he was no longer attentive to casual family discussions. Always first to finish his dinner, asking to be excused, citing a spelling test and a research project that needed work. When asked about the paper due, his response was vague. "It's about how governments around the world differ from one another. It's interesting, but needs my time."

"It's Juicy Sushi Day, Jon," Nori called out. This day was distinguishable from others because the pair teamed together to make sushi in the kitchen— usually the first Thursday of the month. It had been tradition for at least two years, finally naming it the tongue twister: Juicy Sushi Day. What made it special was that Jonathan found pleasure in helping her spread sushi rice over seaweed wrappers (even when he got his hands slapped for eating the seaweed wrappers) and chop veggies. He marveled how she could slice the fish paper thin then layer it over the rice. Early on Nori set up a rule: During these days they'd simply chat, keep it fun and light . . . nothing consequential, just random topics like "If you could, what animal would you be?" Or "Would you pick your nose in a fancy restaurant?"

They could only talk about silly things; that was the rule, which usually branched off to other ridiculous topics. Jonathan usually came prepared with thoughts. "Who do you know that reminds you of a TV character."

Nori popped up. "ME! I'm just like Sandra Oh?"

"Who?"

"Sandra Oh. She's cute and petite with shiny black hair like mine. And she's fun and funny."

"Yep, that's you."

With that, the two laughed to tears.

Nori began gathering the ingredients and called for Jonathan once again, to remind him it was Juicy Sushi Day. After ten minutes and he hadn't responded, she walked the hall and rapped at his door. "It's Juicy Sushi Day, Jon."

He finally appeared at the door. "Nori, I'm not up to making Sushi rolls tonight. Might have a cold." He sniffled into a Kleenex, "Sorry."

"Again? You sick again? Oh, Jonathan, poor boy. Best you stay away from kitchen for now. I make you special tea . . . "

As she turned, he called out to her, "Hey, Nori, did you ever eat Emma's dog food?"

Back in the kitchen, she brought together another Asian concoction from her homeland, specifically for early symptoms of a cold: Ginger, dried tangerine peel, and a tad of brown sugar all boiled into an herbal tea. Once prepared, she hustled to his room and knocked. She could hear papers rustling and quick footsteps hustling about the room. "Jonathan?" she called softly.

He opened the door only a crack, again.

"Here, ancient miracle tea I make. Clear your head. Still hot. You try."

"Thanks," he whispered.

"Rest, you feel better. I bring you plate of sushi."

"Truthfully, I'm not hungry."

Not hungry for sushi? Now *that* alarmed her. Nori saw his preoccupation with his project becoming an obsession, isolating him not only from friends, but now it was encroaching on his family life. And now his love for sushi. *Child needs challenge. He must go to high school.*

Chapter 5

DEADLY INTENTIONS

H E ARRIVED NAKED, RIDING aboard his massive, snarling black wolf. Stretching his large, feathered wings out from his Adonis body, he dismounted the beast at the gates of Hell and turned his raven-like head to acknowledge the guard at the gate. "Take him to the kitchen," he ordered, extending out the wolf's bridle. Once the sentry looked down at the animal growling up at him with bared teeth, he shied away.

"Take it!" shouted the Archduke of Hell.

"Yes, sir. What do you want me to do with your beast, Lord Andras?"

"Feed Shadow mortal meat from the kitchen, but not too much. I need him hungry to keep his edge." The wolf issued another growl in compliance.

"As you wish, my Lord."

"Where is the Emperor?"

"He is expecting you and waiting in the private sector, M'Lord."

"Excellent."

Andras travelled down the cavern toward the complex lava tubes leading to Lucifer's sanctuary. As demon passersby met him, they stopped and bowed. The pungent smell of sulfur wafted about him, and he stopped to inhale its invigorating essence.

"Ahh, the sweet smell of sulfur. Smells like home!" he laughed, paraphrasing a quote from his favorite movie.

He proceeded down the lava tube to be met by two sentinels standing guard at the black, opulent door, showcasing old, gold patina skulls. A blood red pentagram symbol branded the center. One guard clasped the door handle, made from a human hand-bone, and opened the door wide to escort Andras inside only to be greeted by an imperial sentinel demon bowing. "The Emperor awaits you, Lord Andras. Follow me."

The sentinel accompanied Andras down a short corridor to Lucifer's inner sanctum, his exclusive room designed for only a select few to discuss matters of utmost importance. The two entered the room, the sentinel halting to trumpet, "Lord Andras, Archduke of Hell, leader of thirty legions of royal troops, Master of Assassination and Sower of Discord and Dissention!"

Slouched on his throne, Lucifer raised his head from his brooding posture and, with a strained smile, beckoned Andras to him. Andras sauntered to the throne, bent to one knee and bowed his head, "Oh, great and powerful Emperor Lucifer, you have called me to your throne. I am here to serve you."

"Ah, my trusted friend, Lord Andras. Come, stand before me."

"So glad to see you again, Your Majesty."

"Yes, it is good to see you, too. But enough pleasantries. I have an important assignment for you; it is only you, with your fearsome tools, that is empowered to accomplish the mission I set forth."

The swaggering demon puffed his chest at the compliment and replied, "I eagerly await to serve you."

"A while back, that infernal Creator bestowed on mankind a Glory Child. The child is destined to gift the living world a contribution to alleviate suffering, thus making all our undertakings much harder. As time goes on, the child grows closer to grant the Creator the gift so anticipated."

"Bastard!"

"I need you to intercede and remove the child from the face of the Earth."

"Send him to the afterlife?"

"Exactly, but . . . " Lucifer trailed off.

"But what, Master?"

"The more I think of it, the more I'm considering the aftermath of it all. You see, while it will be beneficial to us for the boy to perish, I don't want to incur the wrath of the Almighty and be blamed. So, instead of *you* landing a mortal blow to the boy, I need you to inspire an earthly mortal to do the job for you."

"I can do that."

"Excellent! It will benefit our campaigns and protect us from the repercussions which will ensue."

"Where does my next victim reside?"

Lucifer handed Andras the scroll Envio delivered to him. He unrolled the paper and surveyed the information, he asked, "How old is my mark?"

"He should be eleven, maybe twelve years old. Oh, and before I forget, most important for you to know is that he is guarded by an angel called Evangelina. Quite resourceful and a ferocious warrior. Since we plan to use a proxy for the strike, she should pose no problem. She'll never see it coming. I'm sending the imp who found the boy to help you. His name is Envio and will meet you at your arrival point."

"This angel is a 'she'? I did not know of any female angels in Heaven."

"Well, there is at least one and she can be vicious. She has defeated many of Hell's fiercest warriors. You must be very clever and stay undercover. She can't be allowed to know it is you who is involved."

"I understand, my liege."

"Now go and return to me with good news."

"As you command, Your Majesty."

Once removed from the throne room Andras proceeded to retrace his steps to the gates of Hell with his ill-tempered wolf at his heel. He paused to allow the beast to gnaw on a mortal leg.

"Hustle, Shadow, it's time for us to leave."

The black demon wolf growled and snapped the leg bone in two. He rose defiantly and shook his black, spiked fur, unhappy his meal had been interrupted. His eyes burned red, and saliva dripped from his mouth. Baring his teeth, he issued a low snarl, lowered his body and inched to his master. Andras flapped his wings and leapt upon his back. Shadow turned his head and snapped, but Andras clutched onto the fur of his neck and leaned in to bite the canine's ear. The animal whimpered in submission. The winged demon directed his wolf down the corridor and out of the gates of Hell. With a wave to the demon sentinel, Andras and his beast raised up and galloped off toward to enter the mortal world.

Chapter 6

Blisdon, Guns, Burgers, and Mom

H IS CAR CLOCK TICKED to 5 a.m., marking the end of his workday. He checked for surveillance cameras, before maneuvering into the dark, corner recesses of an empty parking lot of a 24-hour restaurant. Reclining back in the driver's seat of his cab he sighed heavily and pulled the bill of his Tiger ball cap over his closing eyes, hopeful for one night of peaceful rest that didn't include thoughts of his former life. But, as usual, he was trapped in those memories holding him hostage, always travelling back to the events which led to his current condition.

Blisdon's Burden

I think back to how honored I, a lowly minion, was invited to travel to Earth with Prince Beelzebub to kidnap the Glory Child, an Earthly child destined by God to rid suffering throughout the world.

In theory, we would nab the Glory Child and drive him to an opening in the earth, and from there escort the 2-year-old Jonathan deep into the bowels of the earth and hold him hostage as a bargaining tool with

God. What a naïve fool I was. That's when my world changed. Once having kidnapped the boy, Beelzebub and I recognized we knew nothing about caring for a mortal child. Neither of us could stop the annoying creature from screaming. Either he was hungry, or his diaper was wet, or he needed a burp . . . What did we know? We needed someone to care for the boy as we drove him to Hell. We needed a babysitter to ride in our camper to the gates of Hell.

It was dumb luck I encountered Nori, a tiny Asian bar worker, in a parking lot. This sweet, naïve and fearless Nori agreed to care for Jonathan, believing we were his uncles, returning him to his parents. At first she was reluctant, but once she saw the wailing two-year-old, she agreed. I watched her tenderly care for his needs. In time she determined we were not who we said and yet, for the sake of young Jonathan, she persevered to care for him. Overtime, however, a feisty, unafraid Nori turned up to rule the trailer, defying the ruthless Beelzebub in the name of what's best for the child. Unbeknownst to her, she gradually restored my sense of dignity; she had reached a tender spot in my heart. I asked how a lowly demon such as myself could form feelings for a mortal woman, knowing she would never reciprocate. Over time I found the courage to break with Beelzebub, Prince of Hell, and quietly work alongside Nori and Evangelina to bring the child to safety. Nori, forevermore, extended kindness, respect, and a special kind of love to me.

My betrayal of Beelzebub, the Prince of Hell, earned me the position as the top deserter of the underworld. Demons across Hell and Earth seek me even today, after ten years. Their dogged determination haunts my every waking hour. If found, I am promised a life of eternal torture for betraying my demon master, Beelzebub. But for the last decade I have persevered.

As the number one fugitive of the underworld, I am a demon without a home; but I don't need a home. I do not eat, nor drink; I have no need to eat or drink. Alone, with few allies on Earth, I face a multitude of demons all looking to collect the bounty hanging over my head like an angry, murderous cloud.

Now, my stomach cramps knowing Nori and I can never be together. While I'm no longer hiding in caves in the Rockies for months at a time, trying to elude mortal authorities and bloodthirsty demons, I am still on the run, always assuming disguises that allow me to mingle with everyday citizens. I keep an assortment of wigs, mustaches, nose prostheses, and cabbie caps in the trunk of my taxicab.

Free, but Not Free . . . craving the company of a friend. I stay away from Nori because I fear bringing those demons hunting me to her doorstep. I cringe at the sound of sirens, a screeching car, even an odd-looking stranger crossing my path.

I laugh thinking back to the night, sitting in my cab, waiting for the light to turn green and a swarthy man in a black tux and red bowtie crossed in front of me. I ducked down and, before the light turned green, I was out of there, zooming to my secret hiding place in the forest, certain I had just seen Beelzebub. A few days later, I saw a poster board from the local school play of *The Great Gatsby*. I realized my "Beelzebub" was merely a student playing a role in the play, dressed in a tux and red bow tie. I've been reduced to being a skittish little gerbil.

Metallic tapping on glass startled Blisdon into jerking forward. His head made a swift swivel left to see the barrel of a gun pointing directly in his face.

"Really? Really? Get that thing out of my face," he uttered, rolling down the window.

"Shut up and give me your money!" said the hooded teenage perpetrator.

"Son, you really don't want to deal with me."

"Shut up, you fat pig, and hand over the cash."

"Last chance. Go away while you can, boy."

"Boy? Hand over the money now or I'm going to shoot you in the face, old man!"

The boy stepped closer and placed the gun directly on Blisdon the Quick's forehead. In one swift move, Blisdon ripped the pistol from his hand, turned it around, and pointed it back at the teenage menace. The boy's eyes grew wide as he hemmed and hawed, raising his hands.

"Da . . . da . . . don't shoot!"

"If I wanted to kill you, you'd already be dead."

Blisdon opened the cab's door steadily with the muzzle trained steadfast on the young menace.

"Put your hands on your head and get on your knees, punk."

He did as he was told, followed by wild sobbing. Blisdon looked at the boy/child and shook his head. He thought, *In the old days Beelzebub would have told me to put him out of his misery and drag his soul to Hell.*

"How's it feel, punk?"

A glint off the metal gun sent him gasping for air.

"Stand up. Wipe your face. And stop your sniveling, *boy*."

The youngster slid his hands from atop his head and dried his face with the raggedy, frayed sleeves of his hoodie. He looked with terrified, pleading eyes at Blisdon.

"What's your name, kid?"

"Billy," sniffled the boy.

"So, Billy, how old are you?"

"Fifteen."

"Fifteen? Did you say fifteen?"

"Yes, sir."

"Where did you get the gun?"

"Somebody from school. His dad's gun. He loaned it to me for half the cash of the robbery."

"Why would you risk going to prison for twenty years for half the cash?"

"I'm desperate."

"Desperate? Why?"

"It's a long story."

"I got nothing better to do. Spill it, Billy."

"Ah, well, everything was great until I turned ten. My mom's car broke down and she needed to get a new car. She got a loan against our house and bought a new/used car. She had it a coupla months and then she got sick. She had to go to the hospital and ended up spending six months there. When she got out, she missed payments on the house, the car, and the medical bills. On top of it all, when she returned to work, they laid her off."

"Wow! That's some really bad luck."

"Yeah . . . but there's more. When I turned thirteen, they took over our house and made us leave. We'd been living on the money Mom could make doing side hustles. I collected bottles and cans, too. When she couldn't make her car payments, they came for our car. Mom and I got away in our car and have been living in it ever since."

"Where was your dad through all of this?"

"Shit. He left us when I was still a baby. I don't remember him . . . I only know what my mom tells me about him."

Blisdon leaned on the back of the cab, removed his hat and scratched his head with the gun barrel and contemplated his next move. After deliberating a bit, he popped the trunk lid to a surprisingly cavernous trunk. Blisdon turned to Billy.

"Get in."

"You want me to ride in the trunk?"

"Bingo, boy genius!"

"I'm not getting in there."

"Well, it's the trunk or the police station. Choose."

Reluctantly, the boy shuffled to the trunk and sat on its edge. With a quick sweep of his arm, Blisdon whisked Billy's legs up and into the boot.

"You stay quiet and don't cause a ruckus. If you do, you'll be happy. If not, you won't."

Blisdon slammed the trunk lid down and approached the driver's side door. He pulled up the boy's revolver and popped the ammunition chamber, dropping the bullets into his hand, then snapped the chamber back, flinging the bullets into the field behind the restaurant and shoving the pistol into his waistband. Returning to the cab, he slid into his seat and started the engine. Putting the vehicle in gear, he drove around to the front of the restaurant and parked. Straightening his ball cap and tossing his spent cigar into a planter box in front of the door he stepped into a near empty restaurant with bright fluorescent lights that made him squint and a loud jukebox playing the old Beatles song "Yellow Submarine." He sauntered to the counter where the matronly waitress stood wrapping silverware in napkins and singing with the music.

"Coffee?" the waitress asked.

"No, just need a to-go order."

"Whatcha want, honey?"

"Give me two hamburgers deluxe."

"Anything to drink?"

"Coffee, cream and sugar on the side and a large milk."

"Coming right up," said the waitress as she danced back to the order window and handed the ticket to the cook.

Blisdon sat on the red leather stool and swung around, taking in the retro décor: A picture of a '57 Thunderbird overhead on the wall; tables and chairs quaintly vintage; booths made to look like classic 1950s vehicles and photos of famous '50s movie stars. One wall near the restrooms featured a glowing, neon outline of Marilynn Monroe. He looked around and spotted a vintage Coca-Cola clock registering a quarter of six in the morning. He had plenty of time before his shift started.

"Here's your order, sweetie," said the waitress, bringing Blisdon back into the present. She put down his order along with the bill.

Blisdon placed a fifty-dollar bill on the check and stood. Taking the order he said, "Keep the change."

The waitress smiled wide as she watched Blisdon walk away. She called out a "Thank you!" and Blisdon waved his hand above his head as he exited into a sky beginning to brighten.

Hopping into the car, he stuffed the bag under his seat and returned to pop the trunk. Seeing the boy curled up, waiting for his fate with a look of terror on his face, brought Blisdon to laughter. "Did you think I was going to take you to the police, kid, or even worse?" Billy nodded. "I wanted to keep ya from running. Get into my back seat," Blisdon ordered, displaying the pistol in his waistband.

Billy breathed easily once out of the trunk and happy to be sliding into the backseat, despite Blisdon locking the door behind him.

"It's smells so good in here. I'm starving."

"Don't worry about the smell, boy. Where's your mom parked right now?"

"Behind a catering place off Wick Road," Billy said through the plexiglass separating them.

"I know the place," said Blisdon driving off toward Wick Road. He continued his questioning. "How have you survived this long in your situation? I mean, how have you not been detained by CPS? Do you go to school?"

"I go to school every day. I get there early and wash up there. They give me free breakfasts and a hot lunch. We dumpster dive for dinner."

"What?"

"You know, fish food out of the garbage dumpsters behind restaurants."

"You kidding me?" said Blisdon. "We're going to end that—and quick. By the way, what's your mother's first name?"

Billy hesitated before answering. *Was this a trick? A scam? Is this odd-looking man a pervert?* "It's Brenda. Her name's Brenda."

It didn't take long before they found the car behind the catering place, alongside a dumpster. Blisdon pulled into the parking spot next to the mother's car and shut off his lights. She jumped out of the car and prepared to run just as Blisdon exited the cab and addressed her by name.

"Brenda, don't run. I have a delivery for you," Blisdon smiled.

"Delivery?" There was something in his smile that allowed her to pause just long enough for him to open the backseat door of the cab and drag her son out by his shirt collar. Billy stood dejected, head down, trying not to look his mother in the eye.

"Billy! What have you done?"

"Seems he wanted to be a cowboy." Blisdon pulled the gun out of his waistband and handed it to the mother.

"What has he done?"

"He fended for his family. Or better, he tried to. Seems he got this gun from a school friend, who borrowed it from his dad. I trust you'll return it to the proper owner."

"Oh my God," exclaimed the mother.

"I have something else for you." Blisdon pushed the boy over to his mother and opened the driver's side door to retrieve the bag of food. "Here ya go," he said, handing the bag to the mother.

Brenda peered into the bag. Her words choked as they spilled from her mouth. "Thank you, thank you, thank you. It smells wonderful, you're so kind."

"And one more thing," Blisdon said. From the inner pocket in his jacket, he extracted one of the last bundles of one-hundred bills he still possessed and handed it to her. "That's about $10,000."

Her face contorted in confusion and disbelief. "For us?" she stammered. "Why?"

When she hesitated to take the money, Blisdon shoved it into her hands. "Take it," he said harshly. "Billy needs a home, and you need a break." With that he made an abrupt spin and returned to his cab.

"Who are you?" she called after him.

Blisdon smiled and waved through the cab's windshield and drove off. Brenda, her clenched fists digging into her hips and brandishing a disgusted scowl, stomped forward to confront her son.

"What were you thinking?"

"We've been eating out of dumpsters too long, Mom."

"You know I have tried my best. I've been to a million interviews, but it's hard to get a job when you don't have a home address and look like a bag lady. On top of that, my driver's license is about to expire. If we get stopped by the police, they'll take me to jail and impound the car."

"I know, I know, Ma."

"This man you met is no man. He was an angel sent by God."

"I didn't see any wings."

"I believe an angel doesn't need wings to be an angel. Whoever this guy is, I believe he was doing God's work. Now . . . Let's eat those burgers!"

Chapter 7

IT'S JUST WHAT I DO

MARY KNOCKED BEFORE OPENING the door, clearly aggravated. "Jonathan, how many times do I need to call you before you force me to come and get you? Your breakfast is ready and getting cold."

When he didn't respond she asked again, her voice slightly more commanding. "Jonathan!" She learned when he didn't respond to her it wasn't that he was trying to ignore her; it was that whatever project he's working on, removed him from all other activity in the house.

Glancing at her watch she saw the time had grown short and soon they would have to leave for school.

"Sorry, Mom. What were you saying?"

"Get your nose out of that magazine and get to the kitchen." She groaned when her eyes caught he was at least dressed for school but still wearing the same clothes from the day before: sweatpants and his favorite Zootopia t-shirt.

"Jonathan, at least change your t-shirt."

"Mom, just five more minutes. I have to finish this article."

"Sorry sweetie, but we have to go. You can finish reading it in the car. I made French toast and it's getting cold."

"Mom . . . " Jonathan whined, "I can be late. We're not doing anything in class I don't already know."

"Same old story. Blah . . . blah . . . C'mon, put your posterior in gear."

In a huff, he earmarked the magazine and tossed it at his bookbag. "I keep telling you, I don't need school. I'm surrounded by little kids . . . "

"Stop, will you? You blabbering about the kids in your class is tedious and immature—a testimony to your intolerant ignorance about mankind. How do you expect to function in the real world where you'll need to interact with those you hope to help?"

Mary grew silent. While applauding Jonathan for his intelligence and good grades, had they been too tolerant of his intolerance of those around him? Having an eleven-year-old boy could be wearing, but an eleven-year-old with a high IQ is demanding. More worrying, however, is the combination of an exceptionally high IQ mixed with a big ego. *Joe and I will work on that.*

Reluctantly, Jonathan got up, squeezed past his mother, swapped his black Zootopia tee for a white one with the same foxy image and trotted to the kitchen. Mary rolled her eyes and sighed.

She reunited with Jonathan in the kitchen sitting at the table, wolfing down his French toast. Sipping the remains of her coffee she watched him suck down his tumbler of milk in record time. *In so many ways he's like any other eleven-year-old . . . awkward, energetic. He has the beginning of teenage pimples, and his hygiene is hit or miss. The only thing that separates him from his classmates is his IQ.*

In childish rebellion to his mom's criticism earlier, he wiped his face with the back of his hand. "I'll be ready in a minute."

"Don't forget to brush your teeth," Mary called after him as he stomped down the hall.

A warm breeze ruffled the kitchen window curtains, bringing promise of another beautiful spring day. Mary anticipated her meeting with the counselor. The one thing she wanted to know was the kind of support and protection her baby would have in the high school setting. In her mind, she revisited her talking points: *One, he's too little to fend for himself. Two, he needs a sponsor to help him adjust to the high school setting. Three, can they guarantee someone would protect him from bullies every day? . . .* She knew there were more questions, but they would come to her at the meeting. As Joe instructed her, she would try to keep an open mind.

Jonathan sat in the backseat of the car having finished the article outlining the losses suffered by the two countries at war in Eurasia. He shook his head, unable to fathom the hardship people on both sides were enduring. It didn't make sense for all those people to lose everything they had because of the ambition of an autocratic leader. Millions of people were displaced and starving because of the war.

"Mom, why is there war?"

"That's a good question, Honey. I don't understand why they kill each other and destroy the beauty of their land and a cultural heritage built on hundreds of years. Mainly it's about power. In the end it's about who controls the most marbles."

She chuckled to herself and compared the power struggle in her own household.

"I wish our government could do something."

"We all do, but reality is they have to work something out between themselves. I know it's hard for you to understand, dear. We can talk later, but right now we have to hustle," she said, having parked. "You need to get to class, and I need to talk to your counselor about your placement for next year."

They briskly made their way inside the school. When they came to the juncture where Jonathan needed to go to his classroom, Mary bent over to give him a kiss, but he dodged and waved her off. "Bye, Ma."

Mary rolled her eyes. *Of course, what was I thinking? He's growing up.*

As Mary made her way down the hall towards the counseling office, she dodged the raucous children scurrying to their classrooms before the tardy bell rang. She passed children's drawings displayed up and down the hallway and wanted to stop to admire their creativity and abilities. *Jonathan needs to appreciate that talent takes form at many ages, in many stages, in many ways.*

As she maneuvered through the bustling hallway, anxiety kicked in, wishing she had better prepared for this meeting. Brought notes. She entered the main office to be greeted by a pleasant-faced secretary. "May I help you?"

"I'm Mary Puro and I have an appointment to see Mr. Bill Person."

"Let me give him a call . . . He's expecting you." Her warm smile put Mary at ease. "Mrs. Puro is here to see you . . . Okay . . . " Turning to Mary, she said, "Mr. Person said to send you in. His office is two doors down on your right. Can I get you a coffee?"

"No, thank you,"

Her nervousness returned at the counselor's office door. Her quiet knock was followed by a resounding "Come in!" Opening the squeaking door, she saw Mr. Person casually slumped back on a vintage, swivel desk chair with his shirt sleeves rolled up, glasses perched atop his head and a stack of files piled on his desk. With one swivel he stood, replaced his glasses, and extended his hand.

"Mrs. Puro, please have a seat. Make yourself comfortable," he said straightening his tie.

His reassuring voice and welcoming smile put her instantly at ease.

"Thank you." She sat back comfortably, put off guard by his easy, relaxed manner.

"You have a remarkable son, Mrs. Puro."

"Thank you, I know."

"He has tested higher than any previous student since I've been here and I've been here twenty years," he said, opening Jonathan's file.

"Yes, he is a very smart boy . . . and it's why I'm against sending him to the high school. He's still a child and I don't want to throw him into a situation which sets him up to fail."

"Academically, he is beyond ready."

"I know, but socially he is still a little boy."

"I understand your concern, but what if we could ensure he is watched over every day at the high school?"

"And how might we do that?"

"Well, I thought it might be your greatest concern, so I did some inquiries at the high school and pulled a few strings."

"I'm listening," said Mary.

"I've spoken with Dr. Mason, the sponsor of the National Honor Society, and he has assured me he would assign a member of the NHS to walk him to and escort him from every class. He or she would act as a liaison and oversee your son on a daily basis."

"Yes, but would they be reliable?"

"He has two potential volunteers who would like to use it as a part of their senior project. Both students are award-winning and exemplary members of NHS."

"Really? Can I meet with them?"

"I don't see why not. I'll contact Dr. Mason."

"I'll reserve my decision until I meet and talk to these young people."

"I understand. Let me talk with Dr. Mason and we'll schedule something for this week."

"That will be very helpful."

"I'll call you when I have something scheduled. Which day would be best for you?"

"Any day at this time. I have prep first hour and the first class I teach is at 9 a.m."

"All right, I'll put it together. Thank you, Mrs. Puro, for coming in."

They shook hands, both optimistic an arrangement suitable for all would be possible.

As an afterthought, she turned to the counselor, and a smile played across her lips. "I want you to know I appreciate all your efforts. I came in here ready for combat, but you've allowed me to freely speak my concerns and you were ready to address them all. You've helped with my decision. Thank you."

"Thank you, but it's just what I do."

Exiting the office, Mary smiled and hurried to her car, checking her watch for the time. She'd have to scramble; she'd never been late for work, and she wouldn't start today. She pushed the pedal a little too hard, and it wasn't until she found herself on the highway she realized she missed the stop sign at the end of the high school parking lot. *Yikes. Calm down.* As she drove, she reviewed her conversation with the counselor, her choices were still jockeying for position. *Yes, having a senior NHS member oversee Jonathan was a great idea, but what about during class? So many things to consider. Would he make friends? Would his classmates accept him in their classes? Would he alienate people with his intelligence? And lack of humility. Are there classes that teach how to be a genius with compassion?* So many questions and so few answers.

I need one more unbiased, independent opinion from someone . . . anyone who understands what's at stake. But who?

She turned on the radio to an old favorite ballad station to take her mind off her situation. Sitting back, she listened to the ending of a hemorrhoid commercial. The first song queued up afterward was a beautiful ballad duet. She didn't pay much attention to the song until the chorus began. *You told me you were ready . . . let him go.* Tears welled in her eyes. She knew what she had to do.

Chapter 8

EVIL ARRIVES

The Angel's Overture

A S THE SUN BROKE through the blackness of night, Evangelina outstretched her body to the edge of the crown of the roof to watch the town of Farmington Hills come alive. Lights in bedrooms and kitchens flick on. Paperboys toss the daily news on porches. Men and women exit their homes to make the drive to their jobs. As Evangelina surveyed the town awaken, she scoped out the neighborhood for any stench of evil in the area. But before all else, she made her routine check-in to Jonathan's room. She giggled to see him, as usual, scramble out of bed, after the *third* call from Nori. "Breakfast, Jon. Hurry up. You be late."

It had been almost twelve years since God gifted the people of Earth a Glory Child—a mortal with infinite intelligence who would one day prevent famine and feed the world. Jonathan was a mere toddler when Lucifer learned of his existence and commanded armies of demons to kidnap him. To no avail. Evangelina, with Nori, diligently bested them all, and continues to do so.

Today, relieved to no longer actively chase and fight demons on a regular basis, she embraced the doldrums of everyday life on the planet as God's emissary to bridge the gap between Heaven and Earth. She loved watching the star-studded night skies, the changing of the seasons, the birds and wildlife, and all the other wonders of the Earth. Above all, though, her happiness centered on being named as Jonathan's guardian, his protectorate wherever he goes. She would continue to oversee him through the complexities of growing up. She is indeed where she wanted to be and yet, always foremost in her thoughts. The probability exists that Lucifer continues to send out his minions on missions to locate the elusive child and nab him. Today, the child remains an elusive, but coveted, prize in the devil's arsenal against God and the people of Earth. He continues to maintain an unrelenting need to capture Jonathan and use him as the cardinal bartering tool with God.

Having learned of Jonathan's proposed promotion to high school, brought a mixed reaction. She anticipated a visit from a messenger angel soon to discuss and guide her regarding Jonathan's advancement. Surely news of the Glory Child's promotion had gotten back to Lucifer and works were being undertaken to make good on God's goal for him.

She continued to follow the sun climb over the horizon while debating the good and bad. *Right now, he spends most of his day in one classroom. In high school he will change location every hour. In elementary school they eat lunch right in their homeroom. In high school he will eat in a large cafeteria with hundreds of other students. That's a problem,* she thought. *An altercation with or an attempt by a demon poses a real dilemma. How do I temper the power of Heaven versus Hell's rage without taking the entire school into to the valley of the shadow of death? If Jonathan does go to the high school in the fall, I'll need to scope the layout and procedures of the building. More importantly, I'll need to learn how to blend in as a mortal without bringing attention to myself.*

"Ah, yes . . . " She inhaled a whiff of Nori cooking breakfast for her family in the house below. Evangelina recognized the heavenly smell of bacon frying and toast toasting. *Fried up eggs, too. If only I needed sustenance, like mortals, I'm sure Nori's culinary skill would be high on the things I love here.*

As Nori scrambled eggs in the pan, she heard a knock at the back door. Excited, Emma barked and ran to the back. But for Nori, always vigilant, even a simple knock brought her defenses on guard. The hair on the back of her neck twitched up. She wasn't expecting visitors today, especially at the back door. Always wary of strangers, she exchanged her spatula for a large carving knife from the block of knives on the counter. Gripping it behind her back, she crept on tiptoe to the door. Evie. It was Evie smiling ear to ear, dressed in street wear. Dropping the knife, she blasted through the open screen door to embrace her best friend.

"Evie! I just think 'bout you. We need talk . . . Need your opinion."

"Yes, my friend, I agree. But first I have to tell you, I happened to catch you in action the other day."

"Huh?"

"The Rottweiler. It was the spunky old Nori in combat again."

"Oh, it was nothing."

"Nothing? Pah! I stood ready to charge that barreling brute, but you stepped in and gave him a good fight. Actually, I got a kick out of watching you put on your show, audience and all . . . Seriously, though, Nori, you're looking good. Being a nanny continues to agree with you."

"Yes, love family. I'm good. Getting old though. Too much grey hair. Aches and pains."

"That will never stop you, Nori. You are one tough customer."

"You right. We took on Bad Bub and we beat him. Together we tough combo!"

"Yes, call us the dynamic duo."

"Like Bat Guy and Bird Boy?"

"Sure," said Evie, cringing at her quirky comparison.

"Nori past excitement. No need more. Nori like dull."

"After all you've been through, I understand." Both voices went silent. "Shh! Your family is beginning to stir. I better go. I'll try to stop by again soon . . . when you're alone. We can discuss Jonathan's placement."

"Yes. We need talk. Important stuff."

Evie scurried away from the screen door and disappeared around the corner of the house to become Evangelina again. She flew to her perch overlooking the house while Nori returned to the kitchen to flip the bacon before it burned. As she scooped the scrambled eggs from the pan into a serving bowl, Joe staggered into the kitchen. He worked a double shift the day before and was feeling the weight of the previous hours and hard work finally overcoming him. His legs gave out as he reached the chair and plopped down.

Nori rushed to set the morning paper in front of him, along with his usual hot mug of coffee and watched him stare down at the table.

"You okay, Joe?"

"Tired, Nori, tired."

"Okay. I make you something."

Nori took the large ginseng root from the windowsill and placed it on her chopping block. She sliced ultra-thin pieces from the root. She filled an empty mug with steaming hot water from the teapot and added the slices to the water, along with a heaping spoon of honey and a hefty pinch of turmeric from the pantry. Stirring her concoction vigorously, she bent down and inhaled the steamy aroma and let the mixture steep awhile. Once cooled a bit, she brought it to Joe.

"You drink. You feel better."

"What's this?"

"Grandma's recipe. Help kill pain and give energy."

"I'll try anything once," he said, slurping a sip. "Mmm."

"Grandma know best."

As Joe filled his plate, Nori began cleaning the counter. She knew Mary and Jonathan would be awake soon and wanted to stay ahead of the mess. It didn't take long for Joe to wolf down his breakfast. He swallowed the last of Nori's concoction and thanked her for breakfast. Rushing, he collected his work supplies and flew out the back door.

As if in a coordinated dance routine, Joe left the house, the back screen door slamming shut with a bang as Mary entered the kitchen, dressed and ready to go.

"What a wonderful feast, Nori. You take such good care of us."

"Nori thank you, Ms. Mary."

"By the way, you'll have to take Jonathan to school today. I have to meet with those two NHS students at the high school. I'm hoping they impress me. Jonathan needs the challenge of the high school. But as smart as he is, he still needs guidance, he needs supervision."

"Okey dokey. I take him."

As the ladies talked, Jonathan sauntered into the kitchen and plunked down at the kitchen table and quickly fed himself two strips of bacon before digging into his scrambled eggs, two slices of rye toast, and a small serving of melon balls. He ended his meal with a long gulp of milk and swiped his mouth on the back of his sleeve. He snuck another strip of bacon off the table, bit it in half and slipped the other half to the tail-wagging Emma.

"Young man, did you think we wouldn't see you? Don't feed the dog from the table. And how many times do I have to tell you, use a napkin."

"Oh, Mom."

"If you go to the high school and they see you doing that, they'll think I raised a savage!"

"Oh, right, Mom."

"Be sure to brush your teeth after breakfast. I've gotta go. Have a great day at school. Love you sweetie."

While Nori finished cleaning the kitchen, Jonathan stood at the counter, grumbling under his breath, not so much about brushing his teeth, but more about being told to do so.

"Jonathan, no complaining. Go brush teeth."

"Not you too, Nori." He griped all the way down the hall to his room.

With the kitchen clean, Nori stood at the window and munched on the last strip of bacon, smiling to herself... *a normal morning for a normal family ... dull and simply the way I like it.*

What a beautiful day, she thought just before a thunderous rumbling jolted the house. She returned to the window to find the brilliant sunshine she admired only seconds before had vanished and darkness now covered the land. Confused by the swift change, she rushed out the back door to see if a rainstorm was eminent. Looking through the trees, she spotted what appeared to be a dark orb covering the bright sun. Captivated, like seized by a spell, she watched it slowly move across the sun and beyond. Within minutes, the sky returned to clear blue with the sun as radiant as before. Confused, Nori returned to the house.

Just down the road, not quite a block away from the Puro home, a large crater smoldered in the Quaker Burial Ground. Arthur Power, founder of Farmington, donated this land to serve as a cemetery back in 1832.

Smoldering sulfur steam rose up out of the crater followed by a black nose edging over the lip of the hole. As a hairy head emerged, its glowing red eyes betrayed its identity. The wolf bared his teeth and gave a low growl. With his master aboard, he bounded from the hole to stand amidst the gravestones. With a signal, the wolf lowered his neck and chest and Andras slipped off.

"Ah, record time, Shadow," complimented Andras tossing a portion of mortal meat to the evil animal. The black wolf snapped the morsel midair and swallowed it whole. "The imp, Envio, is supposed to meet us here. Where is the little cretin?"

Flapping his wings, Andras rotated in a circle surveying his surroundings. A squeaky voice caught his ear. Looking down and behind him was the imp, Envio, staring up at him, shaking his head and looking displeased.

"You're naked!"

"I am Andras, Archduke of Hell! How dare you."

"I don't care if you are Lucifer himself. You can't be running around Earth without clothes. You gotta lose the wings, too. Your raven head is stylish, but it won't play here. You look like an Egyptian hieroglyph. You're supposed to be doing this clandestine."

"You, impertinent piece of cow dung! How dare you."

Stewing at the imp's brazen frankness, Andras realized he was right. Resigned to the facts, he morphed into humanoid form. Dressed in a black, embroidered barong shirt and black slacks, he smoothed back his sleek, shoulder length hair (also black) from his piercing eyes flickering between black and red, and glared down at the imp.

"Is this acceptable?"

"What the Hell are you wearing?" asked the blunt imp.

"It's a barong shirt. Every man in the Philippines wears this shirt."

"This isn't the Philippines. Lose the shirt. Try a black t-shirt. Put a gray sport coat over it."

"Watch it imp! I don't take orders from lowly peons."

"I'm trying to help you fit in."

"Argh . . . I understand."

"Your pet wolf has to go. Mortals see him and they'll call the cops."

"Really?"

"Really! I'm not pulling this stuff out of my hat."

Andras sighed and waved his hand over the head and down the creature's back. Shadow was transformed into a black German Shepherd. "There!"

"Sorry, big guy. He needs a leash. There're laws here."

"Son of a . . . !" With a snap of his fingers, the transformed wolf had a collar and leash which he wrapped around his hand. "Is that enough?"

Envio circled the duo, scrutinizing the pair. "You'll pass. Don't say anything stupid. Don't draw attention to yourself. You should be fine. How long has it been since you walked the Earth here in America."

"Haven't been here since the 1960s, but my favorite time here was during the Salem witch trials. It was a wonderful time. Since then, spent most of my time in Asia and the Philippines reeking chaos."

46

"Things have changed . . . a lot!"

"Don't worry. I'll adapt. Now where is my target?"

"Well, this time of day, he's probably in school."

"Point me in the right direction so I can get started, you squeaky little tour guide."

"It's a straight line." Envio pointed to the direction of Jonathan's school and Andras began his quest.

The imp hopped on a tombstone. Stroking his sparse beard, he shook his head and chuckled. *This guy thinks there're palm trees and an ocean here. He spent way too much time in the Philippines. He may be an archduke but acts like an Arch Schnook. He's going to need a lot of coaching. And I left my beautiful woodland for this?*

Chapter 9

DUCK!

THE ANGEL KNEW SOMETHING was amiss. Things weren't right. While Michigan was not averse to heavy thunderstorms, black clouds don't appear and disappear in a matter of minutes. Evil festered somewhere close. She could smell it. She needed to find it and crush it. There had not been any word from above, so Evangelina held her position.

Usually they would dispatch a warning. No word. Nothing. Evangelina scanned the horizon looking for clues. She didn't know exactly what to look for, but anything out the ordinary would pique her interest. She knew if evil arrived, it would show itself sooner not later.

Her first thoughts were to alert Nori of the suspected evil, but Jonathan was awake and scurrying about, getting ready for school. She'd wait at the school door until Nori delivered him before briefing her of the impending evil. Meanwhile, she felt content to stand guard atop the house until such time she could confer with Nori.

"Jonathan . . . Jonathan! We must go. You be late for school," called Nori.

Jonathan sauntered into the kitchen, reading from his notepad. So engrossed in the article, he bumped into the kitchen chair and staggered backwards. Nori laughed out loud.

"You be first boy in emergency room for reading injury."

"Not funny."

She handed him his brown bag lunch. As he continued to read his article, she ushered him out the kitchen door. When they reached the sidewalk, Nori asked, "What you reading so important?"

"This is a fascinating article about synthetic food. They're trying to make food from chemicals, and it isn't working. They have some real problems they can't solve. If they could successfully do this, it would eliminate hunger all over the world."

"Oh. Uh-huh. Fascinating."

"Okay Nori. I know it's gobbledygook to you. But you know what? I love you for trying. I really do love you. You're my best friend."

Rapidly blinking, she scolded herself. *Don't you dare let him see me tear up.*

The two tarried solemnly along the sidewalk, lost in their thoughts until they reached the school. The students played outside the school door, listening for the admittance bell to ring. When the first bell rang, the mob of waiting children collected their things and stormed the school. Nori looked down at Jonathan, "Be good. Do best."

"Always, Ms. Nori, always."

She watched him trot to the school and eventually mingle in with the student population. He'd once told her that it's not that he didn't like the other students; in fact, he said, "I kinda like watching them. But I don't want to *be* them." Once she saw he made it safely inside, she turned to leave and abruptly came nose to nose with the person behind her. "Oh, sorry, so sorry," she said. "I didn't . . . I . . . Evie? Evie? Why you out here scaring Nori?"

"We have to talk."

"Yes?"

"Did you notice the dark clouds and the thunderclap?"

"Yes, very weird."

"I believe it was evil breaking through to the mortal world. We need to be on extra high alert for anything out of the ordinary."

"Gotcha."

"I'll watch over Jonathan while he is in school. Of course you will retrieve him. Together we'll protect the boy from any of the mischief or threats the demons may pose."

"Nori ready. Just like old times."

"Good. You go home now. I'll take it from here."

Before Nori turned to leave, Evangelina vaporized into a sparkling wisp of mist. Her spirit form traveled to Jonathan's classroom. Over the last several years Evangelina learned a lot about humans simply by spending time with Jonathan in the classroom. The pureness of young children warmed her. Also, she liked listening about science, math, and history. She loved the stories and poems from the fifth grade English class. They added to her "Book of Knowledge" about the mortal world, a world she was becoming an integral part of. With her first charge, Brent, the attorney, she experienced the seedier side of mortals. While the attorney tended to be forthright, his clients and associates were not. This experience with Jonathan restores her faith in mankind.

Before the first bell rang, Evangelina secured her invisibility and relaxed into a corner of Jonathan's classroom, on the inside ledge supporting a row of windows overlooking the playground and the street beyond. Birds flew from tree to tree and squirrels ran across the school lawn. Was it by accident, or her angel's intuition that drew her attention to a man stalwartly leading a German Shepherd as on patrol? She watched him conspicuously stop in the middle of the sidewalk and turn to stare pointedly at her corner.

With the final bell, children settled into their seats. The teacher, Mrs. Miles, stood with her computer notebook and took attendance. Seeing all present, she pressed the send button.

"Jonathan, please pull the computer cart out of the closet for me. Today, class, we have a special online assignment. It's a survey project the school is using to help us make school better for all students. You are fifth graders, and you will be in middle school next year. You have experienced a lot during your years here. We would like your feedback and comments to help those who come after you have as good or better experience. Remember, there are no right or wrong answers. I want your personal opinions. Now, get in line and Jonathan will hand each of you a laptop as you approach. You have thirty minutes to complete the survey. You may put your name on the survey, but it is not required. All we ask is you be honest in your responses. The link you must use is written on the board."

Jonathan pulled the cart from the closet to an excited chitter-chatter spreading through the classroom. The students lined up to receive a laptop. Everyone complied except Manuel, who sat at his desk and stared blank-eyed at the chalkboard on the wall.

"Manuel? Are you alright?" Mrs. Miles noticed Manuel remained at his desk. Concerned, she went to him and stooped to his level. "Did you have a breakfast this morning?" she asked, prepared to escort him to the cafeteria.

With sad eyes he looked to his teacher, "No, I'm fine. I just, just . . . "
His faltering words matched his lackluster demeanor.

"It's okay, Manuel. Go get your laptop; we can talk later." Mrs. Miles'
eyes followed his awkward gait to the cart, and she reminded herself to
check with him after the survey.

On his way, he paused at the window overlooking the street and fix-
ated on what seemed like nothing in particular.

"Manuel? Is there a problem?"

As he turned to face the teacher, all those watching gasped and moved
back to retreat from a brief flash of red glowing pupils. He stood briefly
before turning abruptly to claim the last laptop, obviously unaware of the
chaos he left behind. He stared down at his possession, as if asking why
he held it; what should he do with it? The students huddled around him,
until, once again, fire-red glints sparked out from the pupils of his eyes.
One student whispered loud enough for everyone to hear: "He's cursed."
The aberration lasted a mere few seconds before his eyes returned to their
normal state.

"Is everything okay?" asked Jonathan, stepping forward to help his
classmate who seemed confused and in need of support.

Manuel paused to offer Jonathan a wicked smile and then raised the
computer high above his head to slam it down on his target's face, knocking
him back, stunning him with the blow. Not to be deterred, the aggressor
stepped forward again and pummeled the computer a second time, forcing Jonathan down in a heap. Manuel then flung himself across his fellow
student and began choking him. Cries and loud screams filled the room.

Seeing the altercation, Evangelina shot up to Jonathan's side in a heartbeat. Laying her hand on Manuel's forehead she could feel evil pulsating
rapidly through his brain. With a surge of energy, she expunged the evil
currents attacking his frontal lobe. Manuel batted his eyes and his head
cleared. He looked down at Jonathan.

"What the . . . what happened?"

Manuel felt a hand clench the back of his shirt and he was pulled
backward off the boy. Sitting on the ground he looked into Mrs. Miles eyes,
searching for answers.

"What is wrong with you? Why did you do that?"

Dumbfounded, Manuel stared at his teacher. "I don't know. Why am I
sitting on Jonathan? What happened?"

Jonathan sat sporting an angry bump on his forehead and a small cut under his eye. Gasping for air, he looked at Manuel still sitting on his feet.

"Whaddya do that for?"

Manuel started to cry. He had no recollection of his attack. He tried to explain it to Mrs. Miles, but in his confusion, couldn't put it to words. "I'm sorry, I'm sorry," Manuel repeated again and again.

Evangelina whispered into Jonathan's mind, "Forgive him. He didn't know what he was doing. It's not his fault."

Jonathan tried to stand, but woozily collapsed down.

"Cheryl, go to the cafeteria and get ice," Mrs. Miles ordered as she called the front office for an immediate administrator. Evangelina looked at Manuel with pity in her heart. She knew it was not Manuel who attacked Jonathan. Outside evil took control of the poor boy and now he must pay for this evil's bidding. How unfair for him to suffer the consequences while villainy roamed free. What worried her the most? First, that she had not detected the presence of evil in the classroom. But more, that evil was on the loose, unknown and unchecked. She knew this might have been a first attempt, but it would not be the last.

Evangelina returned to her place at the window. While the others attended to Jonathan, she studied the outdoors. As expected, she saw the same figure of the man and his leashed German Shepherd still standing on the corner. He stood tall to make himself known to her and glared. Once the two connected, he raised a fist, then turned his back to continue his walk away from the school.

Chapter 10

DECISIONS AND ROADKILL

AS ANDRAS LEANED ON a gravestone, the black demon wolf relieved himself on the adjoining grave. The heavy dew created a misty fog as the morning sun hit the cold wet grass. Andras impatiently waited for his demon guide, Envio, to arrive. Off in the distance, movement caught his eye zigzagging around the gravestones and making its way to Andras's side. The imp, Envio, had arrived.

"Well, how did ya do? Find the school? Can we go home?"

"Silence, peon!"

"I take it things didn't go well."

"That shrew of an angel interceded and spoiled my plan."

"Yeah, I heard she was a formidable foe and has beaten the best from Hell."

"That's her hype. But let me remind you, you arrogant pea head. I am an Archduke of Hell. I am the king of assassination. My resumé is star-studded. I took down the Kennedys, King, and Dianna. Russia, North Korea and Saudi Arabia are my favorite places to work, but I gave a master class in Turkey with Khashoggi. This angel skank is in for the run of her existence. I never concede and she'll never overcome my onslaught. I have just begun! No angel shrew can stand between me and my quarry and live."

"You know, rumor has it she took on Lucifer, himself, and bested him."

"Rumors are nice, imp, but I have a track record of proof. She doesn't have a chance in Hell to keep me from my call of duty."

"I hope you're right."

"Hope? Hope! Did I hear you right? Why, you . . . There's no need for hope. It's merely a matter of time. Now shut your face and show me where I can regroup and plan my next attack."

"As you wish. There's the Governor Warner Museum just north of here. It's been closed and now only used for weddings and such. You and your pet can hide out there for now."

"Lead on, you lowly piece of pig excrement."

Andras and his canine followed the imp a mere two blocks northeast of the cemetery to the white Victorian home of Michigan's former Governor Warner. As they ascended the stairs to the covered porch, Andras surveyed the grounds.

"Perfect. It has large grounds with big trees to provide privacy and keep the curious away. And it's vacant."

"Wait 'til you see the inside."

He threw Andras the original set of solid iron keys from the museum and followed the new resident and his black, snarling canine into the vestibule. Stepping inside, it seemed they time-travelled back to the 1800s.

"Ah, yes. This reminds me of the good old days when men were men and women were wenches. I loved this era. It was filled with misunderstanding and superstition. Humans were gullible souls who could be tempted and frightened. I miss those days."

Andras sat down in the armchair facing the grandfather clock in the front room and kicked back to relax. He surveyed the room and noted the carpet and wallpaper.

"This stuff is making my eyes hurt. The taste in décor back then borders on early nausea."

Envio let loose a high laugh and jumped on the piano bench to bang out a distorted sound from poorly tuned piano keys. He belted out "Rig-a-Jig-Jig," a bawdy bar song from earlier days.

"Stop! Stop! You screechy, tone-deaf guttersnipe." Andras put an end to his serenade by slamming the lid on Envio's skinny imp fingers who yelped and ran around the room holding his crushed digits. Andras cackled, watching the imp yowl in pain.

"Ow, ow, ow!"

"I approve of the accommodations. Now get out. I'll call you if I need you. Leave the property."

"Ow." Envio rubbed his fragile knuckles, "You mean I won't be staying with you and the mutt? For convenience?"

"Nope. And just so you know, pipsqueak, call Shadow a mutt again and I'll send him to make impsqueak pie outta ya."

"But . . . "

"No buts. Out!" Andras strutted the room, pleased to possess a historic governor's museum.

Envio trailed him, pleading to stay. "Please boss."

"Find a spot in the woods surrounding the property."

"So, your flea-bitten mutt can stay here and I can't?"

"Flea bitten? Shadow . . . " Andras opened his mouth to call his wolf, when, from the kitchen window he spied a red barn in the back yard. "There you go, Envio. You can stay in the barn out back. It's perfect. I can call you when I need you and you're close. Now, get yourself to the barn, imp, and be thankful you have somewhere to stay."

Envio hung his head and headed toward the door. How could he challenge an archduke? When he reached the door, Andras called to him.

"Shadow is hungry. Find him roadkill to snack on."

"As you wish, Sire."

Envio shut the door and stood on the porch. *Wow, I serve an archduke. My friends in the Woodlands will take notice. They will know my name. When I return to the Woodland, if I return, they'll have a parade.*

"Now, let's find us some roadkill."

Envio's skin swirled and churned a mixture of colors to match his surroundings. He hopped down the wooden steps, raised his nose to the wind and sniffed. "Aha . . . " he said, prancing off in search of fresh roadkill.

With Shadow now fed, Envio puffed out his chest and pulled down on his vest and made way to his first visit to his "Palace of Rest." He opened the door and promptly decided never describe to the Woodland dwellers that his "Palace" was nothing more than a smelly barn reeking of mildewed haystacks and dirt, laden with droppings from mice scurrying the rafters. He looked up as the moon shed its light on glistening spider webs in every corner, housing a variety of Michigan spiders. The one that Envio recognized immediately was the one known as the Wolf spider, and not unlike its canine counterpart, is noted for pouncing out of burrows to attack.

Chapter 11

BUMPS, BRUISES AND
NEWS FROM AFAR

A FTER PLACING AN ICE bag on Jonathan's bump, the school nurse's skilled fingers cleaned the minor cut on his cheekbone and sealed it with a small bandage. Invisible to mortal eyes, Evangelina watched from a bedside chair. *Here we go again. The boy has already gone through so much. Why don't they merely concede? Is it because he is too important or is it because they can't stand that I bested them so many times? Whichever it is, I am ready.*

Once his wounds were attended to, the nurse offered Jonathan a sucker. "You should be just fine. They're calling home to get someone to come get you. Sit back and relax, just don't fall asleep. Stay alert."

"I don't wanna go home. I feel fine."

"That may be true, but the principal feels, as a precaution, you need to be watched."

"Ah, man . . . "

As the nurse tidied her station, she casually asked, "Did you and Manuel have a problem?"

"No, not at all. In fact, I kinda liked him . . . he's a quiet guy."

The nurse documented his statement and prepared to ask more questions in case she was asked, when the door to the station banged open. It was Nori rushing in, out of breath. Her frantic behavior told the nurse this must be Jonathan's nanny. The nurse smiled at her.

"You must be Nori."

"I, Nori. He okay?"

"He has a slight bump on his head and a small contusion under his eye, but he should be fine by tomorrow. I recommend you observe him for a while and if you see anything peculiar, call his doctor. Follow your instincts."

"How this happen?"

"I wasn't there, but if you talk to his teacher, she should be able to shed more light on it."

"Nori, I guess you have to take me home . . . I'll tell you on the way."

"Where your things?"

"I have them right here," said the nurse.

"Okay, we go."

Jonathan gathered his belongings and followed Nori to the door. Turning, he managed a smile and said, "Thanks for patching me up. I feel great. Oh, the sucker, too."

"You're more than welcome, sweetie. Just remember, take it easy. No running, jumping, or fancy dancing. And, one more time, stay awake."

The pair left the nurse's office and moved cautiously down the corridor in silence. Exiting the school, Nori looked ahead, and without moving her lips said, "Tell me now. You tell me what happen." The harshness in her voice confused Jonathan.

"I didn't do anything. Why are you mad at me? I was handing out laptops for Mrs. Miles when Manuel went berserk and hit me with the one I gave him."

"Why he hit you?"

"I don't know, and he even said he didn't know why he did it. If you tell Mom about this, she's gonna flip out. She's so afraid for my safety; she won't let me go to the high school. Let's just say I tripped walking home and fell into a tree."

"Really? Hmm . . . I could believe that story. Okay, tree it is."

"Thank you, Nori. I owe you one."

Evangelina, imperceptible to the mortal eye, travelled above Nori and Jonathan and listened while scanning the horizon for the mysterious man and his large black dog. She felt his evilness but couldn't put a name to his face. He was simply too distant for her to get a good read on him. She maintained a hand on her scabbard, prepared in the event he showed up. She was certain the incident at the school could be traced to this mysterious man and his dog. Both had retreated into hiding.

"Nori, I still don't get it. What happened to Manuel?"

"Nori no know, but poor boy no know neither. Make mistake human, but forgive is virtue. You must forgive boy. Make you better person."

As the two continued their sullen walk home, Evangelina decided. *I think this is the time for Evie to meet Jonathan. I can help him work through this.*

At last home, Emma met them at the door. The gray on her muzzle betrayed her old age, but not even the arthritis in her bones could dampen her love and excitement at seeing her young master. She lived a good long life, but now her various ailments slowed her down. Joe and Mary had talked about sending her "to the farm." *But not yet.*

Once Evangelina saw Nori and Jonathan safely enter their home, she transformed from Evangelina the angel to Evie the mortal and knocked at the door. Nori opened the door, surprised to see her old friend.

"Evie!"

"Nori, so good to see you face to face again."

"You come in, come in."

"Yes, thank you, my fierce tiger."

"Tiger, so happy to see you. I think I know why you here."

"I'm sure you do. It's about time I meet the boy, don't you think?"

"Oh, yes. I look forward to this. Come sit. I get Jonny-boy. You're in for a treat."

Nori left the room and returned followed by a confused Jonathan. "Jonathan, I like you meet our best friend, Evie. She watch over us. She keep us safe."

"Hello, Miss Evie."

"Hello, Jonathan. Please sit so we can get to know each other."

"I don't understand. Who are you? Do you work for the school? You look familiar. Why do I need protection?"

"Let's say I'm there often. I'm here today because of the altercation you had with your classmate."

"You mean with Manuel?"

"Yes, exactly. I happened to be at the school after it occurred. And when I heard Manuel was involved, I was shocked. He's such a good kid. I want you to know Manuel meant you no harm. He was not acting on his anger, but instead was influenced into his actions by an outside force. He wasn't the Manuel you know and play with."

"Yeah, he's the last person I think would imagine losing his cool and attacking someone. 'Specially me. We play chess together every once in a while at lunch. He's cool, calm and very polite. I don't know what got into him."

"That's another matter I will deal with soon. In the meantime, he's been suspended for the rest of the week. When he returns, he'll need your hand in support. Let others see you hold no resentment. "

"I have no problem with that."

"Good. My job here is done. It was about time we met. After all, our Nori talks about you often . . . what a wonderful kid you are." Despite his occasional preteen outbursts, Evangelina saw grace in this young man.

"Can Nori make you tea, Evie?"

"No, thank you; I must return to my duty."

"Come again, soon?"

"I'll see you when I can. You keep up your good work."

After saying her goodbyes, the front door closed, and she took her post atop the family home. It is a glorious day to be on the Earth. She watched a robin scurry along the grass looking for his next snack while a multitude of squirrels busied about searching for last year's buried delicacies. A touch on the shoulder startled her. She turned and came face to face with her friend, Raziel, the messenger angel.

"Greetings Evangelina. Peace unto you."

"Peace with you, Raziel. So good to see you! What news do you bring me?"

"I bring you news from the leader of the Choir of Dominions, Archangel Zadkiel, wanting me to alert you that the solar eclipse you watched recently indicates there is detection of a serious evil presence in this area. Be alert as it poses a threat to the Glory Child."

"Tell me something I don't know. The eclipse has come and gone, *and* I just exorcised an evil presence out of a little boy. Next time, don't wait. We're dependent on you to alert us. God demands that from you. Apparently, Lucifer is continuing to send his minions on missions to locate the Glory Child. It seems he has located our ward and is intent to do him harm. We need to nip this in the bud.

Raziel remained silent, shamed by his neglect in the face of such seriousness.

To change the intense undertone in their conversation, Evangelina smiled and asked, "Anything else? Any news?" angling for gossip. "Any juicy rumors? You know I'm a little out of touch being here 24/7."

"Well," said Raziel, grateful they were on to mood-changing topics. "There's a couple of things going around."

"Ooh, do tell, do tell."

Raziel moved close to Evangelina and whispered in her ear, "St. Peter is taking time off to travel the Holy Land and then vacation at the Dead Sea. Some angels think Saint John the Baptist is going to take over at the pearly gates while he's gone."

"Really?"

"Yes, but even bigger. Archangel Zadkiel is retiring from managing the guardian angels."

"No. Really? Are you sure?"

"Yep, they are going to appoint a new head of the guardian angels."

"Wow! When? Who?"

"Don't know, but it's said he's going to try to finish this earthly decade. Who? Nobody knows. Your guess is as good as mine."

"Ya know, it is about time the old man took some time for himself. Perhaps that's why he missed informing us about the eclipse. He's been overseeing the protection of mortals for thousands of years. Wow, I'm going to have a new boss. But Zadkiel will always be my hero. He gave me my first shot and I'll always be beholden to him for his belief in me. I'll miss reporting to him. I can only hope the new boss is half as good.

"Oh, he will be around, but his load will be lighter . . . Anyway, I've stayed too long, I best be going. I only came to warn you, but I see we're a little late. I have two more messages to deliver. I hope to see you again soon. Peace be with you."

"And peace be with you, Raziel. Remember to convey my eternal gratitude to my mentor, Archangel Zadkiel."

"Well, Zadkiel feels that Lucifer has bided his time for too long. The Emperor of Hell will not be denied. He has an obsession with the Glory Child that borders on the insane."

"They sent their best demons against me when they kidnapped the child a decade ago. Hell hath no demon I cannot handle."

"Archangel Zadkiel advises you to not expect a frontal assault. They are a devious and conniving bunch. He advises you to watch your flanks."

"So noted, Raziel. But pass it on; you need to update your messages."

"So noted, Evangelina." Raziel flapped his wings and in an instant, disappeared. Evangelina looked off to the horizon contemplating who her new boss might be. She ran through the list of possible replacements. Overwhelmed by the possibilities . . . *too many to decide. I'll simply wait 'til Raziel updates me.*

Chapter 12

A CHANCE REUNION WITH A SCOTCH CHASER

NORI PULLED HER FADED red Civic into the parking lot and began hunting for a spot. It was a busy day for the little shopping center in Ann Arbor. She cruised up and down the lot until she saw a car pulled out and zipped into the space. She was late. Grabbing her purse, she ran towards the K-Beauty Salon for her monthly hair appointment. Of all the wonderful things she found in America, getting her hair done on a regular basis was her addiction.

Breathlessly, she opened the salon door and hurried to the counter. The young Asian woman at the counter smiled sweetly and greeted her.

"Miss Nori, so glad to see you."

"Sorry, Young-Soon, I'm late, but traffic, you know."

"Yes, many late today."

"Is Ji waiting for me?"

"I tell her you here."

It took but a moment and Ji stood smiling at the door. She beckoned to Nori and the little Asian woman popped up, grabbed her purse, and followed the stylist to the back. They chatted as they walked along.

"How is Ms. Moon, today?"

"Busy, busy. After hair, must pick up boy after school, make dinner."

"How's boy's family doing?"

"They are all good."

"How your daughter Kim?"

"She working hard at university. Graduate soon."

"You must be so proud."

"Oh, so proud."

"Have a seat and we'll get started."

Nori sat down in the stylist's seat and settled in. As Ji prepared her station the two women customers, sitting not far away, whispered between themselves.

"Is that who I think it is?" asked Duri.

"Who you think she is?" asked Yon.

"You know. Woman who save child."

"Oh. What her name? Ah? I no remember."

"Yep, that her. I remember face from TV."

"She hero."

"She just tiny thing."

"Yeah, but tough like nails."

Ji worked her magic and cut Nori's hair. It took about twenty minutes and Ji swiveled the chair to face the mirror so Nori could see the final look."

"Oh, very nice. You make me look good."

"You know, Ms. Moon, we could rid your head of that grey hair."

"The glory of age is the beauty of gray hair."

"Well, if you ever change your mind . . . "

"I keep for now," smiled Nori.

Nori tipped and thanked Ji for her talented work. She hurried to the front desk and paid Young-Soon. After mulling the coloring of her gray hair, she set another appointment for the following month. Nori waved as she scurried out the door. Checking her watch, she saw she had plenty of time to fetch Jonathan from school, but it was a forty-minute drive. Considering construction traffic, she thought to herself, *I better leave now, just in case.*

Nori jumped into the car, put the key in the ignition and then nothing. She turned the key again, but only heard a click, click, click. *Oh, no,* she thought. She tried once again, but only heard the click, click, click. She pounded the steering wheel in frustration. "No," she yelled. She sat and thought a moment, then pulled out her phone and called Joe.

"Hello, Joe here."

"Mr. Joe, Nori. I in Ann Arbor and car no work."

"What's wrong?"

"I turn key and car goes click, click, click."

"I see. Sounds like you need a new battery."

"What I do? Jonathan needs pick up."

"Well, things are kinda slow here, so I'll pick him up. Meanwhile, you call a cab and go home. Tonight we'll buy you a new battery and install it. I'll meet you at home."

"Okay, Mr. Joe. I see you at home."

Nori hung up the phone and immediately called the cab company. After talking with the dispatcher, he assured her that he'd have someone pick her up within fifteen minutes. Meanwhile she should wait patiently in her car.

The dispatch hung up and checked his board. *Let's see. Who's close to Ann Arbor? Ah, Biz . . . he just dropped off someone at the University of Michigan Medical Center. Perfect timing.* He immediately got on the radio and called Blisdon, hoping he was still in the area.

"Dispatch. 19, Biz, come in."

"This is 19. Whatcha need, Boss?"

"Can you take another run?"

Blisdon, grizzled and unshaven from a string of late night and early morning runs escorting passengers in his taxi, groaned at another call from dispatch.

"What's with you guys? Look at my time sheet. I need to clock out and get rest . . . Where's the pickup?

"Got a lady in the parking lot behind the M Plaza Center who needs a ride to Farmington Hills. You available?"

"No!" was his first response, until he remembered the upscale area of Farmington Hills is known for good tips. "Wait. Yeah, yeah, never mind, I'll take it."

"Look for a late model red Civic."

"Gotcha. I'm on it." As was his routine he swapped wigs after each call to confuse Lucifer's bounty hunters. Today he donned a salt and pepper, neatly cut hairpiece, trimmed just beneath his taxi cap, and blue tinted shades. Primping in the mirror after a quick shave, he was pleased at the old, hip guy with an air of dignity looking back at him. He knew the area well and headed directly for the M Plaza to cruise up and down the aisles of cars until he spotted a lady waving her blue umbrella with large red polka dots and zoomed to her side.

"Farmington Hills?" he asked after rolling down the window.

"Yes, that's me." Fumbling with her oversized tote and umbrella she managed to open the door and hoist herself into the back seat before Blisdon had a chance to offer assistance.

"So, what's in Farmington Hills?"

"Home. My car broke down."

"So why the umbrella? S'pose to be sunny all day."

"Protection," she offered without explanation.

He heard her rummaging in her tote bag. " . . . ah, here," she mumbled, pulling out a sheet of paper. "Rice, tuna, avocado, wasabi paste . . . "

"Making sushi?"

"Yeah," she responded, not interested in conversation, realizing she needed more sliced ginger and soy sauce.

"One of my favorite foods."

"Good."

"Farmington Hills. Nice area. Live there long?"

Ignoring his question, she blurted out, "Hey. You stop at Kroger ahead. Need soy sauce. I be fast; you wait for me."

"Huh?" he asked, but felt obliged to make a quick turn into the parking lot and pull to the curb.

"You be here. Just this place. I leave umbrella in car. You no steal it."

Blisdon shook his head at her bossy command and laughed. So like his memory of Nori, down to her perky, determined steps into the store. Nori incarnate. Even her pronunciations, and clipped way of speaking, mimicked his Nori. He could almost hear her voice in his head.

His passenger's feisty nature sent him brooding into nostalgia for the past. His thoughts settled on Nori. How he missed her. How he would never risk searching her out and exposing her to the vengeance Lucifer would impose on him, her and/or Jonathan and the Puro family. Never certain he wasn't being followed by clever demon bounty hunters, he always reconsidered any thoughts to seek out his dear Nori.

"Okay. Now you take me home," Nori ordered upon entering the cab.

"Yes, ma'am." Blisdon looked into the rearview mirror to support his suspicion. *Swap her grey hair for dark black, erase the minor crow's feet and that's it. It's uncanny. Nori. Yep, my Nori in the flesh.* To verify he wasn't delusional, he asked one final question: "You have family?"

"You too nosy. Raise partition and hush up."

Yep, that's my girl. That quirky brashness answered him without question.

With that, he raised the window separating them and made a U-turn to enter Parker Mill County Park's wooded area and pulled into a secluded parking spot tucked in a grove of trees.

"Hey, hey, what you doing? You turn 'round right now." She pounded her umbrella against the partition.

He made a rapid-fire exit out the cab and opened the rear door before Nori could react. Her eyes popped wide and, in a swift move, her survival response kicked in and she assaulted him with a violent punch to his chest, taking him by surprise.

"Nori warn you. I fierce tiger. You no want to tangle with me. I make you sorry."

Holding up his hand in a defensive posture, he started to say "Hold on, let me . . . "

"You serial killer?"

"Oh, no. Not me."

"You rapist? Why we not on highway? Take me back to highway." She took aim at his belly button, ready to thrust the point of her umbrella when he wrestled it from her.

"Stop! I have a surprise for you."

"No like surprises from perverts."

Maintaining his hold on Nori's weapon with one hand, he removed his cap, then his wig and sunglasses.

"Blisdon? . . . "Ohh, Blisdon. Is it really you?"

"Yeah, Nori, it's me." His voiced trembled.

Nori raised her hands to his face and gazed into his eyes. The years of their separation faded away. Without pause, they closed the gap and embraced.

He whispered, "I've missed you every day since my banishment. And to think a chance encounter in a cab brought our paths together."

As they held on to each other, emotions buried deep inside resurfaced.

"Are you getting the money I'm sending?" he asked, finally breaking away.

"Yes," Nori whispered. "You are giving Kim a college education. You'd be so proud. There's much I need to tell you, Blisdon."

"Nori, I'm gonna beat those demons and one day we'll be together. I want to spend the rest of my days with you reassuring me you are living a good life, but, sadly, we have to move on away from here. I'm being hunted all the time."

Nori placed her hand on his chin and raised his forlorn face. As a single tear rolled down her cheek, she looked deeply into his eyes, "Nori know. Nori understand."

She knew it foolhardy to think the demons chasing him would ever give up. She could only hope he stayed safe and his luck stayed true.

He returned to the front and began a slow drive home in silence. She huddled deep into the back corner of the cab to prevent being seen. He studied her face in repose as silent tears fell into her lap.

Nori sniffled into her hankie. This demon, this man, had done so much for her and her daughter. How could she pay him back? In her eyes, he was no demon. She considered him an angel sent just to her from heaven. *Oh, to only be with him every day and share a life together.*

At the museum Andras relaxed in an overstuffed chair, his feet perched on an ottoman, and sighed. "Ahh . . . " He took a long drag from his cigar and puffed out rings of smoke, filling the air with a musty haze.

"A glass of Scotch would go nicely with this cigar," he said, thinking out loud. I *need it to relax as I contemplate my next move.*

"ENVIO!" he shouted, startling the canine asleep at his feet. Shadow's head popped up, looked around the room and, finding no disturbance or threat, settled his muzzle back between his paws.

"ENVIO! ENVIO! GET IN HERE?"

Hearing his name booming from the house, Envio, with meteoric energy and speed, emerged from the barn and blasted out into the night air. Being an imp, he was thought to be a dreg in the hierarchy of demons. But amongst his community of imps, Envio held considerable prestige. He came from a long bloodline of uncontrollable pranksters and mischief makers. Servicing an archduke would only bring additional celebrity. There were drawbacks, however, as he was beginning to see. He took the chance: the job would be short-lived or possibly deadly. On a whim, an irate archduke could whisk him off to the seventh level of Hell simply because he became displeased with his service. Envio promised himself he would not let that happen to him.

Envio sprinted out the barn door and blasted into the cool spring night. He raced to the museum and entered to find himself standing face-to-face with the Archduke blocking his way, anger etched into his face. The imp stood at rigid attention, despite his wobbly knees. Even his floppy, pointed ears stood erect.

"Yes, Archduke Andras, how can I serve you?"

"What took you so long, peon?"

"Please forgive my tardiness, Sire."

"What is all over you, imp?"

Looking down at himself he saw his sparse fur covered with straw fragments, and spider webs. Envio said, "Looks to be straw from the barn, Sire."

"You dare present yourself to me in such disarray?"

"Please forgive my appearance, Sire, but I thought serving you as quickly as possible was more important."

"You're lucky my need for Scotch whiskey is more important than your substandard service."

"I understand, Sire."

"Fetch me a bottle of the finest Scotch in these parts and make it quick, you piece of farm dung."

At the archduke's command, Envio flew out the door to his mission. Becoming familiar with the area, he recalled Teeny's Liquor was not far away. With his skinny legs pumping, the imp made it to the establishment. Hiding under a parked car, he waited. It didn't take long before a car pulled up and a group of rowdy teenagers jumped out and entered the store yelling and laughing, pushing and shoving as they made a raucous break to the back, to the beer coolers. When they opened the door, Envio slipped in off their heels. The store employee looked up, alarmed by the fracas. It took little brainpower to sense trouble, and he bolted to the back, leaving Envio to jump into action by scaling the shelves. His hand zipped to the Scotch section. Unfamiliar with Scotch, he picked the bottle with the most impressive label. With a snatch and grab he was out the door and slipping into the night at top speed. He thought he heard police sirens in the vicinity of Teeny's and wished he could return to watch the action.

Breathlessly, he raced to the museum and presented himself at Archduke Andras's side.

"I hope this Scotch will please you, Sire."

Andras yanked the bottle from Envio's claw and inspected its label, then removed it. Sticking a cigar in his mouth, he used both hands to detach the seal and swiftly open the bottle. Without hesitation he drew it to his mouth and guzzled a handsome portion down his throat.

"Ah," the archduke exclaimed, wiping his lips with his sleeve, "You made a fine choice this time, Envio. Now get your skinny behind back in the barn. I'll call you if I need you."

"As you wish, Sire," said Envio scurrying out the door, but not before seeing families of wolf spiders rushing across the floor to safety. The vision put a little skip in his step and a smile on his face. *Wolf demon meet wolf spider families moving in.*

Andras settled back in his chair puffing on his stogie and sipping Scotch. *This is a wonderful state of affairs. I could get used to this. Now that I'm thinking about it, Lucifer never gave me a deadline. Methinks I'm going to milk this for as long as I can."*

"Shadow!"

The fiery beast in German Shepherd-guise, trotted to Andras' side and sighed, happy to nuzzle once again into his master's lap.

"You're such a trusted companion, buddy. The demon scratched the canine between his ears; they were two comrades exchanging company and safekeeping.

"Whaddya think, pup? Stay awhile and enjoy the free ride?"

Shadow snipped a bark, affirming the plan.

"Then that's what we will do."

Chapter 13

Gardens, Disappointment and Eureka!

ANDRAS DECIDED TO "SUMMER" at the museum and made no serious attempts on the boy's life. Instead, he enjoyed leisurely lounging as the bedraggled imp indulged his every need. Whatever he wanted, Envio found a way to deliver it to him. With no real visitors to the museum, Andras made it his home. Once he sent Shadow to terrorize the caretaker. Seeing a huge wolf growling at you in the doorway has a chilling effect on humans.

This seemed a perfect summer for the Puro family. Both Mary and Jonathan were off from school and spent much time at home together. Mary got a chance to give the house a thorough cleaning and take time to work in her garden. Jonathan delved into expanding current research: "Creating a Sustainable Global Food Source."

The scenes Jonathan watched on a new documentary, one of the many presenting actual footage around the devastation of war and climate disasters in relation to malnutrition and famine across the world, confirmed what he already knew: he had a long way to go. Recognizing the work he was building on was like snatching one cockroach out of a nest-infested sewer. But these documentaries did nothing to discourage his aspirations to feed the world. To the contrary, it spurred him into action, if only to prove his father's faith in him. He'd already researched the digestive system and how the body processes food and learned about how enzymes and chemicals break down food. Acknowledging he fell short in countless areas, would not deter him. He looked forward to facing each challenge, which included actually getting the food to the people . . . "I will. I can," he said, laughing at his own bravado.

The early morning sunshine found Jonathan half-awake in his bed, thinking about his research from the previous day. Propping himself up, he reached across to his nightstand for his charging laptop, anxious to get an early start. Unable to locate it, he groaned and rolled out of bed to switch on the table lamp. How was it possible? The laptop had vanished. He frantically searched the room, thinking he must have moved it and not remembered. But he remembered that he remembers everything. Running to his desk, he looked under each pile of books and papers cluttering his workspace. The laptop was missing, nowhere to be found. *Had someone taken it?*

Panicked, he slipped into a t-shirt, gym shorts, and unlaced tennies and ran from his room to the kitchen. "Mom! Mom! Nori?" Not only was the kitchen empty, but it also appeared the entire house was vacant. Usually Emma would bounce out at the first sound of his footsteps. His eyes shifted to the kitchen window to see his mother working in her garden with Emma keeping her company. The screen door banged as he bolted to her side, gasping for air.

"Well, well, little man, I see you've found me."

"Where's Nori?"

"She went to the grocery store eggs."

"Mom! Someone stole my laptop last night. I looked everywhere and it's gone."

"Look at you. What's happening? You're as pale as a January moon. This is not the way an eleven-year-old boy should look. Tell me the last time you were outside in the sun and running and playing? Do you ever laugh?"

"Um, ah, I don't know. Didn't you hear me? My computer's gone."

"Look," she said pointing to the picnic table under the big oak several feet away. "You'll find your breakfast in the warming basket."

"And my computer?"

"You'll get it when we're done."

"Done what? What are you thinking? Is this blackmail?"

"Let me finish before you take off. After you eat, you're going to help me garden a bit and then, and only then, will you be allowed to work on your computer." She paused before adding: " . . . in the fresh air."

"Forget *that.*"

"Just come out here and work alongside me. For once you can humor me. Maybe the two of us can play catch a little later in the day."

"Catch with my mother? You've got to be kidding."

"You need physical exercise. If you don't want to toss the ball around with me, then find some friends. Bottom line, you can't spend your summer like a hermit in your room."

"I have important work to do." His lips pursed in frustration as he tramped away. *This is child abuse.*

"I'm sure you do, but today you're helping your mom and that's just as important."

"Ah, Mom, stop bugging me!"

"Do not 'Ah, Mom' me. Go eat." She could hear his whining as he walked off.

From atop her perch on the Puro home, Evangelina watched Jonathan stomp toward the table and plunk himself onto the bench. She chuckled at the obstinate boy who decided to boycott eating.

I'll show her. I'll go on a hunger strike, fade away under the good old oak tree. The image made him smile. But pancakes and sausages were his favorite and hard to resist. For show, he jabbed his fork for a quick bite of sausage, struggling to hide his enjoyment. His eleven-year-old bottomless pit of a stomach took over and he crammed down the contents of his plate. After the last chew and guzzling the remaining milk, he wiped his mouth with his t-shirt.

"Good grief! Why do I even bother to give you a napkin," shouted Mary, watching him from the corner of her eye. "Lace your shoes and get over here." She sighed as he shuffled over, his laces still untied and flopping with every step. *Is this the first sign of teenage rebellion?*

"What now?" he asked, looking down at his mom working on her knees, planting lettuce seeds. He crossed his arms, took a belligerent stance and waited for a response. Mary planted the last seed and looked up at her young, sulking assistant.

"Grab the rake and grade the ground over there. Make sure all the clumps are broken down and smoothed because I'm planting spinach in that area."

"Spinach!? Why spinach? NOT my favorite food."

"Spinach is good for you. It has lots of iron for your blood."

"Spinach tastes like crap. Why not strawberries or melon?"

"I'll make you a deal. Do a good job raking and I'll plant a raspberry bush over in the corner."

"Okay, deal." The sooner he agreed with her, the faster he could go back to his research.

Jonathan manned the rake, chopping big clods of dirt and raking them smooth, all while wishing he hadn't made the deal with his mother. "I think I prefer store-bought raspberries," he yelled out to his mom. She secretly laughed and watered the lettuce bed.

Wiping beads of sweat from his brow he hollered, "Is this good enough?"

"Still too clumpy. Use the rake head to break the little clods, then rake it smooth again."

"Sheesh . . . "

As he worked, his brain addressed the problems encountered from the documentary the night before. For his paper he needed to diagram the equations necessary to keep the calories at 2,500 or higher and the actual volume low. Trying to figure in all the required nutrients and minerals would not be an easy task. Even tougher was how to make the person feel full and satisfied for the day. The thought of a single dietary product which could supply a day's worth of calories, protein, carbohydrates, vitamins and minerals would change the world. How to create and produce it cheaply and make dispensing easy and efficient kept his mind busy as he crushed clods for his mom.

Mary surreptitiously studied her son as he ploughed the ground. *Huh, he's smiling. Sweaty and sunbaked and yet he's got a big, daffy grin. What's he thinking?*

Midmorning and the summer sun continued to blaze down on them. Chopping with the rake made his shoulders ache, but he stayed focused on the task. With no more clods to break down, he raked the surface smooth and hollered to his mom.

"How's this, Ma?"

Mary saw her son glistening with sweat; his face had taken on a quiet pink from the sun. "Jonathan, you're done. Go in the house and take your breakfast stuff. Your laptop's on a shelf in the utility closet. You're starting to burn in this sun. You really should get yourself outside more, prime your skin, son."

"Whatever you say, Mom," he said, rapidly gathering the stuff from the table and speed-walking back into the house before she changed her mind. Depositing his things on the table he dunked his head under the faucet and luxuriated under the cool wetness. He grimaced in pain, however, when he reached for a paper towel to dry it off. Running to the bathroom mirror, he grimaced in disgust to see his face painted in high volume pink. "No more mother/son days." Rather than returning to show her what her good intentions brought, he chased to his room.

Clutching his computer, he raced off, pumped on the new possibilities in front of him. Settling on the bed he waited. And waited. Where to start? After the latest documentary, his imagination, earlier on high, began to fizzle. He wandered from his room, certain a change of scenery could help refresh his thinking. He ended in the living room, plopping on the couch to wait for the "reinvigoration" process to kick in. He threw his head back and stared at the ceiling and waited for his brain to talk to him. Frustrated, he plopped himself face down into the cushions of the sofa, his hands landing in the crevice between two sofa pillows. His fingers touched the all too familiar TV remote wedged there. Pulling it out, he reflexively pointed it at the TV already tuned to the Science Channel from the two nights before. Before falling asleep, he remembered watching a prerecorded program about African drought. He perked up and located the recording and fast forwarded to where he'd left off. An image of a large whale accompanied by familiar singing told him the program now featured whales. Right where he wanted to be. Rolling to his side, he immediately recognized the featured whales were called baleen whales. Moving to the floor, and inches from the screen, he focused on the whale opening its gaping mouth, forcing plankton through finely fringed baleen, a filter-feeding system used to sieve prey into its belly.

That's it, he thought. *It's serendipity* . . . finding the controller when he did and all by the happy miracle of chance.

Rolling off the couch, he dashed back to his room eager to open his computer. He spread out a rudimentary blueprint put on hold until he felt ready to begin the next stage: how to manufacture the patties. *I have to change everything! This is all wrong! What better way than nature's way. It's been tried and true for thousands and thousands of years. I can't design it any better than what nature has already produced.*

He studied his early blueprint and began to make changes by pulling components from one spot and integrating them into others. He modified the collection component to match what he saw on the TV.

"Clever, clever whale!"

The boy focused on the task at hand and worked well into the night. Emma, his ever-present friend and protector, lay on the bed watching in complete disinterest. With configurations near complete, Jonathan jumped from his desk and threw up a fist, startling Emma, "That's it, buddy!" Emma leapt up barking and wagging her tail, anxious to share Jonathan in this rare show of exuberance. "We're gonna do it." With that he tackled his best buddy down on the bed and into a hug. "We did it, girl! We did it."

Chapter 14

WHERE IS HE?

I N A STATE OF increasing fury, Andras stood glued to the bay window, glowering out into the black night while the wolf lay on the floor whimpering.

"Where the hell is that miniature piece of dung? He's nearly three hours late. He knows you need your evening snack before bedtime."

Shadow responded with a menacing growl in agreement, followed by a loud wail.

"Stop your . . . Hold on, buddy, I see movement outside . . . eh . . . sorry, just a branch blowing across the yard." Frustrated, he slammed his fist on the side table and gritted his teeth. "When I get my hands on that little imp, he'll have hell to pay."

Sitting upright on his haunches, Shadow stared at his master.

"Stop looking at me. I know you're starving, but I can't help you. Maybe I'll feed you the imp when he gets home."

The wolf barked in agreement. Andras threw his hands up in frustration and plopped down in his overstuffed chair. Shadow followed to rest his head on his master's lap and stare up pathetically with a look that begged for his missing meal.

"You're annoying me. Get down!"

The ravenous beast whimpered in reply and clawed roughly at Andras's leg.

"Argh! You're wretched to be around. Go find a dark corner and stay there."

As the clock struck midnight, a knock at the door broke the silence. Andras, sunken into his chair and deeply asleep, dragged open a single eye. He thought, *If it's Envio at the door, the little bastard will wish he never returned.* He shuffled to the door to find his servant huffing and puffing with sweat dripping from his brow.

"Where have you been, cretin?"

"Uh, I was recalled to Hell. I hurried back as fast as I could," Envio said, breathlessly stepping inside.

"For what?"

"Lucifer," he said, trying to regain his breath, "wanted an update on what we were doing, and he wanted to know why the Glory Child was still alive."

"And what did you tell him?"

"I told him about the attempt at school. He wasn't happy about the failure. Then he wanted to know what else we had tried to kill the boy."

"What did you tell him," Andras's voice cracked nervously.

"I told Lucifer the boy rarely leaves the house. Our only opportunity was when he went to school, but the angel and his nanny always accompany him. With school out now for the summer, there're no real openings to get to him."

"Good, good. What did Lucifer say?"

"He told me to tell you to burn down the house."

"That's a bit rash. I am an efficient assassin. I pride myself in getting my target and not others which are not involved."

"I don't think he cares. He wants the boy dead and that is it. He was very adamant about it."

"Not even Lucifer tells me my business, but I guess all good things must come to an end. You know, I really like this house. I was getting used to this lifestyle. Time to focus on business, though. Too bad."

"Well, you've had time to unwind and relax. He is losing his patience."

"Silence, imbecile! Now go and fetch my wolf some roadkill or you'll be relaxing in the seventh level of Hell."

"As you wish, Sire." Envio gave a deep bow and backed out the front door.

Truly an honor for Lucifer to appoint me as Archduke Andras's courier and it surely will elevate my stature among my fellow imps. Although, if I had known how demanding Andras would become and the fury of Lucifer's wrath, I would have respectfully declined the appointment. If I wasn't Andras' attendant, I'd be back frolicking in the forest causing mischief and pulling fun-loving prankster pranks. Like tying the tail of bunnies with twine wrapped around small trees and watching them dance while I play "Country Cha-Cha" on the banjo. Instead, I face an onerous, surly archduke with increasing daily demands. Shadow, the wolf, scares the dickens out of me. I know if I don't keep him fed, the archduke would have no qualms about feeding him an imp. Fortunately, it was a good thing the highways of Farmington Hills are a cornucopia of roadkill.

Envio scampered off into the night. *Roadkill? Seventh level of hell? I'm exhausted to the bone working for that bastard. He's going to banish me. Well, if I'm going to be treated as a lowly peasant, I'm at least going to have a little impish fun first,* Envio thought.

Closing his eyes, Andras began to contemplate his next attack on the boy. What could he do to draw the child out in the open? Without a guardian. Also, he needed a weak-minded stooge to do the dirty work. While he preferred to do the deed himself, he promised Lucifer he would use a surrogate to avoid conflict with Heaven. He shook his head, *why did I agree to such a stupid thing? It makes planning for the deed so much more complicated. I'll shop tomorrow for a sucker to help me carry out my deed. It should be a nice day to take Shadow for a walk and shop for my mark. I'm sure I can find a wino or homeless man who's ripe for the picking. There's no shortage of them.* Andras took a long slug of Scotch and slipped off into blissful sleep.

In the wee hours of the night Envio, the king of impish trickery, returned with a meal for Shadow wrapped in a burlap bag. As the door creaked open, Shadow's ears perked. Envio snuck a look into the room and tiptoed in and passed the snoring Andras to Shadow's food bowl. Shadow stood and growled at the frightened imp, but Envio came prepared and reached into the bag to extract a mysterious oval object which he hastily threw into the demon dog's bowl. The imp jumped back so as not to impede Shadow's attack on his food.

The beast curiously approached the bowl and sniffed its content, extended a paw, then tentatively touched the hard covering of the offering. Unable to discern the creature, he sniffed deep into the bowl. Like magic, a living head popped from under a shell and briefly stared eye to eye with the demon dog before retreating back. Shadow stopped, shocked by the surprise, and crawled away. Slowly he approached the creature again and reached a paw out to smack the crusty casing before him. In a flash the snapper chomped down on the extended paw and attached himself to Shadow, now swirling around and yelping in pain to shake off the vicious beast. At a certain turn he caught a quick sight of Envio's broad smile. Finally, the turtle let loose, and Shadow flung him across the floor to slide under the safety of the china cabinet on the opposite wall.

Envio laughed and rolled on his back holding his sides with laughter. Shadow, realizing he was the butt of the joke, began to viciously show teeth and creep with murderous rage in his heart toward the laughing imp, intent on making him his late-night snack.

"EEK!" The self-satisfied imp sprang to his feet and nabbed the burlap bag just in time to retrieve a real roadkill and toss it to Shadow. The beast stopped abruptly and sniffed at this new snack. He pushed it around testing for another impish trick. Certain it was edible, he sunk his teeth into the carrion and returned to his spot to enjoy his meal. Between each bite, Shadow would raise his head and shoot venom though his eyes and snarl ferociously through his sharp fangs.

But the imp continued to snicker over his accomplishment before slowly shuffling to the exit with the intent to retreat to the barn, but his muscles gave into fatigue, and he slipped to his knees and crumpled against door. The bone-weary imp snored softly with a satisfied grin across his lips as Shadow chomped his late-night snack, with the grinding sound of his teeth crushing the bone of his quarry echoing through the night.

The early morning sun blazed through the museum window forcing Andras' eyes to jolt open. He surveyed the room and saw Shadow sleeping peacefully in the corner and Envio passed out against the door. The sight of Envio in the house and not in the barn angered the archduke.

"What in Lucifer's name are you doing in this house," hollered Andras.

"What?" said Envio rubbing his eyes and fumbling to his feet, "Oh no! I'm sorry, Master. I must have dozed off feeding Shadow his snack. Please forgive me, Sire."

"Don't let it happen again!"

"Never again, Sire."

"Prepare for a jaunt to downtown 'Wherever We Are.'"

"You mean Farmington Hills?"

"Wherever."

"Are we shopping?"

"Shopping for a stooge. We're looking for weak mortal to do our dirty work."

"I understand, Sire."

"Now go and get ready for our excursion."

"It is not far. Will we be walking?"

"I'll be walking Shadow on his leash. You will accompany me but keep out of sight. We don't want to inspire any of those alien sightings."

"As you wish, Sire. When will we be leaving?"

"When do the stores open?"

"At 9 a.m., Sire."

"Well, then it will be our departure time. Make ready and bring fresh food for Shadow."

"As you wish, Sire."

"Begone, imp."

Chapter 15

CIGARS, IRISH WHISKEY AND THOU

ANDRAS, KNOWN FOR HIS vanity, stared at himself in the hallway mirror. Having read about the "perfect man" in *GQ* magazine, he morphed into human form, then primped and posed. Slicking his head of feathers back to resemble the jet-black hair as seen in GQ. *I make a hunk of a mortal man.* He adjusted his grey suit jacket over his black t-shirt, then slipped into his black slim fitting trousers. Finally, he added his belt and tightened it to emphasize his thin waste. Standing back, he looked down at Envio.

"So, whaddya think, imp?"

"You're quite handsome, Sire."

"Of course I am, you little dreg. Have we set a route to downtown?"

"We leave here and stroll down the road out front called Grand River, then proceed about two blocks and we'll be at the edge of downtown."

"Excellent. Is there anything I should know while out amongst humans here?"

"Though you have Shadow downsized to a German Shepherd, you'll still need to keep him leashed. Some will fear him, while others will want to pet him. Be sensitive to it. Also, you will need money to enter some of these places, so I made a trip to Teeny's liquor store last night and made a withdrawal from the cash register," said Envio handing him a wad of money.

"Anything else?"

"I don't think I can accompany you. It's broad daylight and, with my looks, I don't fit in, Sire."

"I don't care. You are coming with me, even if you have to run bush to bush and hide behind garbage cans, you will be there to do my bidding."

"As you wish, Sire," Envio said with a look of worry.

"Get Shadow's leash and put on his harness."

Envio took the leash from the side table and carefully hooked it to Shadow's spiked harness, fully cautious of his killer stare. He handed the end of the leash to Andras, bowed, and quick-stepped forward to open the door and usher his master out.

Andras paused on the wood porch. "Ahh . . . it's a new day. A glorious day. Now let's find us a patsy!"

Anxious to begin their new adventure, the demon dog tugged on his leash and the three stepped out to begin their new mission down Grand River. Not wanting to be seen, Envio scuttled from tree to tree. Like a chameleon, the imp changed his complexion to match each tree he hid behind. His camouflage proved quite effective. It wasn't a long trek down Grand River before they approached the corner of Farmington Road.

Spotting a cigar shop in the first group of buildings, Andras stepped up his pace until he stood at its door.

"I wonder if they carry my favorite Filipino cigar?"

"What would that be, Sire?"

"Bago Especial Cigars."

"Well, you should go in and inquire, master. It seems they have a fine selection. You have money in your pocket."

"Right," said Andras, hurriedly tethering the muscled beast to a bike rack.

A bell jingled announcing his entry to the cigar store door. The smell of exotic tobaccos filled his nostrils with their intoxicating magic. The Jamaican man behind the counter, outfitted in a rainbow striped beret atop his dreadlocks, turned and greeted him with a smile of shiny white teeth.

"Good day, mon. Is there something I can help you wit?"

"Yes, do you carry my favorite Filipino cigar?"

"And what might that be, mon?"

"Bago Especial Cigars."

"But of course, mon. How many do you want?"

"A box would be nice."

The clerk went back to the humidor and returned with a box of Bago Especial Cigars. Andras opened the box, and gently removed one and inhaled its fragrance. He stuck it in the corner of his mouth.

"How much?"

"The box is $375.00 US."

Andras reached into his pocket and pulled out the wad of bills Envio had given him. He peeled off 20 twenty-dollar bills and handed them to the clerk, then snatched the box and left.

"Your change, mon!"

"Keep the change. Buy yourself a good cigar."

"Thank you, mon, thank you," the clerk waved.

The bell jangled and the door banged behind him. Happily, he raised his face to the sunshine while chewing on his fresh cigar, assured he was cutting an enviable demeanor.

"Envio!"

"Yes, Sire?" Envio peered out from behind a lamp post.

"See the Irish pub across the street? Barney's. I bet we can find a drunken stooge there."

The trio crossed the street and stopped at the door to the pub. "Here," Andras handed Envio the leash, along with the cigar box and opened the heavy oak door. "Find a tree in the back and tie him to it. Wait with him until I come out."

"As you wish, Sire."

The demon disappeared into the pub, certain all heads turned to look at this dashing figure entering. He swaggered to a stool and removed the cigar from his mouth and folded his hands gentlemanly on the bar top. In a short time, an aged face with sparking blue eyes under a heavy wedged gray brow stood smiling before him.

"Whaddya have, sir?"

"Give me two fingers of Jameson neat, barkeep."

"Coming right up."

Barney pulled the bottle from the shelf and, with flair, filled a rock glass with whiskey and placed it over a napkin in front of the dashing patron.

"Starting a tab, young man?"

"Yep. Keep 'em coming."

"Will do," he said, returning to drying glasses at his station.

Andras dipped the end of his unlit cigar into the Irish whiskey and savored its flavor. Casing his surroundings, he spotted a middle-aged woman sitting across from him. Her head rested in one hand while the other fiddled with the deep, red curls peeking out from under her blue knit cap. It was her worry-worn face that intrigued Andras. *She's a distinct possibility,* he thought. The woman reached into her thermal vest and pulled out her phone. After checking the screen, her head drooped and she returned the phone to her pocket and drained her rock glass of whiskey.

"Barney, bring me another," the woman called out.

Concentrating, Andras invaded her mind and listened to her thoughts. *He'll come after me, even with a restraining order. I can't believe they're letting him out so soon. I can't let him find me.*

"Barkeep! Put her drink on my tab," Andras called out.

Andras stuck his cigar in his mouth, clasped his drink and strolled to where the lady sat. "I'm Andras."

"Get Lost," the woman said, refusing to look at him.

"Seems you're under a little duress, young lady. Is there some way I could help?"

"I said, 'Get Lost.'" Her scowling face swiveled to pointedly address the intruder and found herself uncomfortably drawn into him. It was his eyes, something about them. *It's his deep, piercing gaze.*

Her face reddened and she turned to hide the angry tears welling around the eyes. He stepped away from the bar to allow her space, but also give him the opportunity to size up his new sucker in his plot. Andras smiled as her shoulders bobbed up and down to the rhythm of her muffled sobs. *Aw, the little lady needs me. Bingo!*

Her humiliating breakdown caught her without warning, forcing herself to gather composure and stand with dignity. She dashed her drink and prepared to escape the bar until the stranger gently touched her forearm, magnetically restraining her.

That she didn't run, he took as an invitation to try again. He raised his fingers and signaled the bartender for two more. The barkeep winked and prepared the drinks, serving them with a stack of napkins and another wink at the smooth operator. She didn't hesitate to swipe her fresh drink and take a slug.

"Let me start again. I'm Andras. Something tragic must have happened. Are you all right?"

"I'm Anna," she whispered, leaning over the bar, cradling her glass. "I'm okay for now . . . but the future isn't as bright."

"Is someone sick? In trouble?"

"That's an understatement. I'm being beaten down physically, mentally and emotionally by the stresses in my life."

"Tell me about it. Maybe I can help."

"You don't want to know. Besides, there's nothing you can do."

"I'll be the judge of that. C'mon, whaddya got to lose?"

"If you insist . . . My ex-husband gets out of prison today."

"Is that a good thing?"

"No! I sent him to jail for spousal abuse. The schmuck beat me with a baseball bat and broke my jaw."

"Anger problem, hmm?"

"He's getting out and looking for revenge, the psycho. I've got nowhere to hide. I'm as good as dead."

"I think we can be very useful to one another."

"How?"

"I know I can get rid of your problem and your problem can help me solve mine."

"How is that going to happen?"

"Here, put your phone number into my phone. I'll call you. Do exactly what I tell you and your problem will be gone for good."

"What's the catch? How much is this going to cost? I don't have money."

"No charge. Believe me, I will benefit, but not at your cost. I might even toss in a little bit to compensate you."

"Give me your phone," Anna said. She quickly typed in her phone number.

"Where's he coming from?"

"Jackson Prison. He gets out today. In fact, he might already be released."

"We don't have much time then. Go home and sit tight. I'll call you and give you the details soon."

"If you can do this, you're an angel."

"Angel? Ah no," he laughed. "By the way, what's your husband's name?"

"Gus. Gus Martin."

"Perfect!"

"Why?"

"I never met a Gus I liked. They all seem to be pompous bullies," Andras said, raising his glass of cheer. "To squashing Gus." The two clinked glasses, tossed down their remaining drinks, and slammed their glasses on the bar.

Andras exited out the back door of the bar with a strut in his step. He found Shadow and undid the leash. "Where's Envio?" he asked the beast, unusually euphoric. Immediately Envio stepped from behind his hideout.

"Right here, Sire."

"Excellent camouflage, pea brain. We need a handgun pronto quick. Find one with bullets. Nothing too big, just a gun. Now go!"

"But . . . but . . . but . . . it's broad daylight."

"And I need it in the next thirty minutes. I'm going to return Shadow to the museum and wait for you in the front yard of the child's home. Do not be late."

"As you wish, Sire," the imp said shaking his head. Luckily Envio remembered a large sporting goods store just south of where they stood. He hoped he could steal the gun without being seen and make it back to the house in time.

Andras pulled out his cell phone and dialed Anna. She took the call immediately.

"Hello," Anna said shaking.

"Listen carefully. Go home and shut every blind, pull all drapes shut and turn off all lights. Get a piece of paper and write this:

> Dear Andy,
> I'm babysitting for a friend at 31415 Gill Street.
> Come over if you'd like. Love, Anna.

"Tack it to your front door. When he comes, find a dark corner and sit stationary and don't make a sound. When he finally leaves, call this number immediately. Your problem will be solved within the hour."

"That's it?"

"It's all you have to do."

"I hope you're right."

"Goodbye, Anna. Enjoy your new life." Andras terminated the phone call and an evil smile stretched across his face.

Chapter 16

FIERCE LITTLE TIGER

NORI STOOD AT THE sink wiping dishes and putting them away in the cupboard. With Mary at the market, Joe at work, and Jonathan secluded in his room, a peaceful calm filled the home. The late summer breeze brought wafts of sweet honeysuckle through the kitchen window, and she could hear the rustling of the leaves with the occasional gusts. Sunlight dappled through the swaying backyard trees creating a kaleidoscope of shadows and shades of green on the backyard lawn. Peering through the kitchen window, she reminisced. *Kim, me, we come long, long, way, but it worth the pain and suffering to get here.* Content her tasks were done for now, she sat down at the kitchen table with her tea and gazed off into the afternoon's backyard world.

Jonathan sat in his room at his computer straining to create a diagram for his solar powered food manufacturing machine, while Emma slept comfortably on Jonathan's bed. From his research he solved the problem of designing an intake system which filtered plankton from the sea water, but now the plankton must be washed from the filters into a collection basin. High pressured jets of air were one option, but it would take more electrical power to run the compressor. How and where the extra solar panel would be affixed posed another problem.

Anna, the red-headed bar patron, ran room to room in her home doing as Andras instructed. All drapes and shades were drawn, and the lights put out. She locked and bolted all the doors and pinned the note to the front door as dictated by the strange man at the bar. Huddled on the floor in a dark corner of the room, glued to the tick-tock of her grandfather clock pounding out with the seconds of her heartbeat, Anna prayed. *If he finds me, he will return with vengeance against me.* She knew if he was coming, it would be soon.

Evangelina sat on her perch atop the Puro home, reveling in the beauty of her surroundings. She knew fall, her favorite time of the year, was at the doorstep and that meant the beginning of the school year. *Am I confident I can protect him in his new environment?* The thought led her to another concern she had with herself. Throughout the summer she experienced strong feelings indicating evil was approaching, but nothing ever materialized. She wondered, *Has my evil perception gone awry? This would be a terrible time for it to go on the blink.*

As the angel contemplated her short comings, Andras hid behind a tree across from the Puro home waiting for his minion, Envio. Closing his eyes and concentrating, he assumed the physical attributes of Anna. His replica proved uncanny, down to the braided, heart tattoo on her arm. As a final touch, the demon pulled down the knit cap and brushed the curly, red hair from his eyes. He smiled, congratulating himself on his devious plan. He became AndrAnna. Andras and Anna as one.

Envio arrived huffing and puffing from his trek. Bent over and unable to speak, he raced forward only to be met by a woman greeting him in a salty voice. "Hello, baby, my sweet Envio."

Envio jumped a foot high and ran off, screaming "Yikes . . . yikes . . . yikes" all the way back to camouflage behind the nearest bush until he heard the uncontained, wicked laughter of Andras.

"Meet AndrAnna."

Envio peered out from around the shrub, and slowly ventured toward AndrAnna, holding out her hands out to him.

"Now hand me the gun, you sissy imp."

Envio pulled out the stolen .38 caliber snub nose revolver and turned it over to his master, yanking it from him. He popped open the bullet chamber and gave it a whirl. The chambers were fully loaded. Stuffing the gun in the belt of his jeans, AndrAnna looked down at the little imp.

"You have done well, little one."

"Thank you, Sire." Envio puffed up his chest, proud to receive a rare compliment from his boss.

"Now return to the house and watch my beast. I'm sure he's hungry by now, so hopefully you can scavenge a snack for him on the way."

"As you wish, Sire." The imp turned and trotted away toward the museum.

Gus sat in the passenger seat of his friend's rusty, old truck as they drove the highway to Farmington Hills. With a cigarette dangling from his lips, he kicked back with his hands behind his head. After spending five years in prison, he celebrated his new freedom. He looked over at Brad, his oldest friend.

"Kinda funny."

"Whaddya mean, Gus?"

"We're driving down Freedom Highway. How appropriate. Let's stop at my old house and see what's cooking."

"You know that's asking for trouble."

"Whaddya mean?"

"Dude, she's got a PPO against you. You're going to break the law and you haven't been out but 45 minutes?"

"We'll merely drive by. No big deal. Simply wanna see the condition of the place. That's all."

"If you insist."

"Didn't she divorce you?"

"Yeah, and the greedy broad took me for everything I owned."

"Ya can't blame her."

"She deserved everything I gave her. She deserves more! I should . . . "

"Should what?"

"Nothing," Gus trailed off. They drove in silence the remainder of the ride. Brad navigated his truck down Highway 5 and exited at Farmington Road, travelling north to Gus's old house. Brad idled down the road, and slowed to a near stop as it approached the house. Gus hung out the window for a better look. Seeing the paper pinned to the front door, he ordered Brad to pull over.

"Are you out of your mind, Gus?" said Brad, reluctantly complying to the command.

"There's a notice on her door. She could be in foreclosure. I just want to check it out. I'll only be a minute."

Gus jumped from the truck and sprinted up the walkway to the porch and bent to read the note pinned to the door. He swiped it to memorize the numbers, then tore it into shreds, tossing it across the lawn before bounding back to the truck.

"Take me to Gill Street."

"What's on Gill Street?"

"Don't ask questions, just drive."

After a few minutes Gus pounded his fist on the dash and roared, "Who the hell is this Andy she's writing notes to?"

Brad put the car in drive and headed toward Gill Street. Being close, just a mile away, it took a mere few minutes, and they were there. Brad looked over to Gus.

"Where're we going?"

"Drive slow," Gus said quoting the address from memory. "31415 Gill Street."

Anna took a stealthy look out the front window and trembled as she watched an angry Gus with the same savage face that frightened her for years, take the note and rip it to pieces. Once she heard the truck squeal around the corner, she dialed Andras's number to give him a heads-up her ex would soon be there. She identified the truck they were driving. Although skeptical of his success, she wished him luck and expressed her gratitude. Once again, Andras assured her of his victory. After the demon ended the conversation, he stared at the Puro's house. *Showtime!*

He spotted the truck Anna described rolling down the street toward the home. He timed his approach perfectly, making certain Gus saw her moving across the front lawn toward the house's front door.

"There she is! Pull there!"

"Are you nuts? She's gonna call the cops, dingus."

"I don't care. I have to talk to her."

"No."

Gus bailed out of the rolling truck and began running toward whom he believed to be Anna. AndrAnna slowed her steps to give Gus a chance to gain ground on her. With Gus thirty yards behind, she began to run, screeching like a little girl.

Evangelina took this all in from her roost. The angel held off intervening, confused because the screaming woman gave off vibes more evil than the man chasing her. Finding the front door locked, AndrAnna, ran around to the back. Evangelina watched the scene transpire. *What in God's name is happening here?*

Rounding the corner of the house, AndrAnna surveyed the yard and concluded the solitary screen door an easy target. She blasted through, startling Nori standing at the sink. As the demon confronted the Asian woman, he shoved her to the floor. Gus, not far behind, ran through the same door, hot on her tail. He side-stepped Nori and entered the bedroom hallway to face a line of closed doors. Fueled by rage he blasted each door open in search of his Anna and her lover. At the last closed door in the hallway, Jonathan's bedroom, he slowly he turned the knob to eyeball inside. To his surprise, his AndrAnna was prepared for him, holding a snub-nose .38 with both hands in front of her, aiming at the door. "Get behind me, kid," she demanded of the young boy. Jonathan, so startled and confused, obeyed, uncertain this a smart move.

"Go ahead! Shoot! C'mon shoot. You've ruined my life; you might as well kill me while you're at it."

"Go away, Gus. Leave me alone. You're crazy!"

Emma barked non-stop at the intruder responsible for the ruckus. Gus looked down at the dog distracting his interaction and kicked at her. Undaunted, Emma sank her teeth into the convict's ankle. As the pain shot through his leg, his anger boiled over and he vigorously shook the dog off his leg, took a step and, without pause, dropkicked Emma against the wall. She laid motionless on the hardwood floor.

Returning to his former wife, he watched her trembling hands, which he took for weakness, and taunted her. "You don't have the guts to pull the trigger, do you?"

He stepped closer and closer until he stood directly in front of her. Cautiously raising his hand to the gun and with one finger, lifting the barrel to eye level he reached to take it from her softly saying: "Pull the trigger, Anna. I dare you. C'mon, do it! Do it!"

AndrAnna began to cry. Crocodile tears streamed down her cheeks. Gus cautiously moved forward to remove the gun from her hand and point the barrel at her. Jonathan, quiet until now, shouted from behind the woman.

"Nori! Mom! Help! You get out of my house!"

Gus laughed wildly at Jonathan's command. "Sorry sonny, with just one bullet I can get you both."

As Gus began to squeeze the trigger, AndrAnna dissolved into a gray mist. In an instant the demon was gone, leaving the unprotected boy to face a confused Gus's wrath.

Without warning, a bone-crushing thud erupted, and Gus contorted to the floor, revealing an angry Nori waving a cast iron skillet. The convict's eyes rolled back in his head as he passed out.

"You no come in my house and hurt boy," Nori said, intentionally heaving the skillet on Gus's face. "Jonathan, you okay?" She stepped over Gus sprawled on his face to embrace the boy.

"Not really. Where's Emma, I saw . . . " Before he could finish his sentence, his eyes flashed to where his beloved dog lay motionless. He broke from Nori to run to her side. Easing down, he gently patted her head and delicately raised her snout to look into her eyes. "Emma. Emma. Emma!" Instinctively, he knew she had passed away. He clutched his lifelong buddy, his protector, to his chest and whimpered, tears falling fast and hard.

Nori dropped to his side and massaged his shoulders and whispered, "I know, Jonathan. I know. It hurts." He threw his face deep into Emma's fur and gave way to heart-wrenching sobs.

"Poor Emma, sweet Emma," Nori choked.

An astral Evangelina stood holding Emma's essence in her arms and shared their grief. She transferred her thoughts to Nori. *Grieve not, Nori, and reassure Jonathan that Emma will be cared for in Heaven. She will have fields to roam and balls to chase. She was a brave and loyal soul and will forever live in the house of the Lord. One day you all will have the chance to play together again.*

"You safe now. We call police," Nori whispered.

Evangelina communicated with Nori once again. *I am here and proud of you and Jonathan. I will get to the bottom of this. It will never happen again.* She felt ashamed she wasn't the one to foil this invasion. *How could I allow two vessels of evil enter the home of the Glory Child? My evil detection is subpar. I should have intervened before they got to the back porch. What's wrong with me?*

Embracing Emma's spiritual essence, Evangelina ascended to a hearty limb of an oak tree overlooking the area. Lost in thought, she despaired over the loss of Jonathan's friend. *Oh, Emma, Emma. I'm so sorry.* Emma turned to lick the angel's comforting hands. Evangelina smiled down on Emma. *It's time to go, pup.*

In a flash, she was gone.

Chapter 17

Frustrations and Frying Pans

L UCIFER SAT ON HIS throne, ready to unleash his erupting rage. How is it that Andras can't complete a simple assignment? Disappointed by Envio's recent progress report he questioned Andras' true ability. He contemplated whether or not to send reinforcements. Until now the archduke was a proven and capable demon soldier. Lucifer did not want to usurp his authority, nor mar his reputation as archdukes tend to be sensitive about their personas and he didn't want to start a pissing match. Yes, he was the Emperor of Hell, but his rule proved less problematic to manage lower allies with those like Archduke Andras, one of his oldest and most loyal subjects, at his side offering his support.

"Lilith! Lilith! Where is that infernal woman?"

Lucifer bellowed his wife's name over and over until she breathlessly ran into the royal chamber, dressed in her floating, jewel-studded gown, gaudy headdress and bearing her sapphire-studded scepter in her right hand. She approached the Emperor's throne and stood before him scowling, obviously annoyed at his constant beckoning calls.

"What do you require, oh majestic one?" she asked facetiously.

"Recall the imp, Envio. I want an update on Andras' progress."

"As you wish, Sire."

"But wait. Why are you always dressed in such garish attire? You spend too much time pampering yourself. When I call, you must be ready to attend my needs."

"You know, Lucifer, I am the Queen of Hell, not your servant, nor your minion. I'm tired of dealing with your whims and wish you'd find another demon to do these menial tasks. I have better things to do."

"Silence, trollop! How dare you be so impertinent. You do as I say. Queen? You're just lucky I saved you from your Neanderthal, Adam."

Lilith huffed, turned on her heel and stormed out of the room trudging with angry steps down the hallway. As she passed a random demon, she swung her scepter and whacked him in the head, knocking him to the floor. Without looking back, she continued to travel until she entered the demon dispatch cavern. Quickly standing as she approached the desk, the clerk respectfully bowed to Her Majesty's presence.

"How can I serve you, Queen Lilith?"

"I need you to dispatch a speedy demon to retrieve the imp, Envio. Lucifer wants to speak with him."

"As you wish, my queen."

As Lilith took leave, the scratchy voice of the dispatcher could be heard calling out, "Demon to deliver . . . Who's next?"

Envio skipped sprightly into the door of the museum with a dead raccoon slung over his shoulder. The ravenous wolf lay splayed out in front of the fireplace. Hearing the front door open, the beast's ears perked. Sniffing the air, he knew dinner had arrived and charged the front door, nearly knocking the imp on his backside.

"Okay, okay, sit down hound and I'll give you your dinner. Give me a second here."

Given a little space, Envio threw the carcass into a corner of the living room and Shadow chased it down. While the demon wolf ripped the corpse limb from limb, the imp plopped himself down into Andras's favorite overstuffed chair and waited for Andras's return from his mission.

Sinking into its plushness and closing his eyes, the imp sighed, "Ah, I could get used to this." He imagined himself throwing a gala for his fellow imps, serving super-hot, mashed wasabi dressed up as a favored avocado dip. *That'd be an eye opener!*

With that image, his eyes popped up, blasting him from his dream state. Looking around, he noted a discarded cigar in the ashtray and a few inches of Scotch left in a rock glass. An image of himself dressed in a grand, red smoking jacket holding court over lesser imps, provoked him to bring the half-smoked cigar to his lips. His spiked teeth bit down and, as any lord of the manor might do, flicked the flame with aplomb, just as he had seen done many times by his master. He closed his eyes and slowly inhaled a deep drag. The effect, however, was not as he expected. A quick squeal gave into fierce sputtering and choking and he watched his entire "impness" turn a pale green. Reaching for the glass of Scotch, he took a swig to clear his throat. When the burning liquid hit his palette, he gagged and spit it from his lips. Looking down at the cigar and glass in his hands, he thought, *What does he see in these things?* Envio replaced the putrid items as he found them. When he looked up, a demon messenger stood before him.

"Envio, right?"

"Ah," he choked. "Right."

"Emperor Lucifer requires your presence immediately."

"What now?"

"I don't know, but I wouldn't keep him waiting."

In a flash, the demon messenger disappeared. *He wants to know if the boy is dead. I won't know until the archduke returns. I should wait.* Nervous, he jumped from the chair and paced the living room, hoping to delay his trip until Andras returned with good news and thereby clear his head from his jaunt into smokes and booze.

Personally, while his moods were generally nasty, he had never seen the Emperor angry, but his tirades were legendary. He did not want to become an anecdote about what not to do when Lucifer calls. He was torn, but he hoped if he waited, he could bring a success story to the Emperor. If not, he could expect to find himself somewhere on the seventh level of Hell, shoveling pig excrement.

The front door slammed open, rattling the glass in the front window, and Andras stomped through the entrance. Visibly upset, and muttering under his breath, he rushed to his chair and fell back into its comforting arms. He quickly downed the remaining Scotch and closed his eyes to wait for its calming effect. "Unbelievable!" He threw the glass against the fireplace spewing broken shards across the room.

Andras stewed over his second misfortune. He puffed on his stogie blowing clouds of smoke into the air. After a time, he calmed and Envio, feeling safer, stood before him and assumed a slumped-shouldered, subservient posture.

"Oh, great and powerful Archduke Andras, I have been called to Hell to report to Emperor Lucifer. What would you like me to report?"

"You little scuzzbag, are you kidding me? Can my day get any worse? I just got bested by an old Asian woman who spoiled my perfect plan. Incredible!"

"Then I should tell him the boy is still alive?"

Puffing his cigar, Andras mused for a time. "Tell the old goat we have the target on the run and should be finishing him off soon. Do not mention what happened today. If he asks, explain to him that using a surrogate to do the deed is making it extremely difficult, but I will find a way."

"As you wish, Sire."

Andras sat back in his chair, seized the Scotch, and chugged the remains from the bottle. "What a mess. I need a new stooge," he said, slinging the empty container at the fireplace just above Envio's head. Narrowly missing the imp, it crashed against the mantel and more pieces of glass rained down on the floor. Envio did an abrupt turnaround and ran off tiptoeing through slivers of glass.

I don't need this! I'm an archduke. It's not like any of this will improve my position. Sure, the reward and prestige would be nice, but my reputation is made. "That meddling angel and her Samurai shrew are making my life miserable. They gotta go."

Chapter 18

HEADACHES AND
FLASHING LIGHTS

M ARY TURNED DOWN GILL Street, heading home from the market, to see red and blue flashing lights a short distance ahead, appearing to be in the area of the elementary school. *Damn crazy teenage speeders getting out of school. Lock 'em up. Get 'em off the streets.* A police car, working its lights and siren raced past her.

She followed it with her eyes and realized it had stopped close to her home. "Oh, my God, please don't let it be my house. Not again."

Approaching her house, she saw three police cars and an ambulance sitting on her front lawn. Panicked, she pulled the car to a halt and jumped out, leaving the door ajar and charged towards a figure strapped to a spinal board being carried out by two paramedics, loading him into the ambulance. As she muscled her way through the crowd she demanded, "Who is he?"

"Sorry, ma'am, you need to stand back."

"YOU stand back, I need to see who's on the gurney. Outta my way; this is my house."

She barreled the paramedic out of her way. Satisfied she didn't recognize the man on the stretcher, she pivoted and raced to the wide-open front door.

"Jonathan, Jonathan! Nori! Nori!" she screamed, charging into the house, frantically visiting each room until she heard Jonathan yelling back, "In here, Mom. The kitchen." She stumbled in to see both Nori and her son standing at the kitchen counter talking with an officer who immediately moved to block her entry. "You can't go in there, ma'am."

"Try and stop me. I'm his mother! I live here!" With a hard shove, she moved him back and entered.

"Hey, Sarge, what do I do?"

"Let her in," said the sergeant rolling his eyes. " . . . and check the crime scene tape . . . Pardon me, ma'am, can't be too cautious. You must be Mrs. Puro?" he said, setting aside the preliminary report taken earlier from Nori and Jonathan.

"What's going on? Who's on the gurney?"

"Please have a seat. I'm Sergeant Frank."

Ignoring him Mary stumbled to her son and swallowed him into her arms. "My baby, my baby!"

"Mom, you're killing me." . . . *and embarrassing me,* he added to himself. "Let's just sit down as we're told."

"Mrs. Puro, do you know a Gus Martin?" the sergeant asked, diverting her attention from her son, clearly uncomfortable with her snakelike vice.

"Who?"

"Gus Martin."

"Never heard of him. Should I?"

"Well, he invaded your home and held your son at gunpoint."

"Oh, my God! Are you okay, Jonathan?"

"No, I'm not okay, Mom," Jonathan said, but offered nothing more. He pushed his chair back to avoid his mother's next round of crushing clutches.

"Well, thanks to your nanny here, she prevented an even greater tragedy. You won't ever see this guy again."

"What exactly happened? What are you not telling me?"

"This Gus fellow, fresh out of prison, charged into your home and held your son and a mysterious woman at gunpoint with a stolen gun. Nori, here, took him out with a cast iron frying pan. He'll have a headache for a month and most likely spend the next fifteen to twenty years back in prison, depending on the judge."

"Oh, my God! But why? Why *Jonathan*?"

"Yeah, why me? You're asking me?"

"That's a question you need to help us answer. Why an eleven-year-old?" asked Mary, not mentioning it was the same question everyone asked ten years ago. "Why a child?"

Do you know a curly, red-haired lady, about thirty-five to forty years old? She was wearing a knit, pull-down hat, jeans and a green plaid jacket. She's bit taller than Nori."

"No, can't say I do."

"She's another witness. She stood in front of your son, we assume to protect him from the intruder. Don't worry. We'll find her."

"Why was she here in the first place? How did she get in? How did she leave? This whole scenario is nuts."

"Give us time. We promise to keep you up to date on our progress," said Sergeant Frank gathering his materials and preparing to leave. "Our team of examiners will be here to conduct the bulk of the investigation. In fact, our crew is following leads as we speak."

Mary swooned after a quick flashback again took her to the day Jonathan was abducted years ago. Fingerprints. Evidence. Blood work. Police. Detectives. And now an unknown woman and a man named Gus surface to add to the confusion and anxiety of the past.

"Fair warning, you'll be contacted in the near future by the detectives assigned to the case. Be prepared for more questioning. Other than that, Nori, you're a bona fide hero, one tough cookie, lady."

"Oh, no big deal. Now I gotta clean pan," Nori quipped.

"Ah-ah-ah-" said Sergeant Frank, removing the pan from her hands. "Lucky for you, you won't need to clean it. We'll need this for evidence." He smiled, as if doing her a favor. "I'll be sure it's returned," he said.

"You be sure!" said Nori politely escorting him to the front door.

In the meantime, parked under a tree to avoid the summery sun, Blisdon relaxed in his cab, puffing a cigar and listening to the news on the radio. Today's workload was light; he had not gone on a run in over three hours. Pushing his seat to the reclining position, he laid back just as a fine rain began tapping on the cab's roof. He found the gentle peppering of raindrops comforting, allowing him a perfect moment to rest his eyes and revisit his time with Nori.

Three loud, harmonic tones preceded the radio commentator's voice, *"Breaking News! Police in Farmington Hills have arrested a Jackson State Prison parolee in an armed home invasion attempt merely hours after his release. It seems the maid fought him off with a frying pan. The suspect was rushed to the Ann Arbor Intensive Care Unit. Talk about having fried egg on your face! More after these commercial announcements."*

The words "maid fought off parolee," "fry pan," "Farmington Hills," clicked instantly with him. He doubted it was coincidental. Churning dust and gravel, Blisdon left his parking spot and headed to the Puro home and maneuvered himself in with the accumulating cluster of cars just in time as the innocent raindrops grew heavier and faster. He focused his eyes through to the increasing pummel of drops, hoping for a sign, anything that would signal life inside the home.

It was then Nori, ushering the sergeant to the front door, opened it to see the heavy storm.

"Oh, dear, me get you an umbrella," she offered, quickly recalling she had left hers in Blisdon's cab.

"Nah. I'm parked just down at the end of the driveway. I'm a speed walker."

She followed him out to stand under the awning of the porch for a brief moment. "I write down all I remember for you. Keep journal."

"Yeah, that's good. We'll keep that in mind." He quickly moved off the steps, mumbling on the way down. "She's an odd duck, but I like her."

She remained on the porch to watch him hightail to his car. Her true intent, however, was to identify Blisdon's cab, certain he would be in the crowd of vehicles and lookie-loos waiting for a sign that she and the family were safe. It wasn't long before she recognized her blue umbrella with red polka dots billowing above all others in the crowd, with Blisdon hoisted up on the running board of the cab, his smile shining through. She threw a deep nod his way, indicating she could see him. He grinned back. They'd connected.

As the chaos settled and Nori returned to Mary fidgeting at the kitchen table, wanting to believe today's event was random; it held no connection to Jonathan's kidnapping from years ago. That the two events could be linked, terrified her.

Mary folded her arms and took a serious look at both Jonathan and Nori. "Speak up. How long do I have to wait for details? You're leaving something out. Something crucial. What is it?" She studied her son's sullen face, looked around and thought to ask, "Where's Emma?"

After a long silence, Jonathan offered the statement dispassionately. "She's gone."

"What? What are you saying? Our Emma dead?" she asked, wondering why they'd taken so long to tell her. "How? What happened? Tell me step-by-step."

Jonathan turned to Nori and nodded for her to take over.

"Emma followed man to Jon's room, barking and attacking leg. She bark and bite him hard on leg. He kick her, but she no stop. She was fearless, giving me an opening to whack his head. That when he kick her hard and she hit wall. Me so angry, I use frying pan and thump him in head again. Jonathan ran to her, and she die in his arms. So sad to watch. She fight for Jonathan. I call Police."

"What happened to the woman?"

"Me no know. She must have run away while I knock crap out of man."

"Wow! Thank God you were there. You saved my Jonathan again."

"Yes Jonathan, but not brave Emma. It over in few seconds. At home, me fought soldiers. They shoot at me. This man no match for Nori. No one ever hurt our Jonathan."

Jonathan rose and reached for Nori. "What would I ever do without my Nori?" With that he lowered his head and left the room leaving heavy sobs trailing behind him.

"I know what you think, Miss Mary. The kidnapping. I think back, too."

Snapping up, she shouted. "My God, what am I thinking? Joe. I need to call Joe." She scrambled in her purse for her phone and waited. "Joe . . . ?"

Chapter 19

MASH POTATOES AND COLD NOSES

I T HAD BEEN THREE days and so far, the detectives had not visited the family as Sergeant Frank promised. Little came from Joe's calls to the police department other than they were making progress. They offered no reassurance the case was still open. The family had not been questioned outside the preliminary interview taken by the earliest officers. Media endlessly contacted them for updates. Nothing. Needless to say, the family felt out of the loop and Joe, in particular, felt inadequate as a parent and showed it with angry aggression: shouting, slamming doors, even swearing at both home and at work. Calls to the station went unanswered. Surely the department could offer *anything* to show their interest on the case. He was seeing his family crumble. What preyed on Joe most, however, was the ineptness of the department. His disdain for them went back to Jonathan's original unresolved kidnapping which he declared they bungled.

"Jonathan, dinner's ready." Mary called down the hallway, expecting another clash with her son over his recent resistance to food and almost everything else in his life.

Emma's death left a hole in every aspect of his life. He missed rolling on the bed with her, watching documentaries with her snuggled under his chin, sharing his joy when he made a breakthrough on his project, offering random sloppy kisses, slipping her food under the table. Theirs was a two-way dependency.

"I'm starving, Nori," she said, watching Nori place a heaping bowl of buttered mash potatoes in the center of the kitchen table next to the roasted chicken she was about to slice and quarter.

"Joe said he'd be home a little late; has to pick up something on the way. A surprise. We'll start without him if he doesn't show soon. He'll just have to eat it cold."

"Cold food never slowed Mr. Joe's appetite before."

"You right. We've all seen him eat whole cold pizza for breakfast."

"Jonathan! Get your butt in gear. The food's getting cold," Mary called out again and listened for his footsteps.

Turning to Nori she asked, "Is something wrong, Nori? You don't seem yourself today."

"I okay, saw old friend out in the crowd the day of crime. He help me out years ago," she answered, keeping it vague. "It made me remember how much I miss his company."

"I understand. You know, I'm still off school for a few more weeks. If you'd like to take time off to visit your friend, we can work something out."

"No . . . It no work out. Thanks."

"Jonathan! If you're not in this kitchen by the . . . "

At last Jonathan strolled into the kitchen, more somber than usual and took his place at the table. Nori scooped a spoonful of mash potatoes onto his plate, but he only stared at it.

"C'mon fella. You have to eat. Nori, cut him a piece of chicken. Jonathan, there's corn on the table too. Don't forget to get some . . . "

"Sure," he mumbled scooping a tablespoon of corn along with his potatoes.

"Eat up or you'll waste away! I know you miss Emma. She was loved by all of us. I miss her too, but she went to doggie heaven. She died defending her family; there is no nobler calling in this world. Think of her playing in the fields of heaven as we speak."

Jonathan closed his ears to his mother's clichés. He wanted to scream: *Stop. The more you talk, the more alone I feel living here.*

Finally, the arrival of Joe in the house, dropping a noisy box on the landing, and hustling to the table broke the growing tension.

"So, Joe, whatcha got there?"

"Just some tools they were throwin' out at the factory."

"Is that the surprise? You said you had a surprise for us."

"Yeah, I did. I meant the box of tools, they're relics, probably antiques and worth a lot of extra money for us. That's all. Man, I'm famished," he said, followed by a chorus of groans.

Jonathan lifted his plate to scrape off the remaining food into the sink.

"Hey, you, you're not finished. Sit down and keep me company."

"Can't Dad. Too busy."

"Oh, did I mention the little something else for you out in the car?"

"Me? What's the occasion?"

"No occasion. Another small surprise to pull you out of your funk and into the fresh air."

"*Really?!* Probably a Frisbee . . . I'm done. I'll be in my room."

Joe raised his hand to slam it on the table and said, "Freeze, partner. Sit down and clean your plate and drop the sarcasm."

Jonathan returned to the table to watch Joe take his time loading his plate with a chicken leg, a helping of mashed potatoes and corn.

Squirming, Jonathan proceeded to clean his plate, hoping to move his dad along. "Ahh . . . almost finished," he said, opening his mouth for all to see an empty hole.

"Great, Jon," said Dad, who grinned, continuing to leisurely chew the meat off the bone of his chicken leg, extending the suspense a little longer. "I'll be done shortly."

"Where'd you get it, Joe?" asked Mary, no longer a spectator.

"A guy at work was going to get rid of it and I thought it'd be perfect for Jonathan."

"Well, what is it?" asked Mary.

"What did I tell you? It's a surprise."

With that, Jonathan turned his chair away from the table and folded his arms, tired of the game playing.

Once everyone had eaten their fill, Joe excused himself and headed outside to retrieve a box and place it on the floor near the table. Strange squeals called out from inside. Mary gave Joe her "this-better-not-be-what-I-think it-is" look.

"Okay, partner, have at it."

Jonathan slid on his knees across the kitchen floor to the box and deftly removed its bindings. Pulling the flaps wide open, he jumped back as a black nose followed by floppy ears popped out of the box. Its long, pink tongue made quick ends to the mash potatoes stuck to Jonathan's chin.

"What are you thinking, Joe? I'm still allergic to dog dander and Nori doesn't need to vacuum dog hair all day!"

"Ah, that's the beauty of this dog. He's hypoallergenic, just like Emma, and doesn't shed. It has hair, not fur."

"Is he house-trained?"

Jonathan's reaction was not as his dad hoped. Instead, he stood and scrambled out the kitchen to his room, crying, leaving his parents puzzled.

It was Nori who understood his reaction. "Give him time."

Her comment enlightened Joe and he immediately followed his son to his slamming bedroom door and barged in. "Jonathan, I get it. I understand my mistake. It's not like I want to replace Emma. I loved her too. I wanted to distract your grief with something else. Nothing can replace your friend. Please understand, I meant well. Besides, Emma was getting tired and old. She was going to leave us sooner or later and that's the sad thing about our doggy-friends. You know she would want you to be happy again and that means for you to move on in honor of her memory."

Jonathan took a sustained minute to digest his father's words. "I know, Dad. I'm struggling. I need to get back to my project, but Emma was always an integral part of the process. In her way she cheered me on just by her company. Her emptiness has left my brain confused and too depressed to concentrate. That scares me. Her loss is unbearable . . . but maybe you're right; I can only try. So, what do you say we go meet that distraction in the kitchen."

"Sure."

Joe grinned, but inwardly chastised himself for not recognizing the depth of his son's grief. Emma was Jon's best friend, his only friend. It was like he was asking him to change allegiances. Now, however, he was grateful Jon was willing to give the new pup a chance.

The two returned to the kitchen with half smiles.

"As I started to say, in answer to Mom's question before we left the room, 'yep, he's house-trained and we have a young man to feed him, collect his doggie doo and walk him every day.' Whaddya say Jonathan, you want him?"

"We'll see. Trial run. In the meantime, I promise to feed and walk him."

"Doggie doo?" Joe questioned sternly.

"And doggie doo, Dad."

"Okay, then it's settled. I'd like you to meet Baillie, a soft-coated Wheaten Terrier wonder dog. Smart as a whip and faster than a bunny rabbit. Which reminds me. Outside you have to keep him on a leash at all times. He loves to run. Good thing our backyard is fenced. If you're going to take him somewhere, he has to be on a leash. Do you understand, Jonathan?"

"Aye, aye, sir."

Mary sat awestruck by the sudden mood transformation in the room, not understanding what had transpired and why she wasn't included.

Jon's demeanor softened as he held his new wiggly, face-licking buddy. Inside he cried. *Emma, You're still my girl, Kiddo. I won't abandon you for this interloper. That's for sure.*

"He's a beautiful dog," Mary conceded. "How old is he?"

"He's almost a year and has all his shots."

"Why would anyone give away a dog like this?"

"The owners are older and they're moving into a condo that doesn't allow dogs."

"That's too bad."

"It was for the best. They didn't have the energy for a dog like this, and as you can see, this dog needs a young man to take care of him and Jonathan is the perfect owner."

Baillie gave Jonathan a final lick before breaking loose and chasing around the kitchen table, sniffing for scraps of food and greeting each person in his new family. Joe reached down to sneak the dog a piece of chicken from his plate.

"Joe!" said Mary exasperated, "don't feed the dog from the table. You're worse than your son and set a bad example. And don't use your sleeve to wipe your mouth."

"C'mon Mary, it's his first day here."

"Yeah, and that's why we need to train him right from the start."

Here you go again, Ma. The mood buster. Anything that might make me happy.

Joe sat back and smiled as his son cavorted around the kitchen with Baillie, knowing his heart wasn't in it. He predicted his relationship with Jon would improve daily. As will his son's relationship with Baillee. "*They will be okay.*"

He hoped the security system he ordered would arrive soon. This new one was state of the art with many other perks. It cost a pretty penny—anything to protect his family. But dark and deep in his thoughts lived the mystery of the toddler Jonathan's kidnapping. The kidnappers were still out there. Never been caught. Periodically, he'd contact the detectives in charge of the first case; but there was never anything to report. Although years had passed, the mystery still bounded into his thoughts. *And now this.*

Chapter 20

FRUITLESS QUERIES

ROLLING UP HIS SHIRT sleeves, Detective Steve Sheppard entered the break room and announced, "Ready to work? " He poured stale coffee into his coffee cup proudly bearing a "Blue Pigs" sticker and spotted his partner. "Hey, Jonesy," referring to Detective James Jones, already at the table downing a hoagie sandwich and flipping the pages of the Gus Martin report. "What's this about a missing eyewitness? What do we know?"

Swallowing his mouthful he read aloud her description. "White female, thirty-five to forty years old, red curly hair, wearing a knit cap, blue jeans and a plaid shirt jacket."

"So, where do we find her?"

"That's just the point, the other two eyewitnesses claimed to not know her . . . never saw her before. Apparently, she ran off during the scuffle, just disappeared. Actually, they said she vanished into thin air. Whoosh. One is the minor boy the perp held at gun point and the other is an Asian woman who speaks broken English. She was too busy assaulting the offender with a frying pan. Claimed she had a brief flash of her before she vanished."

"Hmm. Shows Martin did time, huh? What was Martin in for?"

"Attempted murder, assault, spousal abuse."

"And he was just released from Jackson?" Sheppard questioned, taking a sip of coffee and wincing at its bitter taste.

"Yep, merely over an hour prior to the confrontation. What kind of an idiot do you have to be to get released and immediately commit multiple crimes?"

"Do we know how he arrived at the site; did he drive? Have help? Find his truck? How about the dame, did anyone see her car in the area? Anyone canvas the neighbors? Looks like we're behind schedule."

"Seems to be a crime of passion. Now who could anger someone enough to incite them to do such a thing? Sounds like we have to find Mrs. Martin," he said, dumping his coffee in the sink.

"Ex-Mrs. Martin," Jonesy corrected.

"Divorced?"

"Yep. Wouldn't you be if your spouse broke your jaw and put you in a coma?"

"Mr. Martin seems to have some violent tendencies, don't ya think? Where did he get the gun? We need to talk to him first," said Sheppard.

"The boy said our female witness had the gun with her and Martin managed to steal it away. We checked the serial number and found it reported stolen from a local sporting goods store earlier in the day."

"Well, it's what the kid said on the police report. We'll test for prints. Both should be on it."

"We need to grill the kid more thoroughly. Jog his memory. He's really our only witness. What all did go down?"

"Where's Martin now?"

"He's still in intensive care."

"Intensive care?"

"Like I said, the little spit-fire maid at the scene knocked him out cold with a cast iron frying pan. He's over at Ann Arbor Hospital on 12 Mile. I don't think we'll get much from him for a while."

"I like this maid already. Well, we have to give it a try."

"Finish your sandwich. We got places to go and people to see."

Jonesy took one last bite and tossed the rest in the garbage, followed by a long swig of Coke and slipping on his suit jacket covering his service revolver. He snatched the case file and chased after Steve out the door.

"Jonesy, you drive," said Steve, tossing him the keys. "I want to go over the file again. Let's check out the hospital first."

"Right."

The men drove the short ride to the hospital in silence. An on-duty security guard jogged over and addressed the men as they pulled the unmarked, black sedan to the inside semi-circle just outside the front entrance.

"You can't park here, gentlemen."

Sheppard flashed his badge and moved past the guard, ignoring his attempt to object. Jonesy followed close behind, smirking at the flummoxed guard standing with his hands on his hips. Entering the foyer area, the two approached the information desk. Sheppard tucked the file under his arm and leaned on the counter.

"Gus Martin?"

"I'll check it for you. He's in room 1022. No visitors allowed."

"Oh, I'm sure he'll be happy to see us," Sheppard said, flashing his badge.

"You can go right up, gentlemen. Use the elevators to the right."

They travelled to the tenth floor and followed the directional arrows to the room. A wooden chair sat outside the door, but where was the police officer assigned to guarding the suspect? Upon entering, they found an empty bed with the restraints undone and hanging from the guard rail.

"What the hell," Jonesy said aloud.

"Go check the nurses' station."

Sheppard surveyed the room noting any details which might help. Everything seemed in order. *Hmm, something's missing.* He plopped into the cushioned visitor's chair and waited for Jonesy's return and took time to flip through the case file again, looking for any new clues about this mystery woman. Certainly they'd have to bring her in for questioning. When Jonesy and a nurse entered the room, he closed the file and gaped.

"Where's Martin? What's going on?"

"Detective . . . ?"

"Sheppard, ma'am."

"As I told your associate, the gentleman you're looking for is in surgery. He'll be there for the next three to four hours, depending. Then he'll be kept in recovery for quite some time. You might want to come back tomorrow."

"Was he conscious? Did he say anything?"

"He's been in a coma since he arrived."

"I see. Well, thank you for your time. C'mon Jonesy."

The two exited the room and headed for the elevators, talking along the way.

"I can't wait to meet the maid, dude. She must have a swing like Miguel Cabrera," quipped Jonesy.

"She certainly put a lick on him."

"Do we arrest the maid for assault and battery?"

"Oh yeah, that'll go over like a lead balloon. I could see the headline now: 'Hero Maid Saves Boy. Arrested for Assaulting Ex-Con With a Fry Pan.' Be serious."

"I was kidding."

"Not funny."

"Chill, dude. Your underwear too tight?

"Let's go meet this maid. What's her name?"

"Nori . . . Nori Moon. She's an Asian refugee, granted political asylum about twenty years ago. She's a widow with a daughter in college."

A loud knock at the door startled Nori folding laundry on the kitchen table. She swiftly put down her chore and tiptoed to the front window to discreetly peek from behind the drapes. She scrutinized two men on the front porch holding badges. Deciding they posed no threat, she propped open the door with her foot and scrutinized their credentials as they introduced themselves as Steve Sheppard and James Jones.

"Are you Nori Moon?"

"Yes."

"May we come in and ask you a few questions? We need to go over your previous statements."

"Yes, but you take off shoes."

Sheppard nodded and said, "Of course," while Jonesy nudged Sheppard not too discretely and rolled his eyes.

Nori led the men to the kitchen table, moved the folded clothes, and motioned them to sit. "You like tea? Coffee?"

"No, ma'am. After reviewing the police report we see we have follow-up questions, if you don't mind."

"Okay, but what take you so long? Mr. Joe wait for your visit to the family. Afraid you bungle case."

Jonesy, about to jump out of his chair, only to be held back by Sheppard responded, "We're doing the best we can."

"You're best is slow as egg running uphill. It's been four days, and we no have contact."

"Yeah, yeah, ma'am, let's move on. We're here now. Did you see the woman with the red curly hair?

"Yes. But short time."

"About how old would you say she was?"

"I too busy looking at man with gun."

"Was she holding a gun?"

"When I get to room, only man. He point gun at her."

"Are you sure?"

"Positive."

"The boy, Jonathan," Sheppard said flipping through the file, "said she had a gun tucked in her waistband and pulled it out when the man entered the room. Is Jonathan here?"

"Joe and Mary told officers before, no want you talk to him without them here. Don't want him forced to talk about it . . . force him to remember watching his dog killed. They be here for that."

"I understand, but this is an important point we need to clarify."

"You no hear? No talk to boy without Joe and Mary. You go!"

"Ma'am . . . "

"No! You go now."

Detective Sheppard sighed and looked at Jonesy. He shook his head. "Well, when will they return?"

"No get home 'til 5–6 p.m. We eat dinner. We finished by 7 p.m. You call. You bring back Nori's frying pan? It cast iron."

Befuddled, Jonesy looked to Sheppard, "Frying pan?"

"They must have taken it for evidence. I'll see what I can do for you."

"Good. Now go!"

The two detectives collected their file and their shoes at the vestibule. Making their way out the door, they thanked her for her "cooperation." Once outside, they heard the front door slam shut, and locks click into place.

"She's one tough customer," said Sheppard containing a burst of laughter.

"I wouldn't mess with her. She may be short, but she is tough."

"We're lucky she didn't have another frying pan handy," he said, this time choking on his words.

After listening to the conversation, Evangelina floated atop the gable and watched the men leave. She, too, chuckled to herself and thought, *Nori is one unshakeable soul. Not even the police can make her crack. They don't understand they are dealing with things beyond their control, and I hope they never find out. If they ever come nose to nose with this demon, I don't see a good outcome.*

She maintained watch on her perch as lookout and combed the horizon. *You're out there . . . somewhere. I will find you and dispose of you.*

Such a cowardly demon, but why would I think better of you? The last thing you'll see on this Earth will be my blade piercing your heart.

Chapter 21

BUDS, SEAWEED, VIDEOTAPE, AND STAKEOUTS

THAT NIGHT HE RETURNED to his room. And, per usual, sat on his swivel chair in front of his computer and punched a few keys, opened the document and stared. While believing in haunts does not coincide with his work as a scientist, he succumbed to the possibility when he thought he heard Emma snoring at his feet. Holding Emma's photo, he remembered his dad's comment, which he discredited as trivial, but *may* have perhaps a possibility of truth. "Emmie, help me. Is Dad right, do you want me to be happy again?" Incredibly, her photo, the same photo he looked at daily for years, took on a new expression. Or was it his imagination? She looked happy. "It's true, you *would* welcome the company, even enjoy, a new pup. He'd be like a rambunctious little son to you. The two of you would have my back."

Was it true or only an imagining of what he wanted to be true?

Frustrated by his depleting desire to continue on with the research so important to him, he gave in. The next morning, after breakfast, Jonathan made the slow trek to his room with Baillee under leash.

"Well, Baillie, kid, let's do this." He lowered himself to his knees to hold Baillee's jowl in his hand. Looking directly into his eyes he lectured in a low, commanding voice: "Be a good boy, buddy. And remember, this is Emma's room."

Jonathan's hands trembled as he twisted the knob. Holding his breath, he opened the door to his sanctuary to be met with the same old lonely gloom he'd been despairing over. After the two stepped across the threshold Jonathan looked down at Baillee wagging his tail and looking up at him as if for further instructions.

"Okay, let's go." Jonathan proceeded to lead this new outsider around the room, past a corner of Emma's toys, a table of her photos, a stray bone. With each stop, Baillee sniffed, wagged his tail and moved on without disruption. Oddly, he remained calm, almost reverential alongside his master.

That is until he was shown the enlarged photo of Emma. Before Jon could hold him back, Baillee reached out and licked the glass, followed with a short bark.

"Okay, let's back up and turn around, there's more." And as he began to explain Emma to him, the dog sat complacently. "Sure, boss, I get it." He listened with seeming interest, that is until he spotted the stuffed replica of Emma on Jonathan's bed. It was then Baillee turned and, without pausing and straining at the leash, galloped towards Jon's bed, skidding to a stop. He reached his head up over the edge and whined.

"Not yet. We'll get you your own toy."

But Baillee was having none of that. He wanted Emma's replica. He barked continuously to show it.

Jon tried to explain Emma to him, and while the dog stopped barking and sat only momentarily complacent before bursting out in a combo of 'bark, bark, whine, whine, bark.'"

Jon pulled him away, ready to exit the room until Baillee broke off to land on Emma's old bed, still on the ground next to Jonathan's, and refused to move.

OK, I don't believe what I'm thinking, and I'll never tell a living soul about this, laughing out loud at himself. *But am I to believe the ridiculous theory of re-embodiment? Soul migration? Rebirth?*

At the end of the day, he had no doubt about inviting this rowdy pup into his room. *Knowing Emma, she'll enjoy the kerfuffle and approve of the new energy Baillee would bring into his life.*

With the Baillee/Emma issue behind him, he worked diligently every free minute to make up for time lost. His eyes watered continuously from straining at the computer screen as he delved deeper into researching the minimum daily requirements for adult food intake. His proposed machine could efficiently produce the minimum protein and fat requirements from the phytoplankton processed. The carbs and fiber could be supplied by the different seaweeds available, but how would he collect them? If he couldn't solve this problem, he would have to restrict the placement of his invention to places where seaweed grew plentiful. He decided to research different types of seaweed and their locations. He chuckled to discover the most common edible seaweed was "Nori."

Bursting with this new information, he had to tell somebody. He swiveled around in his office chair to find Baillie on his bed, cuddling with the toy replica of Emma and chewing a rawhide bone.

"Baillie, wanna laugh?"

The dog cocked his head and perked his ears.

"Arf . . . arf." He stood and barked in response to Jonathan's enthusiasm, his tail now wagging.

"Our favorite nanny's name translates as 'Seaweed Moon.' I can't wait to tell everyone at dinner. They're gonna laugh."

Jumping from his chair, Jonathan tackled Baillie and the two rolled around atop his bed. The dog playfully fought back, mouthing Jonathan's arms and hands. The spirited bout culminated when Jonathan squeezed the dog tight, and Baillie licked his face. The two had become the best of friends.

Detectives Sheppard and Jones studied the sporting goods store before heading to the handgun counter. The clerk behind the counter immediately addressed them.

"How can I help you gentlemen?"

Flashing his badge, Sheppard said, "It was reported a snub nose .38 caliber pistol was stolen from you this week?"

"Yeah, and for the life of me I can't figure how they did it."

"What do you mean?"

"One second the gun was in the showcase and the next second it was gone."

"Who was in the vicinity of the gun case?" asked Jonesy.

"That's what is really weird. No one."

"Where were you when this happened?"

"I was at the other end of the counter helping a customer."

"Did you leave the vicinity of the counter at any time?"

"No, I didn't need to go into the back, nor did I leave the counter during my shift."

"Was the door to the display cabinet locked?"

"It was, but the customer asked to see another model next to it in the case and I unlocked it."

"Did you happen to see or notice a curly, red-headed lady, thirty-five to forty, wearing a knit cap, blue jeans and a plaid shirt coat anywhere in the store?"

"No, I can't say I did."

"Do you have video surveillance of this area?"

"Yes, sir. I have it in back."

"Can we check your footage from that day?"

"I already have it queued. Come in the back and I'll play it for you."

The three men walked into the back room and sat next to a monitor. The clerk reached over and hit the play button. The men kept a keen eye on the footage focused on the display case. In utter disbelief, they watched the back of the case slide open and "Poof," the gun vanished before their eyes. No human, nor shadow of a human, appeared in the frames. They ran the sequence over and over but could not identify anybody stealing the gun. It seemed like magic, one second there, the next gone.

"The tape has to have been altered," concluded Sheppard.

"I'm sorry, but it hasn't left the store and if you look at the time stamp on each frame, it runs continuous."

"How the hell can that be true? Do you have a ghost in the store?" Jonesy asked.

"I don't know either. The only explanation I can figure is we have something supernatural going on in the store."

"That's really creepy," said Jonesy.

"So, you found the gun in the hands of a crook? How in the Hell did he get it? What about prints?"

"It's what we're investigating. The fingerprints don't match our alleged thief. Right now, the gun's sitting in the evidence room. Don't worry, you'll eventually get it back."

"Well, as far as we can see, there is a conundrum. We'll take your tape into evidence, let the tech guys figure it out. I'm certain they'd find it interesting, even perplexing. If you ever see a redhead with curly hair in the store please give us a call," said Sheppard. "Here's my card."

Envio hefted the dead raccoon across his shoulder and proceeded down the road toward the museum. Having returned from Lucifer's throne room where he suffered a severe tongue lashing, he wanted to relax for the night. But he still had to feed the ravenous beast and report Lucifer's outrage to Archduke Andras. Relaying Lucifer's message was not going to be fun. The old barn never seemed so good to rest his skinny bones. Arriving at the museum he plopped the carcass on the front porch and took a moment to breathe deep and steady himself before taking on another abuse. He thought to himself, *This too shall pass.*

Envio gathered the dead raccoon from the porch and entered to find Shadow pulling on his chain and howling vigorously. As he dropped the carcass in the vestibule, Andras shouted out.

"Well, it's about time, my useless idiot!"

"I brought dinner for Shadow."

"As well you should. Get in here. What did our Emperor have to say?"

"He was angry, to say the least." Envio slowly entered the front room to face his master. "Uh, I never saw him turn such colors before. He sarcastically wanted to know if you might need some help. I told him you had everything handled and he should expect you to complete your mission soon."

"Good . . . good. Hmm. Now, I want you to stake out the boy's house. I want to know everyone who comes and goes. Don't stare at me. Go!"

"Now? I was hoping I could rest a bit before . . . "

"SILENCE! Rest? There is no rest for puny imps. Go!"

"Bu . . . bu . . . but I'm an imp."

"Imp? How about a shiftless shrimp. Get your behind in gear and get out the door or I will . . . "

"As you wish, Sire."

"But hold it Dum-Dum. What about Shadow? Are you going to let the carcass rot in the vestibule?

"No, Sire."

Envio assumed the proper nighttime camouflage and shuffled out the front door of the museum, plodding forward to the Puro home to stake himself out in the bushes lining the front of the house. Once again, he mutated himself to blend with his new surroundings. Confident he could not be detected, he kicked back, closed his eyes and drifted into visions of the woodland where he was born, recalling the freedom and simplicity of those bygone days where mischief, jokes, and naughty pranks were considered, as with all imps, the lifeblood of his life. By inhibiting them, he was afraid of waning away. Envio missed those days before working for Lucifer.

Of late, his dreams focused on his first and only love, remembering the day he first saw her. It was down by the little creek that flowed through their home in the forest. He waved to her, but she blushed and ran away. He spent days tracking her down. It was only this focus and determination that led to finding her under a towering sunflower where she busily gathered its seeds. He eyed her from a distance and quietly wound his way through the tall weeds to finally take the opportunity to introduce himself.

Alerted to the sound of footsteps and crackling of bramble, she turned to face a stranger. Her fear caused her to stagger back and fall into a patch of prickly nettle.

"Oh, my," she said.

"Stop, I mean you no harm." He introduced himself with a bow and flourish. "I'm Envio. I saw you gathering seeds and thought maybe I could help. It looks like fun."

She stood silent.

"Actually, I've been wanting to meet you since way back, when I saw you picking berries in the forest. You looked so serene."

"My name is Freya. Thank you for your offer." Her face blushed as she whispered the words.

Taking her words as an invitation to help, he moved closer to retrieve her basket from the ground.

As the two talked and laughed, Envio revealed his long-standing crush on her and how he often returned to the creek where he first saw her.

But the budding romance waned once Envio learned of Lucifer's message to all his followers: Hunt for the Glory Child. A decade ago, he took it upon himself to improve his lot within the community of demons. It became his personal quest to find the toddler, believing that once found, he could report it to the Emperor and return to his blissful woodland with status. Freya would see him as a hero. But that was not to be as he was then assigned to Andras, an opportunity and detriment, but not something one could refuse. Lucifer does not accept "No."

His one fantasy was that this adventure be over soon, and he would return to his home. He prayed he could find her again and she was free. It was the single ambition urging him forward, giving him hope. Imps are born without gender and must earn their place in the woodlands. It took many years for him to earn a gender, and he hoped Freya was still there waiting for him.

The screen door banged, startling the imp out of his nighttime dreams, into a sunny day. He knew he had overslept when he saw Nori walking to the street to retrieve the late morning mail and return to the house. The remainder of the day was long and uneventful with one exception. After settling himself comfortably into his lair, he spotted a family of toads at his side, playing in the dirt. Hooray! This energized him to prank. He dug a narrow, deep hole in the ground and layered nettle needles at the bottom. He scooped the happy toads into the nasty nest of nettles and sat back to watch them struggle to climb out. They looked up at him with pleading eyes. Usually a prank such as this brought him joy. But not today. Instead, he sighed and lifted them gently to their freedom. "Sorry, guys."

Chapter 22

WHITE CHILI AND
RED-HEADED LADIES

MARY PULLED INTO THE driveway, popped out of the car and pulled her bulky bookbag and files from the backseat. She struggled to shut the car door and headed to the back porch stairs. The new school year hadn't started, yet the preparation for the work ahead overwhelmed her. The daily load of preparation and bookwork were collateral for the job she loved, but sometimes the paperwork asked more from her than actual teaching. She entered the screen door and plopped her load down in the vestibule. Baillie tore around the kitchen corner and bounced off Mary, causing her to stumble. Scooping the puppy, she moved into the kitchen area.

Nori looked up from the stove and smiled at seeing Mary cradling the pup. "Miss Mary, looks like you have a special buddy. Do you need my help?"

"No, I'll come back for these after dinner. Whatever it is, it smells delicious!"

"Me try something new . . . white turkey chili," Nori said stirring the pot.

"Oh, Joe is going to love it."

"Me hope so."

"Where's Jonathan?

"In bedroom."

"Did he walk the dog today?

"Yes, twice."

"It's good we got Baillie. He has no choice but to go outside."

"Yes, but Nori always follows. Make sure he okay."

"How long 'til dinner?"

"When Joe gets home."

"Great! I'm going to take a load off my feet. Maybe nap until dinner. Lord knows I need it."

"Detectives come today. Want to talk to Jonathan. I say 'no.' Wait for Joe and Mary. They come back after dinner."

"Really? I have so much to do today to prepare for the new school year. I guess it's no nap for me."

Mary released the puppy and trudged back to the pile left in the vestibule and dragged it across the kitchen floor. "I'll be in the living room. Call me when Joe gets home."

Nori smiled and returned to stirring the pot of chili with her wooden spoon. As she stirred, she thought about Mary. *Miss Mary work so hard. She such good teacher. Students lucky to have her. I am truly privileged to be here with this family to care for. Plus, I can still fight demons and kidnappers. Each day is a blessing. Life funny thing.*

Nori hummed an old Asian song her grandmother sang to her. Glancing at the clock, she knew Joe would be coming through the door soon. With the table set and side dishes steaming, Nori turned off the flame, began ladling chili into bowls and placing them on the table. With the last bowl filled she entered the living room and found Mary fast asleep on the couch. *Poor thing,* she thought. She gently shook Mary's shoulder until she awoke. "Time to eat," she said.

Groggy, Mary bobbed up and rubbed her eyes. "What time is it?"

"Joe be home any minute."

"Oh God, I must have passed out there."

"You needed rest. Time to eat."

Mary flopped back on the couch and Nori left to call Jonathan to supper. She rubbed her head looking at her work spread across the coffee table. *So much to do and so little time until the school year begins.* One way or another she would get it all done. That's not what worried her. What kept her awake at night was how her Jonathan would adjust to being at the high school. She worried how the other students would treat him and whether or not he would make friends. Although he said friends didn't matter to him, Mary knew in her heart she didn't want him to lead a lonely life. She hoped this new environment might produce someone Jonathan could bond with.

Shuffling into the kitchen she saw the table set with steaming bowls of chili, but no Jonathan. "Where's my boy," she asked Nori.

"Still in room on computer."

"It's okay, Nori, I'll get him."

She quietly knocked at his door and waited for a response. She knocked again, but he still did not answer. Mary opened the door, not surprised to find her son hunched over the computer, engrossed in something or other beyond her understanding, or interest for that matter.

"Whatcha doing, kiddo?"

"I'm finishing my proposal to submit to Dr. Pravir Singh, Director of the Government Global Food Research Agency, for funding. If they adopt my idea there won't be starving people in the world."

"What?"

"Yep, my design here will produce eight-ounce bars of edible nutrition which contain everything humans need to sustain themselves on a day-by-day basis and, once in operation, will produce 180 bars per minute. Daily, it's over a quarter million bars per day. The cost of making these bars would be minimal, but the making of my machine could possibly be a million dollars."

"You're asking this doctor for a million dollars?"

"A small price to pay for a solution to world hunger."

"You never cease to amaze me. But dinner is ready. Your doctor can wait an extra half hour to receive your proposal."

"But Mom . . . Mom . . . "

"NOW, mister. Dinner's getting cold. It's not fair to Nori," Mary said, cutting him off.

While proud of his intellect and his capacity to analyze facts and use new information in positive ways with a promise to end world hunger, she still wished for a more typical boy. A boy, like her own brothers, who loved sports, fishing, hunting and the outdoors. *We don't get to choose our children's likes and dislikes*, she thought.

Reluctantly, he closed out the computer and shuffled behind his mom to the kitchen. He folded his arms and slouched into his chair to make known he was disgusted by the constant interruptions. Looking down at his bowl of chili, he wrinkled his nose, wary of the new dish. "What's this stuff?"

"This 'stuff' is chili," said Nori.

"Chili is red and spicy. This is white and creamy. Are you sure this is chili?"

"It chili. *Taste.* You like," she said, crossing her arms, priming for criticism.

"Lifting the bowl for the smell test . . . "

Mary spoke up. "Jonathan! Your rudeness is unnerving. People don't like . . . "

"Yeah, yeah, sorry," he said, scooping a spoonful to his mouth and swallowing it in a gulp. After letting it sit on his tongue, he smiled up at Nori. "This is really good as always, Nori. You've done it again!"

"Thank T.V. food show."

The back door opened, and Joe rushed in to drop his lunch pail on the sink, wash his hands and eagerly join the table. "What do we have here?"

"White chili."

"This is new."

"Try it, Dad. You're gonna like it."

"Um, dis is wunderbar." The family continued to gorge on this delightful meal until everyone sat back stuffed and satisfied.

"May I be excused. I have to finish my proposal for Dr. Singh."

"I forgot to tell you the detectives come tonight. Want to ask questions of Jonathan, family too."

"What time?" asked Joe.

"Half hour or so," Nori said.

"I was going to relax," said Joe.

"JOE, you've been crabbing they don't communicate and now they do and you bi . . . , um. Grouch," Mary said frustrated.

"I clean. Hope they don't stay long."

The family retired to their corners of the house while Nori hurriedly washed the dinner dishes. As she finished wiping the chili pot, she heard a knock at the door and hurried to the door to greet Detectives Sheppard and Jones. Baillie charged around the corner and bounced off the leg of detective Jones, pushing him off kilter.

"Baillie, down . . . Ignore him, he's just a puppy."

"Cute puppy," said Sheppard, smirking at his partner so addled.

"Gentleman, come in. You hungry? Take off shoes."

"Thank you, but no Miss Moon."

Once the men reached down and slipped off their shoes, she directed them to the kitchen table. "I get folks. You sit."

Nori retrieved the family, and they gathered around the kitchen table. Mary, a bit perturbed, sat down and scowled at the two men.

"Mrs. Puro, you look unhappy. Is something bothering you?"

"Well, I have a lot to do and this unscheduled meeting we're having here is cutting into the little time I have. Besides, you guys should have contacted us days ago."

"We'll try to be brief."

"My first questions are for you, Jonathan. Young man, when the woman entered your room was she carrying a weapon?"

"I didn't see anything at first, but when the man came in, she pulled a gun out of her waistband."

"Did it look like this one?" Sheppard produced a photo of the gun.

"Yep, that's it. I remember because I thought to myself it was too small to stop that big guy."

"When the woman fled your room, how did she get out?"

"I don't know. She was here one second and gone the next. I never saw her leave. All I remember is this sparkly haze she left behind, and the man standing there with the gun aimed at me."

"Sparkly haze?"

"Yeah, kinda like glitter floating as mass in the air and then dematerializing."

"Hmm . . . Are you making this up?"

"Excuse me detective, but my son doesn't make things up."

"Hmm . . . I apologize, son. But it sounds so . . . . . . well . . . weird, almost mystical."

"Yeah, I agree with you," offered Jon, "but it happened, I assure you."

"Well, we have the perp and we have the gun. What we don't have is the lady who invaded your home. If you recall anything else about the red-headed lady please call us. Mr. and Mrs. Puro, we appreciate your time. I'm certain we'll be back at a later date with follow-up questions based on what we've learned. Promise to have more information for you, too." After thanking the family again, they exited.

The detectives paused to chat on the stoop outside the door, and lingered while Jonesy lit up, and inhaled this welcome breath of smoke. "Ahhh . . . "

"It's odd those parents don't seem alarmed . . . ask more questions of us."

"I agree, I guess. But that's it for me tonight. Gotta put my brain to bed."

Envio's pointed ears struggled to listen as the two began their walk to the car.

"Drop me off at Barney's tavern. I need a drink, a strong one. Maybe two. How about you?"

"Nah, sorry, the wife's got plans for me tonight. If I don't go, my life will be miserable for a week."

"Fine, I'll get a cab home."

"Anyway, do you buy the boy's account?" asked Sheppard.

"No, sounds like a fairytale he heard or a dream. I wish we could put him in an interrogation room and do a thorough interview."

"Not going to happen without parent's consent."

Envio's head popped up, "The archduke is going to love this. Yip! Yip! I've got to get back and tell him."

The two slipped into the car and Jonesy's phone rang. He fumbled in his pocket to retrieve a call from the precinct officer stationed as security at Martin's hospital room. Jonesy took the call and listened intently.

"Got it. Okay. Thanks for the update." Jonesy ended the phone call and turned to Sheppard. "Seems our perp died on the operating table. Are we going to charge the maid with manslaughter?"

"Not our call. That's a prosecutor's decision. Looks like we're done here for now. Tomorrow we interview Mrs. Martin."

Chapter 23

CRYING IN HIS BEER

A S WAS HIS ROUTINE, Andras sat back in his overstuffed chair and held his glass of Scotch eye level, admiring the glint of the golden liquid. He reached down and picked his lit cigar from the side table and took a puff. Laying his head back, he puffed out smoke rings one after the other. He was going to miss this comfort when his assignment was over, but it served as a relaxing break from his normal agenda of assassinations.

As his heavy eyes began to flutter shut, Envio blasted through the door and burst his relaxation bubble. The demon canine jumped to his feet and began to bark at the intrusion. Startled, the archduke dropped his glass of Scotch which shattered on the wood floor.

"What in Lucifer's name possessed you to come through my door without knocking?"

"I never had to knock before!?"

"Well, you knock from here on out, you brainless imbecile!"

"As you wish, Sire."

"You better have good news."

"Indeed, I have. I believe I have identified your next stooge."

"And who might that be?"

"Well, from the aura I detected, he's a troubled soul and, the best part, he's required to carry a gun at all times. Plus, even better, he's angry with the kid."

"Interesting . . ."

"And he has official access to the boy."

"Really?"

"Where would I find this troubled soul?"

"Last I heard from his conversation, the same bar you found your Martin gal. And he's there now."

"Excellent!

"You should go. His name is Jonesy."

"C'mon Shadow, looks like you need a walk."

Jonesy threw back a shot of Irish whiskey and chased it with a hefty chug of beer. Slamming the empty bottle down next to his building collection of dead soldiers, he wiped his mouth with his sleeve, and called out to the barkeep.

"Bring me another, Barney!" The bartender reluctantly poured another shot and pulled a beer from the cooler, setting both down. Standing back, he wiped his hands on his towel and shook his head in concern for his favorite regular.

"You know, Jonesy, you can't drink her back into your life, son."

"Mind your business, Barney."

"I'm simply saying that drinking yourself into a stupor won't change the fact she left you."

"I said mind your business!"

Before the conversation could continue, Barney looked to see the stranger enter the establishment once again and stand at the entrance. The few patrons paused their drinks to gawk at this gentleman, suited up in a black velvet suit jacket over a black t-shirt. His matching black hair, slicked back and shiny, added to his appearance of a mobster straight out of a gangster movie. Andras had arrived. With suave nonchalance, he stepped to the bar and flagged Barney for a Scotch. Casually examining the room, his eyes rested on Jonesy, head down, peeling the label from his beer bottle. Feeling the man's eyes upon him, Jonesy looked up with a scowl that gave way to an anger.

He threw back his whiskey and guzzled the beer down. "Whaddya looking at?"

"Barkeep, bring this man another," Andras called out. "He's obviously a man in pain."

"Pain? You don't know the half of it."

"Wanna tell me about it?" Andras asked, casually making his way to the empty stool next to his next stooge. "Confession is good for the soul."

Jonesy let loose a long, loud belch and laughed. "She was my life. We were going to get married. Settle down. Have some kids. Buy a house. All that good stuff. She left me. She up and left me. For what? For what?"

"Well, you tell me. For what?"

Jonesy hesitated a moment. He scratched his ear trying to again make sense of what she said to him. He rubbed his eyes and then blurted out, "She said I wasn't Christian enough. Can you believe that? Considering the scum of the Earth I deal with on a daily basis, it's a miracle I even believe in God."

"It's a hard pill to swallow."

"Sshtoopid bitch, *hic*."

"It's better you found out now rather than later, after you've invested years of your heart, time, and money."

"Th . . . thas right."

"Well, young man, I wish you better luck in the love department."

Andras raised his glass to the troubled detective and finished his drink. Having identified his mark, he smirked, *This is going to be easier than I thought*. He threw money on the bar and exited the establishment.

"C'mon boy, we have a new lackey to turn into our henchman," Andras said with joy in his voice as he untethered his canine beast."

The two strolled along the sidewalk back to the museum, Andras mulling his strategy. "You know, Shadow, he's in emotional distress. I scanned his mind and he has a lot of things he's worried about. It's not just his girlfriend leaving him. The guy has trouble at work. He's been suspended twice for insubordination and wavering from official protocol. He's a wannabe cowboy. He hates rules. He hates to be told what to do. My mark wants to get things done by any means possible. He's just the man for the job."

Shadow barked and wagged his tail. "Com'on fella, I'll take you back and order the imp to bring you food."

Envio met Andras leaving the museum, just in time to be told to fetch Shadow's dinner. "I'll be back later, after I do reconnaissance around areas the kid may visit, like his school. My new plan may take a while to orchestrate, but it'll be, shall I say, 'bulletproof,' once it's set up.

"Aye, Aye, sir." Envio entered the museum with his bag of carrion and slammed the door shut. Weary from his recent tasks he collapsed in the overstuffed chair Andras considered his throne. Shadow eagerly approached him, tongue out, panting, and drooling in anticipation of his next meal. He clawed at Envio's leg to reach the bag. The imp smacked his paw to keep him at bay. In retaliation, Shadow gave deep growl behind his sharp fangs and nipped at his food-finder's fragile fingers.

"Ow, you sack of pig excrement," Envio yelled, pulling his hand away. "You ungrateful, ornery canine!"

The scolding did nothing to deter the beast and he continued to claw furiously at the overmatched imp. Finally, Envio pulled the dead animal from the bag and threw it into the furthest corner away from the chair. Shadow galloped to the carrion and began his feast.

"After all the times I worked hard to find this imbecile his dinner, he still attacks me? He needs to behave when I deliver him dinner." The imp fell back into the chair and closed his eyes. He was totally exhausted from the day's tasks. He rubbed his eyes and when he opened them, he spied the fifth of Scotch he procured for Andras the night before, sitting on the side table. *I'll calm that cretin canine down and show him who's boss*, thought the chuckling imp. *I'll tame his bum right down.*

Envio reached for the Scotch and uncorked the bottle. One sniff and he cringed at the odor. *I don't know how the boss drinks this stuff.* The devilish imp prowled to the beast's watering bowl and poured a heaping splash into the dish. *Hope this is enough to do the trick. If not, I'll whack him with the bottle between the eyes.*

Envio returned to wait and watch Shadow finish his meal, certain the stuffed, thirsty wolf would drag himself to his bowl and drink a mighty share. It took but a few moments before the beast began to sway. He took a few clumsy steps to sit up, but his front paws slid out from under him, leaving the lump of fur splayed across the floor. Envio tiptoed to the prone body, hoping his foe he had passed out.

"Well, that seems to have done the trick. Hmm," he said, contemplating his next move.

Returning to the table, he retrieved the Scotch bottle and, laughing back to his comatose nemesis spread out across the floor, he doused him with the golden liquid. Then, for the pièce de résistance, he tucked the uncorked bottle under Shadow's paw. Standing back, he framed the scene from the door. This is what Andras would see when he returned. He couldn't wait for his prank to come to fruition. *Poor Shadow—I tried to befriend you! When Andras sees this, he's gonna bust your behind. I don't want to be anywhere near when he returns. I'll be at the barn.* He whooped continuously as he returned to his shelter, pleased Shadow would get his comeuppance.

Chapter 24

BUBBLE BOUNCERS AND GYM

"Hurry, Jonathan, you no want to be late first day," Nori called, heading out the front door to her faded red Honda. Jonathan and his backpack came rushing out the front door and flew off the porch. Noting he neglected to shut and lock the front door, she remained stationary and glared, her hands on her hips.

When he arrived at the passenger door and found it still locked, he asked, "I thought we were in a hurry?"

"We go after you lock front door. You smart, but absent-minded professor."

"Oh shoot," Jonathan said racing back to secure the lock. "Good grief," he said, plopping into the front seat. "I'm exhausted already."

"You excited?" asked Nori, turning the engine.

"I hope it's everything I've thought about. No more dumb kids who only talk about Facebook, Instagram and YouTube. Hopefully there'll be kids who talk about science and math."

"I certain you not be disappointed. Many smart people in high school."

"Well, at least the subject matter in class won't be baby stuff."

"Just try to fit in. Not so uppity."

"Today is freshman orientation, so I don't think I'll meet any of my classmates today. Remember today is a half day, so please come get me at noon."

"Me remember."

The little red Honda Civic pulled in front of the high school and idled while Jonathan gathered his backpack and papers. Before he could shut the door, Nori issued him another warning.

"Remember, be careful. Stay away from problem. Only talk to nice boys and girls." Nori could hear Evangelina's voice in her head, *I'll take him from here.*

"Oh, Nori, of course I'll stay out of trouble. *You* drive careful. See you at noon." Nori's eyes followed him as he headed to the front steps and watched him encounter a group of football lettermen horse-playing on the steps. Upon seeing the baby-faced freshman, they decided to have some fun. One of the football players nabbed his backpack and lifted him like a mama dog carrying her pup and looked him eye to eye.

"Well, looky, looky. What do we have here? I believe we have a world record for smallest freshman."

"Put me down!"

"He's kinda cute, Todd. Sorta like a lost puppy," said Sam, the football team's tight end.

"You're gonna make a great gofer for us."

"Gofer?"

"You know. Go fer this. Go fer that."

"Put me down. I'm not your slave."

"You're gonna be or you might have a few, how shall I say it, accidents."

Hearing the bully's nonsense, Evangelina had to think fast. She needed to find a way to insulate Jonathan from these boys. Too late for her to intervene as a human adult, it became clear that Jonathan's assigned escort was nowhere to be found on the premises. She scanned the growing crowd and found his designated National Honor Society escort preoccupied with a cheerleader out in the parking lot. Evangelina fixed his mind on the job at hand. The six-foot-eight power forward snapped to attention and broke through the crowd to address the bullies.

"Put 'em down!"

"Hey Tommy (aka the bubble bouncer)! How you doing? Have you ever seen such a small freshman?"

"Put him down, Todd."

"When you going to play a real man's sport like football. Chasing around with that orange pumpkin on a court is sissy stuff."

"I'll tell you what. Come to a practice and we'll see how much of a sissy sport basketball really is. Now put down my semester's project for NHS!"

"He's *your* project?"

"Yep, the boy's a genius. He skipped sixth, seventh and eighth grade. He's in ninth grade for I don't know how long, but I'm entrusted with his well-being. Now, put him down."

"Or what?"

"Tough decision . . . I could bounce your pumpkin head off that wall, or I could report you to the office for bullying. Wouldn't that get you suspended from the team for a couple of games? Or . . . you simply could put my best friend, Jonny, down."

"You're such a buzzkill, Tom."

"Put the boy down!"

Todd let go of his grasp and his prey fell to the ground.

Casually Jonathan brushed the dirt from his clothing, then faced his bully with a smile. "Seems the bully got bullied."

"Why you little . . . "

Jonathan hurriedly jumped to Tom's side to watch the crowd disperse and the frustrated gang scuffle away. He craned his neck skyward to look at the six-foot-eight Tom, his protector. "Thank you. You saved my life. I'm Jonathan Puro. You're Tommy . . . ?

"I'm Tom Decker, senior and class president."

"Well, you took care of those boys in short order."

"Actually, they're nice guys. They were merely having a little fun at your expense. Now they know you're my project, they shouldn't give you any more problems."

"I hope you're right."

"You're to report to the auditorium for orientation. Follow me."

As the two turned to leave, the first bell rang. They entered the front door to a jam-packed hallway. Jonathan followed his protector like a puppy dog follows his master carrying a treat. Tom, a tall, stocky young man, created a hole through the crowd which Jonathan navigated. Once they reached the auditorium doors, Tom turned and faced his charge.

"Listen, kid, I've got to get to my class. I'll be waiting for you when you get out of orientation, right at this door. Be here. I'll get you to the front door and your ride should be waiting. Remember Jonny, be prompt because I have another class to go to after I see you off. By the way, I'm not your only escort around here. There's a girl who will share the duties. Her name is Beth. You'll meet her tomorrow. Don't be late."

"Gotcha. I want to thank you again for rescuing me."

"No problemo. Now go get a seat."

Tom turned and disappeared into the crowd. Jonathan entered the raucous auditorium and headed down the aisle to the empty front row and sat. It seemed odd to him that he was the lone body in this row. Looking behind him he saw the back of the auditorium swamped with students. *Weird*, he thought, *you'd think they'd want to sit close to see and hear all the details*.

He reached into his backpack and retrieved a clean notebook and a pencil to take notes. Just prior to the principal arriving on stage another student quickly stepped around Jonathan's outstretched legs and sat in the seat next to him.

"Hi, I'm Pedro. My friends call me Petey. Who are you?"

"I'm Jonathan. My friends call me Jonathan." It was then he remembered Tom referring to him as Jonny, twice. He'd never considered using a nickname for Jonathan. His folks sometimes referred to him as the shortened "Jon," but he admitted to himself, he kinda liked the moniker "Jonny." Turning to Pedro, he added, "A few call me Jonny."

"When do we get our schedules?"

"I believe we get them at the end of this assembly."

"Cool biz."

Principal Hodges took the stage and greeted the incoming freshmen. He proceeded to go over the mundane, day-to-day, hodge-podge of expectations of students at the school. He also emphasized the school's code of conduct (which included bullying). After he completed his talking points, he wished all the freshman a good and fruitful year, then directed them alphabetically to their appropriate counselors to receive their schedules.

Since their surnames started with the same letter, Jonathan Puro and Petey Pabon stood in the same counselor's line. Inching forward in the line, they made small talk.

"I hope I get all the classes I asked for," said Petey.

"I know I will."

"How do you know?"

"Well, my mother negotiated with the principal last June when they sent me here from elementary school."

"How old are you?"

"Eleven."

"I thought I was young at thirteen, but I'll be fourteen at the end of September. I'll bet we're the two youngest kids here."

"You're probably right."

"I hope you're in my classes."

"I doubt it," said Jonathan. "I'm in all AP classes."

"AP?"

"Advanced Placement, like AP Math, AP science and AP English."

"Wow, you must be a brainiac."

"Let's simply say I'm no slouch."

The boys received their schedules and stood against the wall comparing classes. As expected, they did not have any periods together except one. They both were scheduled for last hour gym.

"Ugh, gym last hour," Jonathan said with disappointment.

"No, that's great. We don't have to take a shower at the end of the class. We can just go home and take our shower. Won't be naked in front of everyone!"

"The time would be better spent in the library."

"C'mon, you'd rather read than play football, basketball and baseball?"

"That's right. It's a waste of time and sweat."

"Well mi papi always say, 'Sound mind, sound body.'"

"Your dad's saying originated with the Roman poet Juvenal somewhere between 50 and 130 AD. It appeared in English in a book by John Locke in 1693. I don't buy it. Your body wears out, but your brain never does. I'd rather build my brain."

"Well, it's a required class for graduation."

"I need a schedule change. Maybe I could become a lab assistant during last hour."

"What do you do for fun?"

"I like watching documentaries."

"You must be a blast to hang around. Well, I hope to see you last hour."

"That's not going to happen."

"Whaddya gonna do?"

"I'm going to talk some sense into my counselor. He's going to change my schedule."

"I wouldn't be so sure. Your counselor is the same as mine. You're gonna need a lawyer to make him get you out of a required class.."

"My irrefutable logic will convince him."

"Good Luck, buddy," he chuckled. "You're gonna need it."

Chapter 25

BIGGER THAN SCHOOL

IT PROMISED TO BE a beautiful fall day from the bright sunshine streaming through the Puro's kitchen window. Nori sat leisurely finishing her tea and biscotti, contemplating how easy it was to pull off Jonathan's first morning in high school. She saw this as a tip-off to how the transition would go seamlessly. She was certain.

Looking to the clock, she jiggled her keys to notify Baillee it was time to leave.

"C'mon buddy. Time to go. We'll get there early to park up front. We don't want our boy wandering the lot, searching for our car."

Once positioned in the lot and with time to spare, she relaxed into her seat and pulled up her hand-worked needlepoint—portraits of Emmie and Baillie on a plaque for Jonathan's bedroom door. The school bell rang, startling her to ram the needle into her hand. "Ahhh . . . OUCH." She looked down at spot of blood spreading out across Emmie's needlepoint tongue. Baillie, scrambling to watch the explosion of students streaming out the front door, barked nervously at the window. Nori craned her neck to scan the herd dispersing in every direction. Finally, with no one remaining, instant panic gripped her. In desperation she reached for the door handle, only to be startled by a hand seizing her arm. She turned to see Evie in her FBI uniform sitting next to her.

"Evie? Where Jonathan? Where my boy?"

"Don't worry. He's sitting with his counselor trying to get out of last period gym."

"Oh, I feel better. I should know you there to take care of boy."

"Well, he's fronting a good fight, but the counselor is as stubborn as he is."

"Boy need exercise. Spend too much time on computer and reading. Needs fresh air."

"I think he's met his match. The counselor won't budge."

"He no be happy."

"Well, it's something he has to learn. He can't always get his way. Who knows, he might learn to enjoy gym class."

Nori laughed out loud. "Me no think so."

Evie spotted Jonathan out of the corner of her eye, then looked back at Nori. "Well, I gotta go. But I must say our boy is scowling." With that said, the angel vanished to her usual lookout point.

Nori studied Jonathan's defeated face as he approached the car and yanked open the door.

"Something wrong?"

Choosing to ignore her question, he slammed his knapsack on the floor and fastened his seatbelt. "Let's go!"

"Tell Nori."

"My stupid counselor won't let me change my gym class."

"Why not?"

"He said it's a required class for all ninth graders and I've gotta have it. I told him I won't even be back for tenth grade because I intend on going to a university next year and he laughed at me."

"He laugh at you?"

"Yes, he did. He said I should take things one year at a time. Stupid old man. I'm telling Mom!"

"Maybe you try class for a week. You might like it."

"I don't think so."

"You talk it over with Mom and Dad. See what they say."

"You bet I will!"

Nori gave a chuckle and drove off. Jonathan clenched his jaw, crossed his arms and glared at Nori. "It's mean to laugh at someone in pain, Nori."

"Oh, yes, Jonathan. You in so much pain," she said, followed by another laugh, only louder. *This be interesting night.*

Once in the drive, he waited impatiently for the car to come to a full stop before jumping out and racing to his room with Baillie snapping at his heels. His confrontation with the counselor was history as he fired up his computer to scan for new incoming correspondence. There, nestled in and lost with all the others was an email from Dr. Singh. Clicking it open revealed a relatively short text. Squaring his shoulders and pulling himself closer to the print, he took a deep breath and began reading Dr. Singh's reply to his new proposal.

> Dear Mr. Puro,
> After reviewing your proposal, we are very interested in your machine design and food product. We would like you to come to New York and present your project to our Board of Directors at your earliest convenience. Please contact me at my office number to work out a date for our first meeting. We will provide of all your travel costs. Thank you for your time. I look forward to meeting you.
> Best Regards,
> Dr. Praveer Singh
> Director of Government Global Food Research Agency, NY, NY

Jonathan leaped from his seat and danced around the room, hollering like a male banshee at the top of his lungs. Hearing the commotion, Nori hurried to his room.

"What's going on, boy?"

"They want me to present my design! I'm going to New York!"

"What design? New York?"

"My machine! You know, the one I've been working on all these months. I designed it to feed the world."

"You make machine? In no see it. Where?"

"On paper. It's my blueprint. They want to build it. It will change the world!"

"Why New York?"

"It's their headquarters. I can't wait until Mom and Dad get home."

"But school . . . "

"This is bigger than school! Especially gym class."

"I no know if Mom and Dad let you skip school."

"It would only be one or two days and most certainly they'd want to come. Wouldn't they?"

"They no let you go alone, that for sure. You minor. Need parental consent and protection."

"You could come with us."

"Me? Little Asian lady?"

"I watched you blitz that Rottweiler. Really, Nori, you rock. Why would I need protection, anyway? Think you'll have to punch out an army of Rottweilers?

Me need to talk to Evie. She know best.

Chapter 26

UNSOLVED MYSTERIES

J ONESY MUNCHED ON HIS second burger while the two detectives sat in the unmarked car watching the woman's house and its surroundings. They'd been waiting for a potential witness and/or perpetrator to return home from her job at the local supermarket. She was a potential lead to resolving the Martin break-in mystery. At last, the woman pulled into her driveway and hurried into the house.

"Lose the hamburger, Jonesy."

"Christ, she could have waited another five minutes."

"Quit your complaining. You eat enough for two people as it is. How do you stay so thin?"

"Nervous energy, I guess. Some people say I'm a little high strung."

"Yeah, and it's your high-strung personality that's gotten you into trouble more than once on the force."

"I'm trying to be a good boy."

"Well, keep trying. You're on thin ice as it is."

"Yeah, yeah."

Jonesy wrapped the remnants of his burger and hurriedly wiped his mouth, straightened his tie, and popped the passenger side door to trail behind Sheppard to the front door of the white frame house. They gave a moderate knock and waited patiently. They could hear shuffling behind the door, so when she didn't respond, they gave a hard pound.

Sheppard called out, "We know you're in there, Ms. Martin. We're Farmington P.D., Detectives Sheppard and Jones. We have a few questions about the death of your former husband." The pair heard shuffling from behind the door. After a long pause, the door behind the screen opened a crack.

"Can I help you gentlemen?" Obviously wary of the two men, they heard the screen door lock before further opening the wood door to speak with them.

"Detectives Sheppard and Jones, Farmington Hills Police Department." Sheppard flashed his credentials. "We'd like to ask you a few questions regarding your ex-husband, Gus."

"I'd really like to forget him," she seethed.

"Well, he died in an altercation recently."

"I saw he was arrested again on the news," she said. "But I wasn't aware of his death. Why am I not surprised? He always had a violent, mean streak." Her tone lacked emotion; her demeanor detached.

"We'll be brief, but we need to clarify a few things."

"If you must."

"Can we come in?"

Anna unlocked the screen door and escorted the men to the living room without offering a seat.

"Ms. Martin . . . "

"Call me Anna."

"As you wish. Anna, did you know your ex was being released from prison?"

"Yes, I did, and it scared the hell out of me."

"Have you ever been to or shopped at The Big D Sporting Goods store?"

"Wha . . . what's that got to do with anything?" she stuttered.

"There was a stolen firearm at the scene."

"I don't even know where it's located."

"Farmington Hills."

"Never heard of it. Is it a big store?"

"It's located on Grand River."

"I can't say I've ever seen it. Maybe when I was driving, I might have passed it, but I don't remember seeing it, let alone go in that store."

"I see."

"Do you own a gun?"

"A gun? Ah, no. Should I?"

"Have you ever shot a handgun?"

"No, never. Where's this going?"

"Do you know the Puro family?"

"Other than what I saw on TV? I can't say I do. No."

"Do you know anyone who lives on Gill Street?"

"I pass the street all the time, but I don't know anyone who lives there. So how did he die? Something about a fry pan. I saw on TV he was taken to the hospital."

"He suffered a blunt head trauma and died in the operating room."

"I can't say I feel sorry for him. He was an evil person. He drank too much and always let his temper get the best of him, but well, you know," she said with a catch in her voice.

"I understand."

"Other witnesses say they saw someone who matched your description at the scene. Were you at the Puro's house?"

"Actually, that day I was hiding in my house. I locked all the doors and windows, turned off all the lights and hid. I just prayed he wouldn't come to the house. Well, he never showed, thank God."

"Did you, maybe, go out for a walk or perhaps go to St. John's Church the day your husband was released?"

"No!"

"Do you have anyone who can confirm you were at home?"

"Why would I need someone to prove I was home?" She deliberately did not mention the dark, handsome stranger or the note she posted to her door.

"Why would he come to your house?"

"Really? Revenge. He blamed me for putting him in prison."

"I see."

"Am I a suspect?"

"Let me finish my questioning."

"Have you made or attempted to contact Gus while in prison?"

"No!"

"Has he ever tried to contact you?"

"Why does that matter? I was so worried he'd be harassing me I got a PPO. Now that I know he's gone I can go back to a normal life again."

"We're glad you feel safe again," said Detective Donnally looking at his partner. "We thank you for your time. I think we have enough for now. If we have further questions, we'll be back. If you remember anything else about that day, please give us a call. Here's my card."

"Thank you for delivering the good news."

"What do you mean?"

"He's dead."

"I understand."

The detectives exited the home and returned to the car. Jonesy clutched the remains of his burger and took a bite.

"You know she's gotta be lying."

"The boy and the Asian woman described her almost perfectly. She must have been there. There's more to the story. We have the boy's testimony. She brought the stolen gun. We gotta bring her in for questioning and administer a lie detector test."

"But there was only one set of fingerprints on the gun, and they were Martin's."

"So, what? We got nothing?"

"Exactly. We got nothing to tie her to the scene except an eleven year old boy's word."

"We can't just let this go. We gotta get to the bottom of this. Either the boy or the woman is lying. We gotta go back and hammer the kid."

"Not going to happen, Jonesy."

"It's not right. It's our job. It simply doesn't sit right with me."

"Sometimes it all ends in a mystery. We'll keep the case open and maybe something new will be discovered."

"We gotta talk to the kid again." The Asian woman was focused on Martin and said she never saw the woman leave. How did she leave the scene without anyone seeing her? The boy must have seen something. He was standing right behind her. Dissolved into glitter? The kid watches too much TV!"

"The Asian woman can't I.D. her and you know it's not going to happen with those parents."

"Well, what about those parents? A break-in occurs in their house, and they don't want to know the details? Something smells fishy all the way around."

"Jonesy, don't go there. You're asking for trouble."

"Trouble never bothered me. We can get a court order to have the kid talk to us."

"Don't get yourself suspended. You already have two strikes against you and the captain won't hesitate to put you on leave."

"Yeah, well . . . sometimes ya gotta do what ya gotta do to get to the bottom of things."

"You're talking crazy, Jonesy. Keep your nose clean."

As they pulled out of the driveway, Jonesy turned to stare at the house. He knew he saw Anna slide back a corner of the window drape and watch them leave the driveway. Although happy with her newfound freedom, she felt somewhat responsible for Gus' death. Did the mysterious man in the bar factor in all of this? From TV coverage, she learned the maid struck her ex. She now knew he died later of complications, but in all of this craziness, there was no mention of the man she encountered in the bar. All she knew was the note she wrote and tacked to the front door sent him to his death. *Am I an accomplice to murder?*

She slumped into her rocking chair and began to cry. Yes, she hated the man who sent her to the hospital for a month. And yes, she remembered all the pain of her marriage and recuperating in the hospital. Even though he created havoc and pain for her, she did not want him dead. He deserved to be punished, but not to die. She sobbed and shook her head. "He was only thirty-seven. He could have changed his life . . . turned it around and made something of himself. But he'll never have the chance. So sad," she whispered.

She slid a tissue from the box on the table and wiped her eyes, wishing she'd never met the man in the bar. If not for him and his scheme, Gus would be alive today. *If I ever see that guy again, I swear I'll . . .* she thought. The tears flooded her eyes again.

Chapter 27

GRATITUDE WITH A CHASER

S ITTING AT THE PEAK of the Puro home, Evangelina stressed over the latest outpost from Raziel alerting her to a suspicious hotspot of evil nearby. Unable to both leave her post to search the surrounding areas and still maintain unflagging defense of Jonathan at his home or school, frustrated her.

She sensed something afoot but couldn't pinpoint its center. The two recent attempts on the child's life claimed all her attention, leaving her no time to hunt new evil. Could she risk merely sitting back contentedly to monitor the background from the rooftop, hoping for evil to show itself?

The angel contemplated her last encounter with evil. She felt a diabolical presence in both the woman and the convict, yet she failed to act. Luckily, Nori came to the rescue and bailed her out. The woman's hasty retreat confused her, but she knew the evil entity would return. If she would have acted more urgently, she could have identified the demon and snuffed out Lucifer's minion. *Hindsight is 20/20*, she thought.

Disappointed by her own performance, she thought, *I must thank Nori for her quick reaction and timely intervention.* Her wings flapped in the wind and lightly set on the back porch where she materialized into the human Evie. With the parents at work and Jonathan back from his first full day of high school holed up in his room, she knew Nori was basically alone. She smiled to herself when she heard the three chain locks slide back and Nori open the door. *Always watchful.*

"Evie," shouted the Asian woman, seizing her friend. "So good to see you!"

"And I'm so happy to see you too."

"Come in, come in."

Upon entering the kitchen Evie turned to take Nori's hands into hers and smiled broadly. "I can't stay. I'm here only to applaud your vigilance. You protected the family from enormous danger, Nori. If not for your quick reaction, we would have lost Jonathan. Once again, I have the greatest confidence in you to protect the Glory Child. God is looking down."

"You right. Nobody hurt my boy as long as I alive."

"One last thing before I go. Do you remember when I gave you the ability to see demons in their true forms? The woman, did you see anything which indicated she was a demon? Any little detail could help."

Nori thought long and hard, then said, "Everything happen fast. She gone in blink, but me think I see a bird's head shape before changing into fizz."

"Bird's head . . . Are you sure?"

"Pretty sure."

"She could have been Horus . . . No. Or maybe Malphas or Andras . . . either way, thank you, Nori. That helps. You need to know, I've learned Lucifer still actively seeks Jonathan; he hasn't resigned, so be on watch 24/7. Together we will slay demons once again."

"Next time I use something more deadly than frying pan."

"I don't know. Your frying pan is pretty tough."

Evie reached up to stroke Nori's cheek. "Know I'm here with you. If you need help, simply yell my name. We've taken on the evilest of demons and this new one won't stand a chance against us." With that, Evie's form glowed as it dissipated into thin air.

Off duty, a depressed Detective Jones once again visited the vacant bar. He had lost the love of his life, left a case unsolved and been reprimanded by his captain. His job and career were in jeopardy. While tearing his napkin into small shreds and forming a pile, he reprimanded himself. *If only I could talk to the boy again, this time alone . . . If I could crack this case, the captain would get off my back and I could breathe.*

The front door to Barney's opened and the man in the black t-shirt from the other night sauntered in and took a seat at the bar. Andras had returned. Barney, the barkeep, wiped his hands and approached his customer, recognizing him as a regular now . . . an oddball, busy body, but a big tipper.

"Whaddya have tonight?"

"Double Scotch, neat," Andras chirped, "and give the young man across the bar whatever he's drinking."

"Coming right up."

Barney backed away to fetch the order while Andras pulled a cigar from his vest pocket and ran it under his nose and sampled the robust aroma. Barney returned with the drink and halted to eyeball Andras dipping the end of the cigar into his Scotch and place it between his lips, then close his eyes to the combination of flavors obviously pleasing his palate.

"That's some glorified ritual you have going there."

Ignoring Barney, Andras called to Jonesy sitting across the bar. "Your beau return, or are you still out of sorts?"

Jonesy gave a surprised glance at the freshly placed bottle of beer in front of him. He propped it to his lips and chugged down half. Wiping his lips with his shirt sleeve, he looked Andras in the eye. "That woman won't talk to me."

"Yep, sounds like the nature of the beast. Give it time or move on."

"Thanks for the beer."

"My pleasure. I hate seeing a comrade suffer."

Andras took a slow sip of Scotch and returned his unlit cigar to his lips. "I remember when a man could puff his cigar and drink his Scotch inside a bar with no harassment. Today, we gotta kowtow to the whiney masses."

"And it's my job to enforce those silly laws."

"You a cop?"

"Detective James Jones at your service."

"I am Andras. Pleased to make your acquaintance . . . Salut!"

Raising his glass in response, Jones hollered back, "Here's mud in your eye."

"So, do you know anything about the ex-con who invaded that family's home and just died?"

"I'm not supposed to talk about an open investigation."

"C'mon, who am I gonna tell? The reporters said something about a mysterious woman who simply vanished into thin air." Andras took this as an opportunity to move closer to his target.

"We're investigating it," said Jones, his voice lower, more confidential.

"Well, who is she?"

"We don't know, but if we could merely interrogate the boy, a witness, without his parents, it would go a long way to solving the case."

"Well, interrogate him."

"Can't. Protocol and rules."

"Ya gotta break a few eggs to make an omelet."

"You're right. Solving it would put a feather in my cap and get the captain off my back. Maybe even impress my girlfriend."

"Well . . . ?"

"I guess I'm going to have to do a little clandestine detective work. Either I solve the case, or I'll be on a long vacation."

"Simple risk versus rewarding decision."

"Seriously, I have nothing to lose at this point."

"Don't worry if you can't figure this out. You know, word on the street says you guys never do anything anyways. They say if it wasn't for the State Police, nothing would get solved in this town and if it ain't a traffic accident, you guys are useless. Such low expectations. I wish you luck. Go for it, kid." Having planted the seed, Andras finished his Scotch and with a cheeky smile ambled to the door and waved his signature backwards goodbye with his hand high over his head, "Happy hunting, detective."

"Barney, who is that dude? Ya know him?"

"Naw, only seen him three or more other times and you were here for two of 'em."

"Moron," Jonesy yelled, throwing the bottle at the closing the door. "Where does he get off implyin' cops are useless bumblers?"

"Jonesy, calm down, kid," Barney said.

Outside, Andras stopped and listened. *That was too easy*. With Shadow at his side, Andras made his way along the sidewalk considering how best to manipulate his new stooge. It would be easy enough to work him into a frenzy. He was already unstable, full of bitterness, and malleable. Now we need to weaponize him and bamboozle him to do our bidding. "If I could get the boy to laugh at him or belittle him, that just might light his fuse. Add a little alcohol and it could put him over the top. Then we get to go home."

Shadow snarled his approval.

Chapter 28

HOPES AND DREAMS

J ONATHAN PACED BACK AND forth in his bedroom, unable to contain his excitement. With his invitation to New York, he was beside himself. He circled the floor in nervous anticipation, imagining his parent's speechless mouths open in awe when he told them of the committees' interest in his project. He repeatedly stopped to admire the drawing of his design emblazoned on his computer screen. Finally, Jonathan raised both hands above his head. This was *his* personal touchdown. Baillie rushed to the bed and flipped his Emma stuffy in the air. All three participated in his success.

He knew his folks were proud of him, but this letter solidified the reason. Again and again he checked his clock; it seemed to move as slow as molasses in the wintertime. His mom would be home soon, but not soon enough. He wouldn't see Dad until dinnertime. Giving it thought, he'd wait until the two were home together and surprise them both at the same time. *Yep, that's what I'll do.*

Nori came to his bedroom and took a secret look inside the open door to see Jonathan pacing back and forth. The sheer excitement on his face made her smile. She gave a gentle knock and waited. Jonathan abruptly stopped pacing and, upon seeing Nori, waved her in.

"You want snack?"

"My stomach is so tight; I couldn't eat a thing."

"Okay, I make you peanut butter and jelly with nice glass of milk."

"But Nori, I said I couldn't eat."

"Okay, PB&J it is. I be back."

"But, but . . . but . . . " Shaking his head he thought, *It's so annoying when she conveniently forgets how to understand English.* He resumed pacing and checking time. It passed, but not nearly as fast as he wanted. He stopped only with another knock at the door.

With a loud sigh he said, "Come in, Nori."

Nori entered carrying a plate with a sandwich and a glass of milk. Smiling at her trickery, she put the plate and glass on his desk.

"You sit down. Have snack. You growing boy. Need to eat."

"I told you I wasn't hungry. My stomach is in knots."

"You sick? I get Pepto."

He thought better of telling her she was a nuisance and to please let him be. Instead, he said, "No, I'm not sick. I just can't wait to tell Mom and Dad about my project."

"They come soon enough. Eat and it kill time. Come."

He waited for her to leave the room before reluctantly eyeing the food. It did look good to him. *Maybe a bite to calm my nerves.* He sampled the sandwich and washed it down with milk, leaving a few scraps for Baillee. He was forced to smile and admit he knew better than to doubt Nori's third eye for knowing what was best for him. The tightness he felt earlier eased.

Taking his empty plate and glass, along with Baillee trekking down the hallway with his stuffed Emma secure in his mouth, Jonathan marched into the kitchen to find Nori standing at the sink, still smirking.

"Can I have more milk, please?"

"You betcha."

Jonathan plopped at the table with his fresh glass of milk to wait and watch the minute hand circle around the face of the clock.

When Nori caught him staring at the timepiece, she threw up her hands. "You know watched pot never boils."

"What?"

"If watch clock, it take forever. You do something, time flies."

"You're right," said Jonathan. He hustled the dog's ball and tossed it into the living room. Baillie ran after the toy and brought it back. He continued to play fetch with Baillie as the hands on the clock skated around the dial. As he readied to the throw the ball the umpteenth time, the back door banged, signaling Mom was home.

"Mom," Jonathan yelled, running to his mother, nearly tackling her as she took off her shoes.

"Hold on, hold on here, dear."

"Mom, Mom, Mom!"

"What!"

Unable to wait for his dad, he blurted out: "They accepted my design!"

"Your design?"

"For my food producing machine."

"Who did?"

"Dr. Praveer Singh and the Global Food Research Agency."

"Really, that's wonderful."

"Yeah, and they want me to come to New York to present it to their board of directors. All expenses paid!"

"Do they know you're eleven years old?"

"Ah, well . . . ah, no."

"Don't you think you should like inform them?"

"It's all about the idea and the design, Mom. My age shouldn't have anything to do with it."

"I guess you're right, but who has time to take you to New York and what about school?"

"I was hoping you and Dad would be proud to make the trip with me. School? You know I'm already ahead of them. It won't be a problem."

"We're only starting a new school year and your dad is working seven days a week, ten hours a day. I don't know how we could manage this."

Once again, her first response put the kibosh on his enthusiasm. Following a long silence, Mary put her arm around him, but he shrugged it off. "You still don't understand anything more than your small world. This letter should encourage you to look at me, my work, my future and the future of the world. No. Your dream for me is that I take gym class."

Nori stood at the stove stirring the pot, Baillie at her feet wagging his tail, begging for a taste. Nori put down her ladle and wiped her hands on the towel."

"Nori, no busy."

"What?" said Mary.

"Me could take boy. Always wanted to see New York."

"Nori, he'll need a legal guardian with him. Not that I expect a final decision before signing anything. I don't know. It's such a big city. I don't know if you could manage it."

"Me escape to Seoul with little Kim. Nori find her way to America. New York, no problem."

"I don't know. Let's wait for Joe."

"Okay. Beef stew tonight. Hope you hungry."

With new hope in his heart, Jonathan hurried to his room with Baillie and Emma tagging behind. He read and re-read his email from Dr. Singh.

"Baillie, I may be gone for a little while, but don't worry. Keep Emma company and we'll celebrate."

Baillie yipped and wagged his tail in understanding.

"Good grief, if anyone saw the three of us cavorting together, buddy, they'd have me screened for 'dissociative identity disorder.'" He admitted being a genius had its disadvantages and bordered on cuckooness.

Baillie yipped as if understanding. Jonathan reached down and scratched the dog's ear and smiled, full of hope and dreams.

Chapter 29

BIG APPLE PLANS

S CRAMBLED THOUGHTS AND IMAGES collided and smashed into a brick wall as Evangelina contemplated the information Nori supplied her about the vanishing woman during the attack on the boy. Her account of the disappearing demon conflicted with most descriptions she had of demons. But a demon with a bird's head helped her narrow it down to just two demons possessing those credentials with the ability to accomplish Lucifer's evil doings.

Malphas, a lower prince of Hell commanded forty legions of demons, but his forté dealt with buildings and towers. Andras, an Archduke or Grand Marquis of Hell with thirty legions of demons at his disposal, however, was known as one of the fiercest warriors in Hell. His modus operandi tended to be more subtle. He liked to enrage and engage mortals to do the dirty work he intended. Either, or both, were formidable foes and not to be taken lightly. Puzzled, she leaned toward Andras, but she couldn't be sure.

The uncertainty of which demon to defend against didn't matter to Evangelina. While each posed their own unique problems, she felt confident that neither would be a match against her. She fought Beelzebub and Lucifer, himself, and arose victorious. No matter which she encountered, she would send him back to Hell with his tail between his legs. Her powers could not be matched by those demons, and she would use all of them against either to protect the Glory Child. But, her foremost concern centered on where or when they would attack. She had to remain ever vigilant.

Evangelina listened in on the conversation between Mary, Jonathan and Nori in the kitchen. Concerned, she shook her head. Going to New York would pose significant problems for the child's safety, especially if the demon was indeed Andras. Mingling into crowds of unconnected people, posed a high risk. It would be difficult to protect against any weaponized human. Although Nori would be there as a first line of defense, she didn't have even one weapon besides a nail file to defend against demons of such magnitude. She hoped somehow the trip would be cancelled, but the decision remained with the Puros. There was no doubt she would serve her duties as primary guardian of the Golden Child.

The angel watched Joe's truck pull into the driveway. The hardworking man loved his family. He worked at a local tool and die shop in the Detroit area. The business supplied parts to the Big Three. Through hard work, creative ideas, and diligence he rose through the ranks at the shop to become a shift supervisor. He had ten years seniority at the supplier. Recently, a buyer approached him and recommended he apply for a middle management job with the buyer's company. The buyer recognized his talent and told him he'd put a good word in for him. Joe had been toying with the idea of a change but wanted to talk with Mary first.

Ten-hour shifts were draining the life out of him. His usually high spirit was being depleted, and while he was always glad to be home with his family, more often than not these past days, all he wanted to do was eat and go to bed. While he received good pay, this 6 a.m. to 5 p.m. shift was killing him. Living to work, not working to live made less and less sense to him. It made the buyer's offer more attractive, offering, along with more money, free weekends, vacation time, shorter hours, even a few dinners out with Mary. He could build the family unit he and Mary often talked of in their younger years. While grateful this job got the family out of the rental in Hartland, it was sucking the life out of him. Joe trudged to the back door and opened it with his usual chant: "Oh my God, it smells so good. What's for dinner?"

"Your favorite, beef stew," said Nori wiping her hands off on a dish towel. "I call Mary and . . . "

Before she could finish Jonathan, followed by Baillie, peeled around the kitchen corner and almost tackled his father. "Dad, Dad, Dad!"

"Wow, I haven't seen you run that fast since you thought a chipmunk was chasing you."

"Dad, they liked my design for my food producing machine."

"They did? Who?"

"Dr. Praveer Singh and the Government Global Food Research Agency." Jonathan handed him the printout of Dr. Singh's letter.

"Well, that's great." He knew better than to allow skepticism to shade his reaction when dealing with his son, but he needed to point out the obvious. His project was not yet accepted. "This letter is an *invitation* to you to *present* your project. It's the first step in the actual process to endorse your research."

Jonathan, not to be waylaid said, "Oh, that's a minor step," followed with "and they want me to come to New York to present it to their Board of Directors."

"Oh, I see . . . When?"

"As soon as possible."

"We don't have money to send you off to New York, son."

"Did you read the note? It's all expenses paid."

"What's your mom say about all this?"

"She said you and her are too busy to take me, but Nori volunteered to do it."

"Nice, but for now let's sit down and eat. I'm starved. We'll have a family pow wow after my stomach stops growling over our voices.

They gathered at the table; their bowls filled with stew. After saying a prayer of thanks, Joe grabbed a warm, fluffy slice of bread from the breadbasket and passed it along to Mary, who thanked him politely.

"So, Mar, what's going on with this New York thing?"

"I'm not sure. I'll need to call this Dr. Singh. He doesn't know that our boy here is only eleven. So, if after I talk to him, he decides he still wants Jonathan to come to New York, Nori has volunteered to take him."

"But it's New York and, well, can Nori handle it? She'll need a letter of introduction."

"She pointed out how she escaped with her little Kim from her home country and made it to America. New York shouldn't be a problem."

"True. Good point." He couldn't admit he thought it a ridiculous plan, wrought with complications.

Jonathan, leaning forward in his chair, listened soberly to the discussions, restraining to not interrupt unless asked for his input less the talk went off track.

"Well, if you feel comfortable with it, then I'm okay too," Joe said, dipping his bread into his bowl of stew.

"But don't either of you two think one of you accompanying me on this is more important than whatever else you have to do . . . ? Oh, forget it." Jonathan knew better than open a new discussion.

"So, Jonnie-boy, what specifically does your machine do?" Joe's skepticism ran high. "Tell me again."

"It converts readily available waters and seaweed into edible bars which provide all the vitamins, minerals, calories and nutrients necessary daily for human nutrition. It is solar powered, and each unit would cost approximately one million dollars to build and very little to operate. One machine at maximum capacity could produce approximately three bars per second, about 240 thousand bars in a day and requires little or no maintenance."

"Impressive." How could Joe admit he had little understanding of Jon's spiel?

"I hope it will eliminate world hunger."

Dead air prevailed in the room until Joe spoke up. "Son, it was only a few months ago when we discussed this. How can you claim to have found the answer to what other brilliant scholars have been researching for years on end?" With restraint, he left out the word "scam." "That's incredible, but you need proof of concept."

"That's why I'm going to see Dr. Singh and his board of directors. I want him to give me a grant for a million dollars to build it."

"A million dollars! Oh, so you think this guy is going to give a grade school boy that amount of money?"

"Yep, a million dollars. The machine is simple, fast and efficient."

"And who is going to build this machine?"

"I was hoping you and the people at your work would be interested."

"Oh, so now you're dragging us into it. Don't you think you're jumping the gun?" His thoughts, however, sidetracked, admitting his company could build it. His journeymen at the shop would be interested in a project like this and would help build this machine. If this truly could be more than his son's pipedream, Jonathan could be a candidate for a Nobel Prize.

Shaking his father from his fantasy, Jonathan blurted out, "Dad, what are you thinking?"

Joe awoke to the absurdity of his dream and laughed. "Oh, just had a snapshot of you accepting the Nobel Prize for having contributed to the benefit of mankind. My son."

"I don't care about prizes, Dad. What matters is no more children die from starvation. I simply see problems and try to fix 'em."

"I'd have to talk to the owner and he must agree he's on board with it. We may need an attorney to insure you're legally . . . "

"You're so typical, always ready to rain on my parade. I've researched the doctor. He's won awards as a humanitarian. He's known the world over for his good works and my plan fits right in with other things he's supported. *He'll* guide us through this."

Without hesitating, red-faced Joe bounced forward to hover over his son, "Dammit, I'm sick of your sarcastic barbs. You're a boy and, take it or leave it, I have a responsibility to see you don't go into this blindly. Let me say this: You can be sure if this project flies, he will have a cadre of employees legally protecting the plan. But we'll be there to oversee it all."

Jonathan acknowledged he was aware of how his father cleared the way for him to pursue his project. Many times in opposition to Mary's dictates. "Sorry, Dad."

"Okay, family, including Baillie, and especially Nori, do we all agree . . . he has to go to New York?"

"Yes," said Jonathan pumping his fist.

"Hold on. Don't leave me out. I have an opinion . . . I'm still not sure . . . " she said, watching three sets of sagging shoulders, "I know, I know, you're disappointed, but . . . " looking to see a mishmash of anger, disgust, mistrust, incorporated into one ugly Jonathan, she quickly changed course. "But I'll remain open to talk to this Dr. Singh fellow. Nori, are you ready for a trip to New York?"

Excitement rippled across the table. Mary shared her stories from her college days at a New York college. She gave Nori advice about what to expect in her journey with Jonathan to the Big Apple. She wistfully reminisced about the sights and sounds of New York . . . *Those were the days*, she thought looking back, but she would never trade her life now for her days in college.

"So, you'll call Dr. Singh tomorrow and we'll talk about it tomorrow night."

"Yeah, will do."

"And I'll talk with the owner and see if he's interested in it. I can't guarantee it, but it does sound like something he'd be interested in doing."

"Can I talk to him, too?"

"Let's hold off on that, son, until you have the money. If you don't get the grant, then there's no reason for it, but if this Dr. Singh believes in you, you will meet Mr. Ruffini."

"Well, I'm optimistic . . . until then I'm outta here," he said, standing to return to a less combative room to review the package he sent to the doctor. He went through the documents line by line looking for mistakes or omissions, recalculating formulas and data verifying all were correct. Finished with his review, he felt confident of his work, but he realized there always was the chance of outside determinants, yet unknown to him, and which were out of his control. He hoped things like budget restrictions, massive corporate rules, and so much he didn't know about did not stand in the way of his project.

He looked down at Baillie sitting at his side and raised the dog's snout to his and spoke directly: "We got this Baillie; we got this."

Chapter 30

PHONE FLURRY

LOOKING AT THE EMAIL Jonathan printed out with Dr. Singh's contact data, Mary sat in a secluded area in the teacher's lounge and dialed his number. The phone rang a few times before Dr. Singh's secretary answered.

"Dr. Singh's office. How may I help you?"

"Hello, this is Mary Puro, Jonathan Puro's mother. I'm calling about Dr. Singh's invitation to my son to come to New York and meet with him."

"Let me see if he's available. Please hold one moment, please."

"Hello, this is Dr. Singh."

His immediate response surprised her, like he was waiting for her call. "Hello, Dr. Singh. This is Mary Puro, Jonathan Puro's mother. I'd like to talk with you regarding your offer to fly my son to New York to meet with you and your board members."

"Of course, what is your concern?"

"First off, I'd like to inform you Jonathan is eleven, soon to be twelve years old."

After a period of dead air, Mary spoke up. "Dr. Singh, are you there?"

"Twelve years old? That's Extraordinary! His level of intelligence and maturity is quite impressive."

"I've been told that. I wanted you to be aware of that before he presents himself to your board members. Some may not take him seriously and consider his age to be a hindrance and possibly a waste of your time and money."

"Mrs. Puro, do you think we'd invest our time and money to just chit-chat with him? I assure you many on the board have studied every intricate detail of his design to find discrepancies in his work process. His work speaks for itself, Mrs. Puro. His design is innovative and groundbreaking. His drawings are impeccable. The boy is brilliant. If it indeed proves successful after further analysis, it will change the course of human history. You must be very proud of him."

"Yes, we agree he's remarkable, but a mother has to be protective of her child."

"I understand. Now, when can Jonathan meet with the board to answer our questions and fill in the details about his machine? Everyone is enthusiastic. The sooner the better."

"I'll talk with my husband, but soon."

"And you'll, of course, be chaperoning your son? Considering his age, we ask he attend with a legal guardian."

"Well, I'm a teacher and it's a new school year, so I can't attend. His nanny, Nori, will definitely attend."

"Excellent. I want to inform you the board regularly meets on the first of the month, so it would be convenient if you could attend then."

"I'll let my husband know and hope everything goes well."

"Please let me know as soon as possible and I'll make all the arrangements necessary. Also," he said with an open-hearted laugh, "the board needs to be prepared to meet with such a *young* man."

"I understand. Thank you, Dr. Singh. Goodbye."

Mary put down the phone, relieved his response to Jonathan's age did not appear to be a hindrance. She heard the words " . . . *change the course of human history*" repeated over and over in her mind. She recalled the number of times she pushed and pushed and pushed for him to find passion in baseball, soccer, tennis, anything but reading books. Today, for her the word "passion" took on new meaning. Her son's passion for learning was a gift, one she promised herself to support. It was only today she stopped to fathom the importance of this project. Joe had seen it; why hadn't she? He was a bright kid, but change the world? Her baby, change the world? And to think she worked to block his way. She shook her head in disbelief.

Chapter 31

INTERVIEW WITH A MINION

HE SAT PARKED OUTSIDE the high school in his black sedan, nervously contemplating his next daring move. He dismissed his first inclination to liquor up before his interview with the boy, knowing booze and him didn't pal well together. Steve often referred to him as a hooligan on hooch. Pulling up his tablet to review his list of questions to ask only fogged a brain refusing to concentrate. Eventually he convinced himself it would be easier with a nip of Jameson Irish whiskey. Just a nip. A little liquid courage to calm his nerves. Reaching to the glove box he removed the half empty pint, uncorked it and took a slug to become: Super Detective James Jones, Ready For Duty.

Unbeknownst to him, across the street loomed a man in a black t-shirt and suit jacket restraining his German Shepherd on a leash alongside him. Andras grinned widely, proud to watch his plan come to fruition. *Ready-Set-Go* he chuckled to himself as he invaded the thoughts of his duped detective. *It's now or never.*

Jones collected a few mints from his console and popped them in his mouth, then retrieved his cheap cologne from the glove box and gave himself a spritz behind his ears. Straightening his tie, he prepared to interview Jonathan Puro.

The detective entered the school office and approached the counter with an air of authority. The school secretary looked up from her typing and quickly moved to stand at the counter and acknowledge his presence.

"Can I help you, sir?"

"Yes, I'd like to speak with one of your students," he said, flashing his badge.

"And which student would you like to speak with?"

"Jonathan Puro."

Pulling up Jonathan's file on her computer she said, "He's in class now. This is regarding . . . ?"

"He is a witness in a police matter."

"I see. Let me allow you to talk to the principal."

The secretary dialed the principal, and after a brief conversation said, "He'll be with you in a few moments. Please take a seat?"

"No, I'll wait here."

Mr. Kyle, a portly high school principal with affable, jolly features which hid his gruff "don't cross me" side, was known to run his school with the firm hand he extended to the detective.

"I'm Principal Kyle, how may we help you?" He stepped out from his office to the front counter and offered his hand. His bushy brows framed his thick glasses giving Jones the illusion of an approachable, almost comical man, easily persuaded.

"I'm Detective Jones," he said flashing his badge, which he believed accomplished his goal to impress the principal, now raising his wagging brows. "I need to speak with one of your students, a Jonathan Puro. May I see him?"

"What's this regarding?"

"He's a witness in a police matter."

"I see. This is not usual protocol. With such an official request, I'd like to have another adult in the room, preferably a parent. If not a parent, then I could stand in place."

"I understand, but I assure you it's not necessary. I'd be interviewing him as a witness, not questioning him as a suspect. With you in the room could be intimidating. And the sooner we collect his information, the quicker we can close the case. His observations could help put a violent criminal in jail for a long time. May I use an office to speak with him alone?"

Principal Kyle studied the detective smelling of the cheap Old Spice cologne from years ago. Against his better judgment he told Betty to "send a pass for Jonathan Puro." He said a little prayer before opening the door to his office and escorting the detective inside.

Jonathan, slouching in his seat in AP Biology, listening to a lecture along with the other NHS students on mammal gestation, moaned. Having already read the chapter, the lecture merely recapped what he already knew. Also, he had done his own research on the topic, so this rehash tended to be more than a bit boring to him. Evangelina, stretched atop a file cabinet, casually reading from a magazine, stopped and looked up when a classmate raised his hand with a question.

"Is it true human babies go through all the physical forms of the different animals on Earth before they are born? Like, do we have gills and tails when we were inside our mother's bodies?"

Jonathan energetically shot up his hand.

"Yes, Jonathan?"

"Ontogeny does not recapitulate phylogeny in all cases of animal gestation. What you are inquiring about is a pre-Darwinian theory promoted by Ernst Haeckel and disproven in the early twentieth century because embryos evolve in different ways. It has been relegated to "biological mythology.""

"Correct, Jonathan."

The classroom, in unison, giggled at "Mr. Know-it-all."

A knock at the classroom door disrupted the discussion and a student aide entered carrying a student pass. She handed the teacher the pass who, in turn, glanced at it and extended it toward Jonathan, only saying: "They want you in the principal's office."

Jonathan accepted the pass and headed out the door. It felt strange to be in the hallway without an escort and no hustle-bustle of students bumping and jostling him. He liked the newfound freedom.

Evangelina, ever on guard to prevent a replay of her negligence to protect a near catastrophe on the Martin case, flew close behind him, seized by curiosity. In any event, her guard went up and she felt ready for anything.

Upon arriving at the office, Jonathan put the pass on the counter and asked the secretary who wanted to see him.

Principal Kyle stood guard at the office door. "This way Jonathan. Someone needs to ask you a few questions. Won't take long. I'll be standing at the door if you need me."

The boy stepped in and heard the door close behind. Looking to the desk he immediately recognized Detective Jones in the principal's chair.

"I know you from the interview at my home. What do you need from me?"

"Have a seat. I have more questions I'd like to ask, certain things clarified."

"Like what? I already told you all I know." Instinctively suspicious of the squirrelly officer across from him, he added, "And, besides, it's my understanding you need a parent in the room."

"Nah, nah, nah. I have the principal's permission. He's standing right outside the door. You're safe. Now, let's move on and get this over with," referring to his notes. "The woman with red hair, what was her name? Did she know you? Does she know your family?"

"I don't know. I don't think so. Actually, I never met her before. I thought she might be a neighbor. But we told you all this before."

"She was protecting you. Why?"

"She was protecting herself, not me. She came crashing into my room, yanked my arm and pulled me behind her. That doesn't sound like she was trying to save me, does it? I would've been better off hiding in the closet."

"Did she have a gun?"

"Yes, I said she did before."

"Where did she get the gun?"

"How should I know?"

"Did she say anything at all?"

"I don't remember."

"C'mon kid, give me something."

"I don't know what to tell you."

"You expect me to believe she simply vanished?" He displayed his agitation by booming out the question. Recalling the words used in the bar, he added, "Do you think I'm a useless bumbler?"

"No sir, I don't. Yeah, it was weird. She was there and then she wasn't. Just like that, she was gone."

Andras's voice whispered in Jones's ear, *He's lying. He thinks you're stupid.*

"Sparkly mist, right?"

"What?" said Jonathan.

"You said she dissolved into a sparkly mist! You expect me to believe your crap?" Jones slammed his fist on the desk, wincing from the pain.

Evangelina bristled at the anger but held back, hoping the questioning would be over without her intercession. This guy seemed out of control; but he was a policeman. He swore to protect and serve. She waited for him to rein himself back.

"That's what happened," said Jonathan.

"You're lying, you little bastard. Tell me the truth! This ain't no Mr. Pickles TV show."

When Jonathan heard the Mr. Pickles reference, he snickered.

"Are you laughing at me you smug twerp? Wipe that stupid smirk off your face!"

Jonathan pulled back his grin, but still confused by the reference to Mr. Pickles.

Again, Andras whispered in Jones's ear, *You know he's lying. He thinks you're a joke. He's even laughing at you. Time to pull out the big guns.*

"The perp held you at gunpoint. So, you're familiar with this," Jones said, pulling out his service revolver and pointing it at Jonathan. "Tell me the truth, or this time I'll finish what the perp couldn't and shoot, you smart-mouthed brat." His anger boiled over. *Time to finish him off. Do it. Now!*

Whoa, whoa, whoa . . . thought Evangelina.

Jonathan's eyes, wide with alarm, opened his mouth to summon Principal Kyle, but Evangelina immediately snapped her fingers and suspended time. Materializing behind Jonathan's chair, she appeared in her astral form and lunged at the desk to snatch the gun from Jones's hand and slide it back into his shoulder holster. Swooping Jonathan under her arm she navigated him out the office, finally setting him down in the hall amidst a time-suspended student body, while simultaneously reinstating time and assuming her "Evie" form.

"C'mon kid, I'll accompany you back to class."

"What happened? How did I get here? What was that all about? He pointed a gun at me!"

"Calm down, kiddo. Don't worry, he won't bother you again."

"Evie? Where did you come from? How did you know to save me?"

"Let's just say I was in the neighborhood. Nori asked me to check in on you occasionally . . . you know. She told me about your big plans to improve our lives and doesn't want them to be waylaid because of your age. With my background in law enforcement, it's easy for me to check in occasionally. Today is one of those days. So, if you see me hanging around, just ignore me." With that, she pulled in close to Jonathan and whispered, "It's best you don't tell anyone about our little adventure."

As she spoke these words, Jonathan felt a balmy breeze play across his face. Somewhere in his memory bank appeared an image of a spritely silhouette fanning gold, diaphanous wings, shedding fragments of light.

A loud voice broke his trance. He spotted the detective blast out the office door and give chase to the two, followed by the principal, and desk secretary.

"Where do you think you're going? I'm not done with you and that woman. Hey, stop!"

As the detective closed in on them, Evie turned and separated the two with her body. Immediately, she stuck her badge in his face. "Evie Jordan, F.B.I."

Jones stopped in his tracks and scrutinized the badge, "What business do you have here? This is out of your jurisdiction."

"Not anymore, detective. I want to be sure you understand. If you come anywhere close to this school or this child again, there will be severe consequences. You will wish you never were assigned to this case."

With clenched fists and loud mutterings, Jones stormed back into the stunned student body, leaving the principal and secretary standing, confused by all the hullabaloo.

Behind the tree across the street from the school, watching through the detective's eyes, Andras punched the air in frustration. "So, she's the angel I was warned about. She needs to be eliminated," he shouted with spittle spraying from his lips. Looking down at Shadow, he said, "Sometimes, if you want a job done right you must do it yourself."

As Evie guided Jonathan down the hall, she began to put the pieces of the puzzle together. *The modus operandi screams Andras.* She was now fully certain she knew the assassin's identity from tales spread about him. Because no demon is allowed to kill a mortal without permission of the Most High, Andras devised a method to dispose of humans without laying a hand on the victim. He corrupted *others* into doing his dastardly deeds. He simply became a director in his own home movie without lifting a finger. This let him off the hook. However, he'd gone rogue in the past and suffered the consequences. Many years ago, the demon killed a priest in the Philippines with his own hands. His punishment was to be chained in Hell for a century. During the 14th century, another of his dastardly murders banished him from the Earth for even more years. Andras had a history of going rogue (low-down and dirty, defining his own use of power) and there were no assurances he would not try it again when all else failed.

Though facing the demon herself did not deter her, the thought of Nori and the boy facing him alone plagued her. It was what worried Evangelina the most. He was a despicable demon—an unfeeling, murderous rogue without an ounce of honor. She could only hope to face him before their trip. Considering his past, the angel craved the opportunity to exercise his evil essence from the planet. Forever.

Chapter 32

MATH AND SUSHI

JOE STRODE THROUGH THE humming plant, so familiar with the sound of machines pounding out parts for the big three and the smell of hot oil saturating the dingy factory floor. He bypassed sparks flying from a welding station to enter the compact office at the back of the shop. Sleeves rolled, coffee cup in hand, the owner sat studying the plans Joe delivered to him earlier.

"Good afternoon Mr. Ruffini."

"Have a seat, Joe. As you can imagine, I'm intrigued. These are you son's plans?"

"Yes, sir."

"And he's only eleven?"

"He'll be twelve, shortly."

"Incredible. I was not aware of your son's brilliance."

"Yep, that's my boy." Joe let fly the implication that he was only a worker in his plant, never a friend after all these years.

"This would be a staggering windfall for our company. If you can get us the contract to build this thing, we'll be busy for a year, maybe more. What did you cost this thing out for . . . how much?"

"My son has given me a copy of his design and I estimate we could charge between one point two-five million and a million and a half," Joe smiled.

"Our cost?"

"Somewhere around six-fifty to seven hundred thousand."

"When are you meeting with these people?"

"From what my wife said, the first of the month."

"And it's the prototype. There's also testing and if everything goes right, we could be the sole producer. It could be an unexpected bonanza. But we shouldn't get ahead of ourselves. There's much to consider before we can fully commit."

Rubbing his grizzled chin, he looked at Joe and said, "Give me some time and I'll have my lawyers draft something to get us started. You're sure we can build this thing?"

"Listen, we have a bull pen filled with seasoned journeymen who have been plying their trade for twenty, thirty years at this plant. If they can't build it, no one can." He was thinking of the promise this held for his long-time buddies at work. "Oh, to be sure, these men must be included. All of them and I'll see to it."

"You're right. Okay, you book the presentation."

We'll all conduct a due diligence on both sides and take our own steps to verify everything before we fall into a business agreement. I'll have my men take a look at the plans before we invest time and money. For starters, book the initial presentation. I'll put together all the paperwork and presentation tools necessary. You're representing all of us. I know you'll do a good job. If you land this thing, there's a nice, nice raise associated with it, and you'll be the project manager."

"Thank you, sir. I'll do my best. I'll get back to you as soon as I have a definite itinerary."

Joe thought to himself, *I'm so glad I stayed with the company. The offer from the major buyer sounded good, but this was an opportunity I only dreamed about.*

Joe left the office and punched out. As he left the factory, on his way to the parking lot, the yard guard waved and said, "Aren't you leaving a little early?"

"Got things to do."

"It's about time you take time off. You're here all the time."

"Yeah, it's my second home," said Joe with a wave.

Joe took a slow run to his car and jumped in, automatically turning the radio dial to his favorite station. His fingers spontaneously rapped out the tune on the steering wheel. With a lead singer's head bang, he belted out one of his favorite songs. Things were going his way and Joe felt stoked.

Home from school, Mary sat in her kitchen resting her feet, savoring a glass of wine, exhausted from chasing around at school. While Nori rolled sushi for dinner, Jonathan helped. From time to time, Nori would intercept his hand as he tried to abscond a finished piece. "Oh, Nori! Just one."

The back door banged, and Joe set his lunch box on the mud room stoop. After removing his shoes, he entered the kitchen with an unusually loopy smile on his face. Seeing Nori rolling sushi, he snuck his hand in, snatched a finished piece, and popped it into his mouth.

"Oooh, you so bad. Bad example for boy."

"So sorry," said Joe clasping his hands and bowing his head.

"Not funny," scolded Mary.

"Forgive me, but I have great news. The owner is giving me paid time off to go with Jonathan and Nori to New York to pitch the idea we build his prototype. We're going to New York, baby!"

"Yes," Jonathan shouted, giving a little happy dance next to Nori.

"That's wonderful," said Mary, seizing Joe into a crushing hug.

"AND," said Joe, "if I land the job, I get a raise and get to head the project!"

"Good feather in Joe's hat!" Nori said.

Evangelina sprawled atop the home to enjoy the family session below. She was concerned, however, with the slight uptick of evil she felt present. She couldn't dismiss that she hadn't sensed Andras's evil before the chaotic school debacle. She had to consult with Zadkiel. Surely he knew of a measurement to determine her instinct levels. Her lack of confidence confounded her as she visually scoured the grounds from her perch to no avail. She could not pinpoint the source. Unbeknownst to the happy gathering, Envio sat in the bushes outside the Puro kitchen window. Listening to the kitchen revelations turned him giddy. He could bring Andras positive news; news the archduke could potentially act on to complete his mission. "This might be the key to my freedom. Once the archduke completes this hellish mission, I can return with honor to the forest and meadowlands of my fellow imps." His heart ached for his home and fellow pranksters. He hated being under the thumb of the archduke and the voracious demon wolf, Shadow. The information he just gleaned, if completed, would return him home. He would continue to bring additional information.

Chapter 33

WET RECON AND
BURNT HOT DOGS

THE AUTUMN WEATHER TURNED crisp and cold, and a tinge of fall colors touched the boulevard trees. Envio scuttled from tree to tree, maintaining a perfect match as he sped along. It would be catastrophic if a mortal saw him and called the police, or worse, the media shouted out about an alien on the loose. The ensuing hubbub would make his job much harder. The thought of police dogs hot on his trail made him shiver. Better to take the extra time and be safe.

Arriving at the museum, Envio sprinted to the porch and high-stepped the stairs, stopping to wipe his feet on the doormat and straighten his vest before knocking. *How ridiculous is this?* Lately, Andras had a penchant for taunting him over little details, like having him wait outside for long periods, sometimes in a downpour of rain, before calling him in.

"Wipe your feet and come in," Andras barked at the imp.

"What?"

"You heard me, peon."

Envio stomped his clean feet, loud enough for Andras to hear and entered a room filled with paw prints from the archduke's wolf, Shadow. Shaking his head, his enthusiasm gone, the imp said, "I come bearing more vital information about the boy!"

"Spit it out, pinhead!"

"As you wish. The boy, the father and the nanny are boarding a plane on Sunday to go to New York. It would be a perfect time for your next attack."

"Excellent! Excellent! What airport? What time?"

"Uh . . . I don't know."

"You're an idiot," erupted Andras. "That's right, a blithering idiot. Envio, the idiot imp! Has a ring to it, doesn't it!"

"But Master, they didn't discuss details of the trip."

"How would you know? You didn't stay long enough to get the rest of the story. You found a crumb, but missed the meat and potatoes," Andras said, his fists clenched and spittle flying.

Envio, cowering dumbstruck at Andras's fury, whispered, "What do you wish, Master?"

"What do I wish? I want you to go back there, hide in your bush and find where and at what time the boy is leaving for the airport on Sunday. You stay there until either you know the time of departure, or they leave for the airport."

"You want me to stay in the bushes until Sunday?"

"Bingo, you little sissy! If you can't get me the information, then you'll personally inform me when they leave. I will follow them to the airport. Enough of this third-party minion crap. I'll do the job myself. To hell with protocol. To hell with the rules. Before you leave, you need to gather enough roadkill to feed Shadow until Sunday night . . . and be quick about it!"

"It's going to be cold and rain all day Saturday."

"AND how is it my problem?"

Envio dragged himself to the door and turned back in time to see Andras laughing at him. He opened the door to large thunderstorm clouds barreling in. This was going to be an ordeal he dreaded. The simple thought of sitting out in the rain caused his complexion to mutate from its standard ruddy red into woodland camouflage. Ready to take on task one, he trotted off to find feed for the dog.

Andras watched from the museum window with wolf at his side. The canine whined as his belly was hitting his backbone. He hadn't eaten anything this day.

Andras looked down at his lifelong companion. "Don't worry, boy. He'll be back soon."

The demon canine howled in response.

"AND you'll feast on his flesh when we finish this thing for Lucifer."

The black wolf growled menacingly and licked his chops.

Baillie sat on Jonathan's bed and watched him shuffle through his closet, picking out clothes to wear in New York. Hanging on his door was his small man suit with matching tie. He hated his suit. He felt stiff and robotic when he wore it last at his cousin's wedding. The shirt collar choked him, and he detested having to wear a tie; but Mom said he had to wear it to make the board take him seriously.

Having reviewed his presentation slideshow any number of times, he moved on to pack his laptop and electronics in a carry-on bag. His eyes circled the room. "Yep. I think I have everything."

According to his mother, tomorrow's trip would take a little over an hour, so he added his cell phone to play fun, preloaded games. He congratulated himself for having prepared diligently. He just hoped these board members would understand the concepts he planned to present.

"Don't forget your good shoes, Jonathan," Mom called from the kitchen.

"Ah, Mom! I hate those shoes. They make me look like a mini man. Besides, they hurt my feet,"

"You need to look as smart as we all know you are."

"What do shiny shoes have to do with being smart?"

"Pack the shoes, Jonathan!"

Begrudgingly, he tossed the leather wingtip shoes into the suitcase and zipped it. Glancing out the window he saw the pouring rain posing a dilemma. He usually walked Baillie at this time. Perplexed, he called on Mom for instruction.

"Mom, Baillie needs to go outside and it's pouring rain. What should I do?"

"Check the Doppler on your weather app and see if it's going to let up soon."

Jonathan flipped on his phone and saw the Doppler radar showed a break in the storm coming. Calculating wind speed and storm movement he figured there would be a window of calm in twenty minutes, and it should last at least a half hour before the next wave of storms would reach them.

"C'mon Baillie, let's tell Nori."

The pup jumped eagerly off the bed and trailed the boy down the hall to the kitchen where Nori worked preparing dinner. Jonathan sauntered up to Nori as she stirred the pot.

"Whatcha making, Nori? It sure smells good."

"Me make pasta for dinner tonight."

"Listen, the rain is going to stop soon according to the weather app, and I have to walk Baillie. I know you always come with us, but you don't have to come if you're too busy."

"Sauce almost done. I come with you."

"Okay, as soon as it stops, we go!"

Jonathan retrieved Baillee's harness and leash from the landing and returned to the kitchen with Baillie wagging his tale in anticipation. "Stand still, Baillee. Let me strap you in."

Once in gear, the dog broke away to stand impatiently at the door.

"Not yet. We have to wait until the rain lets up."

Baillie barked in response. The boy stared out the kitchen window as the downpour reduced to a drizzle. Outside, below the kitchen window, poor Envio sat drenched and shivering, straining to hear the chatter from inside the house. "Going for a walk . . . ", " . . . rain lets up." Finally, the words he waited to hear: "Looks like the rain has stopped for the moment. Let's rush before the next wave of storms, Nori."

Certainly, they'll talk of the trip, he thought to himself. He shook himself off and readied for his stealth following, knowing he needed to be close to hear their conversation, but not so close as to be discovered.

Nori plucked her shawl off its hook and the trio shuffled out of the back door. "We just go 'round block once, Jonathan."

"Sounds like a plan."

Baillie pulled the lead tight, and they traipsed after him down the muddy, puddled drive splashing up at them. The chilly air filled their nostrils with the pleasant, musky smell of earth. They began at a brisk pace but stopped at each tree to satisfy Baillie's ritual. Meanwhile, Envio lurked in the bushes, straining to listen in on their conversation. As they moved down the sidewalk, the imp, in full woodland camouflage, leapt from bush to bush.

"What kind noodle you want?"

"Huh?"

"You want shell, angel hair, mostaccioli or gnocchi noodles with sauce?"

"I don't know."

"What your favorite?"

"I don't know . . . how 'bout shells. I like how they fill with sauce."

"Okay! Me too."

Baillie caught sight of movement in the bushes and focused his attention on the shrubbery. Barking non-stop, he refused to proceed. *Rats, I've been made*, thought Envio. Cornered between the front of the house and the porch, he panicked. The only route of escape was to crawl to the far corner behind him and scurry across the side of the house. Envio retreated with Baillie on his tail, dragging Jonathan behind him.

Reaching the corner of the house, he ran to the backyard in search of safety from the tenacious, barking dog gaining on him. Envio halted in the open for a brief moment to regain his sense of direction before moving on. But in that short pause, a hungry, red-tailed hawk spotted his wee body standing alone. The large raptor circled, then dove, his sharp talons poised to snatch Envio and lift him into the sky.

The imp struggled furiously against the claws restraining him. Resigned he couldn't loosen the raptor's grasp, he kicked up and navigated his tail to wrap around the hawk's neck. As he squeezed, the red-tailed hawk, caught off guard, panicked and let Envio tumble from the sky and plummet into a neighbor's open swimming pool. Stunned after his splash-down, he floated to the surface. Recovering from the impact, he crawled from the pool and shook off the water, grateful he still lived, until, after clearing the water blurring his eyes, he came face to face with the neighbor's giant schnauzer.

The imp's eyes popped out, and he struggled to back away from the teeth-bared, snarling dog with evil intentions. Slowly, carefully, Envio turned and ran toward the fence with the schnauzer hot on his trail. Jumping up he pulled himself over moments before the dog nipped his tail. Once on the other side, Envio collapsed, panting, grateful to be alive. For the first time ever, he knew anger and directed it at an image of the smarmy face of Andras.

Regaining his composure, he surveyed the sky and groaned to watch another massive thunderstorm rolling in. He decided it best to return to the Puro home and his hiding spot. He took only two steps when a lightning bolt shot from the sky and struck him between his miniature horns. Envio laid on the ground, smoldering and moaning. After regaining his equilibrium, he sniffed the air and uttered a deflated: "Smells like a BBQ gone wrong and I'm the burnt hot dog."

He struggled to a sitting position, shaking his head in disbelief and began patting himself down, extinguishing any smoldering spots on his body. Taking inventory, he decided he was no worse for the wear. "What part of my body hasn't been attacked today?" *I want to be free of Andras, his mutt and this assignment,* he thought. *That's it. I've had enough.* He trotted off, making his way back slowly, tree to tree and bush to bush, arriving at his spot in the Puro's bushes. The clouds opened and a deluge of rain poured down. "I just cannot catch a break."

Chapter 34

PREFLIGHT AND
HUNGRY DEMONS

J ONATHAN SNAPPED HIS SUITCASE closed, slung his backpack over his shoulder and headed to the front door, propping them next to his dad's luggage. With his mission complete he found his way back to the kitchen and sat at the table to find Baillie looking up at him with soulful brown eyes, aware something out of the ordinary was happening.

"Don't worry, buddy, I'll be home Tuesday and I'll take you on the longest, bestest walk."

Baillie turned his head away, shunning his master. His instincts told him something was different. The boy reached down and scratched his friend behind his ears and patted his head. Nori appeared at the kitchen door, pulling her rolling luggage and saw the two at the table.

"You got everything?"

"I'm pretty sure."

"Got toothbrush?"

"Oh, shoot. Thanks for reminding me."

Jonathan scooted off to the bathroom to retrieve his toothbrush. Baillie now stared at Nori and whined in concern. She patted the bewildered animal and then rolled her suitcase to the front door. Jonathan joined her and stashed the toothbrush in his knapsack.

"When are they coming?"

"Don't know. They say before noon."

"Well, it's getting close. Where's Dad?"

"He go to shop to get presentation stuff from boss."

"Well, he better hurry. What happens if they come and he's not back?"

"I call him when driver get here."

Jonathan plopped in the rocking chair with Baillie at his feet and peered out the front window, watching for their ride to the airport. Mary left her bedroom, hoping the driver would come soon as she needed to finish grading papers. When she saw her son sitting alone in the rocking chair, she sat next to him.

"Thank God for such a beautiful fall day. Perfect for flying. Are you nervous about anything?"

"Not really."

"Hopefully, your trip will be smooth sailing. How about your presentation? Are you worried?"

"I worry those grown-ups won't understand the concepts I have to present."

"Are you comparing intellects already, Mr. Know-It-All? Show humility. I'm sure they're all very smart men. Where's your father?"

"Nori said he went to work to retrieve his presentation from Mr. Ruffini."

"I hope he doesn't miss his ride. I know he has his plane ticket and Nori has her ticket and yours, too. If he doesn't make it back in time, take his luggage with you . . . aw, shucks, I'm going to miss all of you." At this moment, for the first time, she had regret about opting out.

"Mom, we'll only be gone for two nights."

"I know, but it's going to be awfully quiet around here."

"Baillie will keep you company."

"Yes, he will, sweetie," said Mary bending to plant a warm kiss on her son's forehead.

"As they say, Ma, 'aw, shucks.'"

Mary left Jonathan at the window, preoccupied with his own thoughts and headed for coffee in the kitchen. Hearing an unusually hyperactive Baillie kicking up a storm in the living room, she called out "What's all the commotion in there?"

"He caught sight of a red squirrel going about his business of burying acorns and streaked to the window to defend his territory; Baillie thinks he's going to steal our front yard."

"Crazy dog."

A limousine pulled into the Puro driveway and parked. A man fully uniformed in chauffeur dress and cap stepped out and moved forward, pausing when he saw the rowdy pup at the window.

"Limo's here," Jonathan loudly announced to the house. Baillie continued to travel back and forth in front of the window maintaining a steady yammer at the squirrels, and now the driver.

"Can't you hush him, Jonathan? He's annoying to say the least."

Nori donned her coat, and beckoned the chauffer to the porch, while Mary handed Jonathan his jacket and waited for him to slip it on before grabbing his shoulders to look him squarely in his face.

"Jonathan, I haven't told you enough how proud I am to be your mother. I admit I was slow coming to your bandwagon, but I'm here now. I-am-so-proud. I'll be thinking of you every minute until you're back. You stay safe little man and listen to your father and Nori, too."

Jonathan, always hoping for this moment, allowed himself to tear up. "Thanks, Mom. Your words are the last thing I needed before leaving. Thank you."

Tripping over Baillie, she opened the door to the limo driver.

"This is the Puro home?"

"Yes, it is," she said, turning to instruct Jonathan to "put Baillie in your bedroom and shut the door."

"Luggage?"

"Oh, sorry. It's all right here," said Mary pointing to the heap.

"Excuse me, ma'am," the driver said, lifting the first of the bags, holding a foot against Baillie to keep him from busting out the cracked door.

"Jonathan! I asked you to take him to your room."

"Got it."

The driver deposited the bags in his trunk and stood waiting aside an open door for the passengers to exit the house.

Mary, meanwhile, scurried about the house, trying to make order out of the chaotic morning mess. Between the concern for the rain, dog, and now Joe's lateness, she worried they were missing something. Taking a last look-around, she followed them out the front door to bid farewell. "Have a safe trip and good luck with 'The Nori,' Jonathan. Oh, and one more thing. Both of you must be careful when you're in New York. I know you're staying at a nice hotel but be wary of people. They're not always what they seem."

"I know very well," said Nori firmly. "I been through this before. No worries, I read people good."

"Yes, you do, I s'pose."

"Thanks, Mom. We'll be cautious. Love ya."

"AND I love you, sweetie."

Jonathan, followed by Nori, moved quickly to the limousine where the driver waited by the open door. The boy scooted into the backseat, followed by the nanny. Mary waved goodbye from the front door and watched them pull away. When she entered the house, she was met by silence. It was then her soft tears burst into a flood. She berated herself: "I could have taken two days off to join my family in this momentous event. Always the contrary one." Her remorse continued until she heard the nonstop yapping from Jonathan's room. Baillie.

Quickly she tidied up. She had to hurry to get to work. She'd taken the morning off from school to see her family off. Time was a premium because she still needed to take Baillie to her neighbor's house. The widow up the road graciously offered to look after Baillie while she was at work.

Envio's head emerged from the bushes and casted an eye over the empty yard and into Jonathan's room. Deciding he was in the clear, except for a few friendly squirrels, and the still persistent yelping mutt inside Jonathan's bedroom, he scampered off to inform his master the group had left for the airport, but not before giving the pooch a defiant salute.

Simultaneously, Mary pulled out her cell phone to call Joe.

"Hello! What's going on?" asked Joe.

"What do you mean 'what's going on?' They're gone. They just left in a limo. How are you going to get to the airport?"

"I'm late because Hank didn't have his presentation ready. I guess I'll take a cab."

"Well, hurry. It's a good thing I prescreened all of you with the airport so you don't have to go through security."

"That's my wife! Always thinking. We're about finished here, so I'll call the cab now."

"Don't miss your plane."

"I won't. Love ya, gotta run!"

Mary shook her head and sighed.

Huffing and puffing, holding his side, Envio knocked on the front door of the museum and dusted his feet. The door creaked a crack and he stepped inside, careful to wipe his feet again. Scraggly, with singe marks crusting his body, he turned to address Andras sitting on his overstuffed chair smoking a cigar. The archduke looked him over and laughed.

"What the Hell happened to you?"

"Not important," said the imp regaining his composure. "They're on their way to the airport."

"Which airport?"

"They were heading toward Detroit Metro."

"Excellent."

"They left a few minutes ago and you might be able to catch them on the highway."

"What's their destination?"

"New York . . . LaGuardia."

"Hmm . . . Methinks I'll wait for them at Metro and take care of matters there or on the plane. Wherever the opportunity presents itself."

"Excellent choice, Sire."

"Now, you get yourself to the barn. Get some rest. You deserve it."

"But what of feeding the beast?"

"Change of plans. I'll be taking Shadow with me. You don't have to worry about it. I'll personally see he's fed when I return. Right, Shadow?" Envio detected a smug smile cross his evil lips.

The menacing wolf snapped his jaws at Envio and licked his chops. The imp felt uncomfortable. Something was afoot. The archduke never acted this nice. Confused, he cautiously backed toward the door and cracked it open a bit, just enough to squeeze his small body through the opening. Once closed, he waited in the shadows for some trickery to be played on him. Eventually he felt safe and shuffled along to the barn where he collapsed, falling face first in a pile of hay.

Chapter 35

THE BATTLE OF METRO

THE LIMOUSINE CAUTIOUSLY CLIMBED the driveway to the airport entrance and the departure doors. It was a busy day at the airport. Bumper to bumper traffic on the approach slowed their progress. Upon reaching the entrance, the driver had no choice but to park three deep away from the curb. Instructing Nori and Jonathan to remain in the back seat, the driver popped out the cab and hustled to the curb to retrieve a luggage cart. Returning to the limo, he motioned for them to exit the cab while he loaded their luggage. Back on the curb, Nori tipped the man from the money Mary had given her for the occasion and rolled the cart through the entrance to the check-in counter to confirm their flight and handle their luggage for boarding. Jonathan followed along with his backpack slung on his shoulder as they made their way to the security checkpoint. As there was a separate line for prescreened passengers, they flew though the security checkpoint. Once in the concourse, Nori studied her ticket and saw they needed Gate 39. They pulsed along with the concourse flow, trapped within the hustle and bustle of the mob of passengers going to their gates.

Evangelina drifted above the airport interior and followed the bustling crowd. Along the way she exercised her powers looking for evil. With all these people, she worried about failing to find a demon or demons led by Andras hiding in the mass. Andras, the assassin, could assemble, within minutes, a multitude of demons or mortals under his control to wait for a vulnerable moment to attack. Though Nori proved herself a formidable force, she couldn't handle a horde of Andras' demons by herself.

Nori and Jonathan made it to Gate 39 and found a seat looking out the window and settled in.

Nori, checking her watch, announced, "We got over hour before boarding."

"Hope Dad makes it here on time."

"He will. You play your game and I read magazine. He be here soon."

At the boarding lounge, Evangelina presented herself. She stood in her astral form at the window and whispered, *I'm here. Relax.* Nori smiled in acknowledgment and opened her cooking magazine, while Evangelina turned to watch a plane taxi and take off. It amazed her to see these behemoths—these giant hunks of aircraft sheet metal—become airborne and fly off. . . . *a true tribute to man's ingenuity.*

Joe stood outside the shop holding an overstuffed valise, waiting for his cab. He chuckled to himself as he thought about his boss, Hank, nervous as a bride on her wedding night, tried to push him to take everything except the kitchen sink for his presentation. He wanted Joe to land the contract so he buried his head to find and include everything he could about his company, dating back to the 1940s. He knew Joe would do a good job and just wanted him to have all the tools he needed.

The cab rolled to the front of the factory to a lineup of employees waving their good-byes, good lucks, and chants of "break a leg, Puro," as Joe stepped in, and the cab moved on.

"Metro," Joe called out from the back seat.

The cabby adjusted his rearview mirror to see his passenger. "I'm Blisdon."

"I'm Joe. Joe Puro."

"Business or pleasure?"

"I think a little of both, but mostly business."

"Where ya headed?"

"New York to give a pitch."

"Well, I wish you luck."

"Thanks."

Blisdon drove off with Mary reminding Joe of his prescreened security pass and that his luggage had already been pre-checked. "All you need to do is get to Gate 39 as soon as possible because the plane is leaving in just a little over an hour from now."

Puro . . . Puro . . . As he drove, Blisdon repeated the name again and again, while taking sideway glances at the passenger. Knowing the answer before asking, he said, "You look familiar. Do you live in Farmington Hills?" he asked, knowing the answer.

"Ah, yes I do."

"Do you have a son, Jonathan? And a nanny, Nori?"

"Ah, yeah, how do you know all of this?"

"Nori and I are old friends. You said your last name's Puro. Right?

"Yeah, Joe Puro. What a coincidence. Both of them are going with me to New York."

"Please give Nori my regards and wish her a safe trip."

"I will."

"It's a small world."

Evangelina stood scanning the concourse crowd. Suddenly, the tiny hairs on her neck rose to attention. *Evil is near.* Scouring the crowd, she eventually spotted a "blind man" standing in the concourse, supported by a white cane and wearing black-out glasses. When her eyes travelled down his side they landed on a robust, harnessed black German Shepherd. A slow progression of bells and sirens sounded off in her head, alerting her. *Evil is here.* Instinctively she returned to the blind man, mentally stripping him of his costume and props to reveal his beaked head and near naked body. With his faithful, powerfully built wolf demon at his side, she knew she was in the presence of the most violent and dangerous of demons. Andras. *Just as I suspected.*

She spoke to Nori's mind. *Snap up Jonathan and run. Get as far away from here as possible! Be aware of a blind man with his German Shepherd. He's here.* Nori scrutinized the busy crowd in search of a man and his guide dog. Her eyes locked on the two demons, and only because Evangelina, at one time, granted her the ability to see demons in their true form, was she able to see behind the blind man's outfit and visualize him as the demon he was. Certain they had not seen her, she seized Jonathan's arm and whispered, "We gotta go."

"Where?"

"We get outta here. Big trouble. We go."

"What trouble?"

"No ask questions. Take backpack; we leave."

184

Reluctantly, the puzzled boy yanked up his things and they speed-walked away from the gate, back toward security. Meanwhile, Evangelina found a restroom to transform into Evie Jordan. She dashed directly to her target, the "blind man."

"Andras. Your cover is blown. It's time for you to leave."

The demon raised his glasses and said, "Who in Hell's name are you to tell me what to do?"

"I am Evangelina, Jonathan's guardian angel and unless you wish to suffer the fate of the previous demons who defied me, you should leave."

"When did they start making female angels? You don't frighten me, you little waif. I'll take care of you and complete my mission here. You should leave while you can."

Evangelina shook her head. "If you insist then we'll do it the hard way."

"Bring it on, feeble fraud!"

Nori and Jonathan ran through the concourse, down the escalator until reaching the doors to the entrance, stopping only for a moment to catch their breath. Confused, the boy looked at his nanny.

"Why are we running away? What are we running from? We're going to miss our flight!"

"No worry about flight. People want to stop you from your mission. They do anything to keep you from flight. Nori see bad guy waiting to stop you. We go. We get away."

"But why?"

"They no want help world. They want destroy world. Your machine too good."

"Why would anyone want to destroy the world?"

"Me no know," she said, heaving with each step. "But you stop talking. We got to hurry."

"What are we going to do?"

"Last question. We go back home and wait. We reschedule trip to safer time."

The two stepped out of the airport, onto the sidewalk to hail a cab. As they approached the cab stand, Joe's cab pulled parallel to the airport departure doors, and he hopped out. He stepped to the passenger side window and looked in on Blisdon. The former demon cabby smiled.

"That'll be thirty-seven dollars and fifty cents."

Joe reached in his pocket and pulled out a wad of bills, peeling off fifty dollars. He tossed it to the cabby and told him to keep the change. Time was not on his side; he took off running into the airport.

As Blisdon turned his head to monitor oncoming traffic from behind, he spotted Nori and Jonathan at the cab stand talking to the attendant. His tires squealed as he rushed to greet them.

"Nori!" he yelled, popping out of the taxi.

"It you, Blisdon?"

Leaping over the curb, he met Nori and lifted her off her feet for a one-sided embrace.

"No Blisdon. No time to talk."

"What is it?"

"We going to New York, but demons intercept us. Bird head man with wolf."

"Andras . . . how d'ya get away?

"Angel lady saw him, and we ran. Can you take us home?"

"Get in the cab. You don't want to mess with that demon. He's a cruel murderer. Let's go."

Evangelina snapped her fingers and suspended time in the concourse. In one fluid movement, she morphed into her lustrous battle armor and released her sword of pure light from its scabbard and her shield from her shoulder. Catching Andras off guard, she took the first plunge. When he turned to recognize Evangelina, he and Shadow converted into full demon form. As a perfectly timed pair, the two circled her to gain advantage.

The black Canis lupus, snarling with bared teeth, jumped at the levitating angel who, in turn, smacked him away with her shield sending him sliding across the concourse. Andras pulled his own sword from its scabbard and lunged at Evangelina; but the angel tied up his sword, reached across and punched him in the face. This infuriated the demon as he backed out of the clench.

"You harlot! I thought I might show you mercy, but now I'm going to cut you into little pieces and feed you to the fish in the lake."

"Talk's cheap, Archduke. You're going to regret this day."

The swords rang with each clash as the two entities tangled in battle. While Andras engaged her, the demon wolf nipped at her heels. She kicked him in the face and sent him flying. Hitting a support column, he laid dazed, only to reengage in the fight once its effect wore off.

Andras charged the angel and pummeled her shield with fierce chopping blows. Each blow pushed her further into the wall. With formidable strength he thrusted his blade point at her torso, but Evangelina rebuffed it away with offensive hearty swipes at the demon's face. Their swords clashed over and over, sparking upon contact. Back in the fray, Shadow snarled and snapped at the angel floating above reach.

Their swords parried and struck back and forth until locking in a pommel-to-pommel bind. Evangelina spun to release her weapon, sending Andras' rapier from his hands to clank against the wall. She moved forward to catch him with a second blow to the temple, dropping him to the ground. Towering over him with her sword pressed to his bird neck, she snapped, "Bye-bye,"

Beneath his furled brow, Andras' black soulless eyes brightened to fiery embers.

"Do it, bitch. But never forget, after I reconstitute in Hell, it will be my sole mission to hunt you down and end your existence."

"You couldn't do it this time, what makes you think the next will be any different, scum?"

As the angel prepared to dispose of Andras in his present form, the wolf leapt and latched his snarling jaws on her sword hand. She tried to shake the animal loose, but he slipped away from under her. Her struggle with the wolf to free her hand opened the opportunity for Andras to scramble away and seize hold of a heavy, detached stanchion. He charged behind her, weakened from their violent exchanges of blows, but still able to bludgeon her head with the heavy steel club. Falling to the floor she rolled in agony and lost consciousness. Andras retrieved his sword.

"Come Shadow, hurry! We much catch the boy. They're escaping. I'll take care of her later."

Andras jumped onto the back of the wolf, and they raced down the concourse. Following the demon wolf's keen sense of smell, they arrived at the airport's entrance and hunted the surroundings to no avail. Concluding their prey had escaped and not to be found on this site, the demon's volcanic anger erupted.

"They're getting away," Andras shouted. Gripping Shadow's back, he flapped his wings and the duo rose into the sky. From his aerial vantage point, he cast about the escape routes. "They're on the highway by now. Which way? Which way? Beast, follow your nose! Follow your nose!"

Rotating his head in all directions, the airborne canine sniffed the air for their scent. He howled to signal his success. He had located his quarry. "Find, Shadow, find," commanded Andras. Shadow snarled and the two flew off toward the highway.

Chapter 36

PARRIED THRUSTS AND
BURNING TIRES

F ROM THE BACK WINDOW of the cab, Nori frantically searched the roadway and skies. Blisdon clutched the steering wheel, weaving in and out of traffic. He knew Andras from the past and remembered his boiling fury when confronted. This demon would never submit to the angel. He would fight her to the death. After all, he was the archduke and would not be denied.

Hot in pursuit, the demon canine raced on, following the scent intensifying with each mile they overtook. There, in the distance, he spotted the cab weaving in and out of traffic along the highway, just beyond the interchange. He focused on his mark and let loose an enthusiastic howl.

Nori bent over and whispered in Blisdon's ear, "I see them. They're coming." Despite her frenzied state, for Jonathan's sake, she struggled to maintain a calm exterior.

To Blisdon, that Andras could be loose and following them, only meant Evangelina had been bested. He set aside his spontaneous reaction to that possibility. *Don't panic. Stay calm.* But he knew he alone could not offer much of a fight against Andras.

Gripping a ball of fire, Andras signaled his wolf to dive at the cab. As the two closed in, Andras pulled back and hurled the fiery projectile to explode directly in front of the cab and force Blisdon to swerve around the crater. The demon launched another fireball, this time the projectile exploding so close behind the cab it raised the rear wheels off the pavement. Losing control, Blisdon began zigzagging in response to the near hits.

Fireball after fireball missed their mark leaving cratered ground behind them. Shadow swooped in and landed on the trunk of the vehicle. Unsuccessfully, Blisdon sharply twisted and turned the vehicle, hoping to throw him off, unaware of Andras dismounting Shadow and skulking on the cab's roof. Taking his sword from his scabbard, he plunged its point into the cover. The blade penetrated through, nearly skewering Nori through the head. Giddy at his success, Andras began quickly sawing through the roof to access the passengers below. Cutting a U-shaped incision into the covering, he reached down and began to peel back the metal.

A loud thump distracted the demon and he turned to the front of the cab. Evangelina stood defiantly, sword in hand, with grim determination on her face.

"You, again?"

"You thought it would be easy to get rid of me?"

"You need to learn to turn and walk away."

"You need to learn I will never go away until I send you back to Hell."

"We had this discussion before, didn't we? And my response is the same. 'Bring it on wench!'"

They charged each other and locked blades, struggling precariously atop the cab. Aware Evangelina had arrived, Blisdon steadied the cab to give her a stable fighting platform. The two tussled on the top until the angel stepped behind the demon and flipped him off the cab in front of the iconic eight-story Uniroyal tire display on the side of I-94. Evangelina jumped from the cab to put an end to the demon once and for all.

Righting himself after rolling down the embankment and covered in filth, he fought to regain dignity. He retrieved his muddied sword from the gutter only to confront that damn angel. It enraged him to see her looking him up and down with a giddy grin plastered on her face.

"Go back to Hell, Andras. You don't stand a chance."

"I'll go back to Hell when your head is on the end of my sword, little girl."

"Ah . . . " she sighed, "typical arrogant demon. Doesn't know when he's been bested."

The two locked swords and tussled for control again. Breaking out of the deadlock their blades rang with each strike. Sparks flew as each competed for control. The angel battled from the high ground while the demon, stuck in the gutter, battled from the mud. Andras tried to advance up the embankment but slipped to the ground. Evangelina took advantage and pinned him down with her blade.

"Yield!"

"Never!"

"Then go back to Hell!"

The angel raised her blade high above her head. Holding her sword at its peak, she felt something tug her wing. Looking behind her she saw the evil canine's teeth locked on her wing, pulling her away from his master. Turning back, she was met by Andras' iron fist. His right cross ripped across her jaw forcing spittle to fly out directly at Andras' mutilated face before dropping to the ground. Noting her disorientation, he quickly grappled with her arm and a leg and hurled her at the 80-foot tire. Her body broke through the plastic hubcap, and she plunged inside of the tire. Throwing a number of fireballs into the hole, set the iconic landmark afire, after which he brushed off his hands and shouted, "Mock me will you?"

"Thank you, beast. I have a special treat for you, Shadow, when we get back to the barn tonight. It's an impish delicacy you should truly like."

The wolf sat on his haunches and happily howled.

He looked up to find the cab had taken off. "Now let's catch up with those humans and finish our mission. I can't wait to get back to the Philippines sipping on ginpom and enjoying the weather."

Andras mounted his wolf and the two gaily lifted off airborne as if in pursuit of a prize. They hit the heights and began to cruise toward Farmington Hills. The demon knew his targets would seek refuge in their home. Humans were so predictable.

Black billowing smoke poured from the large tire and hot, bright flames leapt from the hole in the roadside icon's hubcap. Inside the burning tire, Evangelina lay limp and unconscious. The interior of the tire raged in flames causing the sides of the tire to melt into a stream of black molten goo which slowly ebbed toward the fallen angel. The intense heat weakened the supports and, if left unchecked, the entire monument would collapse. The eight-story iconic structure creaked and groaned as the flames intensified.

Outside the tire, motorists stopped and pulled over to the side of the road. Some watched from outside their cars, videoing the spectacle, while others pointed and spoke excitedly. In the distance a wail of sirens could be heard growing ever closer.

Fire trucks from every municipality pulled onto the grass surrounding the fiery framework Firemen jumped from the trucks and busily unwound hoses and pulled axes and other tools from their storage. A hook and ladder backed into place and a crew of firefighters hoisting hoses crawled up the extended ladder to a vantage point looking into the gaping hole in the side of the tire. Once in position, one crew member waved his hands to the support below and a jet stream of water poured from the hose directly into the tire.

When the flood of water hit Evangelina directly in the face, she jumped to alert and inhaled deeply. *I need to get out of here.* With a flap of her wings, she lifted off and shot out of the hole in the tire. Clearing the smoke and torrent of water, she looked back to acknowledge "those brave people cleaning up after that stupid demon. He needs to go."

Many on the ground looked up to follow a celestial body of light blaze out of the flames into the sky. They followed her trail, dumbstruck.

"What the hell was that?" asked many.

"Musta been aliens living in the tire."

Chapter 37

DEATH AND REDEMPTION

*T*HEY'RE COMING. THEY'RE COMING.

Starting with the day she escaped with her daughter from the labor camps in the old country, without her knowing, Nori was tested and groomed to fight in the face of evil demons. Her appointed role, designated by God, was to protect the Glory Child, Jonathan Puro, from those determined to stop him from fulfilling his quest, those who would discourage him through ridicule and laughter. But most importantly, she prepared to face the demons from hell in avid pursuit. And now, as her charge drew closer to realizing his mission to feed the world, the mighty demon Andras appeared. Having fought evil before, she would do so again. The little Asian lady was fierce and ready to battle.

"Nori, what's happening? Tell me what's happening."

"Hush, Jonathan, hush. In due time."

Her breathing came in short gasps and her trembling fingers wouldn't cooperate to unlock the back door of the Puro home. But finally it opened, and she pushed Jonathan inside. Over the last ten years she mentally prepared for what might come. But those were just thoughts. Pie-in-the-sky thoughts. Nothing like what she faced in this moment. And she was scared.

It was more bewilderment than fear crossing Jonathan's face. He was beginning to understand that it was he, not Nori, who was the target of an unidentifiable presence and this presence wanted to harm him, maybe even kill him. *But why?* Nori dragged him into the kitchen and looked to the butcher block for her chef's knife, always kept razor sharp for such an event.

"Boy, we hide you."

"Where?"

"I no know. Somewhere near door or window so you run if they get close."

"Where do I go?"

"Go to St. John Church behind house and hide. God will protect you."

"Okay."

Although it was early afternoon, the skies outside turned an ominous gray, and the wind whistled through the trees. Debris raced across the backyard and plastered against the cyclone fence. Trees swayed in the wind as the lights flickered in the kitchen. Nori knew it wouldn't be long before the evil would arrive.

"Go now. Hide!"

Before Jonathan could take a step, the back kitchen door exploded into a thousand pieces raining through the kitchen. Decisively, Nori shoved Jonathan against the wall to protect him with her body. Pointing her knife blade out, she waited for the evil to arrive.

The huge wolf bounded through the back door snarling and salivating with teeth bared. His furled lips revealed glistening sharp canines. With one hand holding the butcher knife, Nori used the other to flip the table and create a barrier between her, Jonathan, and the black wolf. She carefully guided the boy to move behind the oak table and then purposely pushed him down to block his vision throughout the fracas.

With bristling fur and fiery red eyes, the evil creature crept tenaciously toward the pair, his hulking body blotting out the light from the kitchen entrance.

"Shadow! Heel!" A command piercing the tense air, spoke to the wolf. Without hesitation the animal ceased his menacing behavior and laid down on the kitchen floor. With graceful nonchalance, Andras, his wings fanned wide, stepped into the kitchen with his sword drawn.

"Well, what do we have here?" Andras chuckled. "A little Chinese nanny and a snot-nosed boy. This is simply too easy."

"Me no Chinese, birdbrain."

Andras reached to smooth the black feathers on his ravenlike head, "Methinks this is a regal look. Don't you? I am Andras, Archduke of Hell, master of assassination, and leader of thirty legions of demons."

"You arch—duck? Look like bad carved Egypt glyph."

"Arch*duke*, not duck."

"You look more like crow, not duck."

"Why you . . . Doesn't matter because in a few moments you'll be accompanying me to the depths of Hell. Enjoy what time remains because I look forward to your suffering."

"We see, birdbrain. I make soup out of you."

"Do you think your little knife gives you even the smallest chance against me and my wolf?"

"Me has taken on bigger, better than you with nothing. You leave before I make duck sorry."

Taken aback by Nori's ferocity and disrespect, Andras shook his head. Looking to his beast, he said, "Would you like a little treat? The young one should be especially tender."

As the words exited his lips, a blur flew between the two sparring enemies. His trailing wind ruffled the kitchen drapes and sent the napkins flying askew. The whirlwind abruptly ceased and Blisdon stood riveted in front of the table barricade set by Nori. Blisdon reached back and took the chef's knife from Nori's hand and pointed it at the demon and his dog.

"Get out," Blisdon shouted.

"And you are . . . ?" asked Andras. "Did someone with a sense of humor send you here?"

"I am the demon Blisdon the Quick. I am your worst nightmare and courier of your demise. Begone or suffer my wrath."

"You're kidding, right? My wolf would be swallowing you before you could ever make a move."

"Like I said, I am Blisdon the Quick and before you could even say Shadow, I will have slain your dog and gutted you like a deer. Now go."

"Listen, you fat little demon, stand aside. Why are you interfering? I am here on a mission for Lucifer, himself, and if I must, I will end you and send you back to Hell to reconstitute."

"I have no allegiance to Lucifer. I'm here to protect these mortals."

"Wait a minute, I know you. You are the demon who betrayed Beelzebub. There's a handsome bounty on your head."

"I'm sure there is."

"This is my lucky day. A twofer. Not only will I get paid for the boy, but I will also take your sorry self to Beelzebub and collect it all."

Andras' response sent Blisdon into action. He swirled and twirled and slit the throat of the wolf. With a choking whimper, the beast rolled over and was reduced to black glittering ash.

Andras bit his own thumb knuckle in white hot anger. He swung his sword wildly, knocking the blade of the knife from Blisdon's hand. When Blisdon tripped backwards, Andras took advantage and jumped forward to pin his target's throat against the table with the point of his blade.

"Not so cocky now, are we? You'd be decomposing now, but you still have value to me."

Blisdon looked despairingly from his compromised position, "I yield to you Archduke Andras, but I propose a solution to our situation."

"You're in no position to bargain, Blisdon the Slow."

"Oh, but I am. If you return me to Beelzebub, yes, he will punish me. On the other hand, he is so dependent on me eventually he will prefer my service to torturing me. Once I begin to service the prince of Hell, I will have time to seek you out and separate you from your vital organs. Every time you reconstitute in Hell, I will again seek you out and gut you. Eternity is a long, long time. You will become my sole mission and . . . I am quick. Ask Shadow."

"What do you propose?"

"I will come freely with you back to Hell, with no resistance, and you can collect your bounty from Beelzebub. In return you will let Nori and the boy live."

"You must be out of your mind. Resistance? What kind of resistance can a peon like you pose to me? I can have it all and I will take it all. Stupid demon! Andras slowly put more pressure on his sword blade which began to pierce his captive's throat. A trickle of blood oozed from Blisdon's neck.

In the next instance, Andras's eyes bulged wide, and his beak dropped open without a sound. Blisdon watched a sword blade pierce his chest from behind. Evangelina wiped black goo from her blade while eyeballing the sprawling, decomposing body. The heap of evil turned to red glittery dust and disappeared.

"It about time," Nori yelled.

"What just happened?" Jonathan said, disoriented. "I missed all the chaos after you shoved me down."

"No sir. I gently push you down. Never shove."

"Regardless, I saw a little and heard even less. All I know was the man in the suit with the dog vanished and left sparkles behind."

Ten years ago, after Nori valiantly fought the hordes of demons at the Lewis and Clark Cavern. A decade ago, Evangelina took it upon herself to give Nori the gift of vision, a rare offering bestowed upon few humans. If she were to protect the Glory Child throughout his life, she needed this advantage. But Jonathan could only see their physical manifestation.

As Nori explained it, "The bad man and his dog ran away when Evie arrived. He was afraid she was going to arrest him."

Satisfied with the explanation, "So Evie comes to the rescue again."

"It's what I do."

"Wow, you must be really scary to crooks."

"Oh, I am," Evie chuckled. "Nori, I need you to take the boy to the church behind the house so I can finish here. I'll come get you when I'm done."

"Who's the little guy on the floor? Is he bleeding?"

"Remember? He was our cabby from the airport. But he's also our friend, Blisdon. He tried to defend us, Jonathan. It's merely a small flesh wound. He'll be okay."

"Okay, we go. Thank you, Evie. You hero!"

"No need to thank me. This is simply what I do."

Nori and the boy hurried out the back door and headed to St. John's Church. Evangelina followed them with her eyes as they faded into the distance, then turned her attention to the shambles the bedlam created, pausing sadly at the body of Blisdon, still sprawled on the kitchen floor.

"Well, Blisdon, it was quite an impressive show battling an Archduke of Hell. It was a little too much for your pay grade."

"I woulda beat him. He just got the drop on me."

"Good thing I showed, huh?"

A radiant light glowing with heat slowly spread across the room, bathing Blisdon in intense warmth. Stunned by the light, he lowered his lids. Evangelina fell to her knees and bowed her head. She knew He was present.

"Blisdon," the voice shook the walls and boomed, "stand!"

Blisdon gathered his strength and, with the use of the wooden table to prop himself, he strained to rise on wobbly knees. He used his forearm to shield out the brilliant light.

"I have been watching thou with great interest since thy actions at the caverns. I have been impressed by thy words and thy deeds. Thou once one of my angels, thy hubris made me cast thou out of the heavens. Since your expulsion, thou hath humbled thyself and dedicated thyself to help mortals through life-altering times. Thou hath openly denied thy allegiance to Lucifer and thou have offered yourself to spare mortals from pain, suffering, and even death. I believe thy views of life and existence have substantially changed. Thou are not the same being thou were many millennials ago. Therefore, I am going to offer thou something I have never offered a fallen angel. I will allow thou to begin again in heaven at the bottom rung of angels."

A flood of unending tears waiting years to be shed, poured out. "I am not worthy of this great gift. I would truly treasure another chance to serve you, Lord."

"Then let it be known, Blisdon the Quick may return to Heaven as my servant."

Blisdon fell to his knees and covered his face and cried in disbelief. Evangelina came to him and draped him in her wings. As the light gradually faded away, Evangelina calmed Blisdon.

"Come, I will escort you."

Blisdon briefly turned his thoughts to Nori. Evangelina understood his conflict and love for his good friend. What leaving her now would mean in eternity? She smiled. Taking his hand, she flapped her wings and the two slowly ascended through the gable and into the crystal blue sky.

"Is this truly happening?"

"Miracles do happen . . . even for little devils," said Evangelina with a mischievous smirk.

Chapter 38

RESET, BAD NEWS AND WELCOME HOME

T HE PHONE RANG IN Nori's pocket. It was Joe calling from the
airport.

"Where are you two? I don't see you at the gate. We'll be
boarding soon. Don't miss our flight."

"We no at airport. We have problem. We go home."

"What problem?"

"All better now. We come."

"There's not enough time for you to get here. The plane will be long
gone by the time you arrive."

"What we do?"

"Let me make a phone call. I'm calling Dr. Singh."

"Okay."

Nori returned her phone to her pocket with Jonathan's pleading eyes
begging for good news. "Nori, we can't miss this meeting. It's too important."

"Your dad find way. For now, let's go back to house, wait for father's
call. Me need clean kitchen."

The two travelled from the church back to the Puro house. Reaching
the back door Nori eyes widened to see the door replaced, good as new. The
kitchen table stood upright and neat. The debris from the exploding door
was swept up and gone. Even the napkins were back in their holder and the

butcher knife back in its block. *It's a miracle.* Nori looked around for Evie or Blisdon and wondered. *Where they disappear?*

Taking stock of the room, Jonathan said, "Boy, Evie is a great housekeeper."

"But she no cook like Nori!"

"Nobody cooks as good as you," said the boy and quickly added, "but don't tell Mom I said that."

Nori chuckled, "Your secret safe with me." The phone rang again, startling them both back into reality. She held up crossed fingers and answered. "Hello, Joe . . . Please say you have good news . . . "

"I talked with Dr. Singh, and they are sending a private jet to pick you up at the airport at 6 p.m., so don't rush, but get here soon. I'm working on getting our luggage from the previous flight delivered to our hotel in New York. It should be all set by the time you get here."

Jonathan watched the anxiety wash from Nori's face. "Good news. Joe. We call cab. See you soon."

The nanny ended the call and looked at Jonathan shuffling back and forth in breathless anticipation.

"Well?"

"They send jet to pick us up at 6 p.m."

"Yes!" Jonathan punched the air and did his little happy dance.

"Hungry?"

"Always!"

"I make you snack. PB&J?" They both laughed. Old habits never change.

Lilith shuffled into the throne room to find Lucifer on his royal seat sipping from his goblet. She truly hated delivering bad news to him. His volcanic temper annoyed her, and she had no desire to deal with his childish behavior. As she approached the throne, he lifted his head to acknowledge her presence.

"Lilith, what brings you to my chamber?"

"Andras has returned."

"Excellent! Show him in."

"I cannot."

"Why not?"

"Because only his anatomical essence, along with his wolf's, arrived this afternoon. He is reconstituting in his cave."

"What?" roared Lucifer. "Who did this?"

"Apparently, your guardian angel nemesis did him in."

"How in Hell's name did a little worthless wench of an angel defeat the Archduke of Hell?"

"I don't have details on that, Sire. Although, if I recall, she has bested the princes of the underworld, an assortment of lesser demons, and Haures' infamous legions of demons over her time on Earth. She even handed you your head. She is a force not to be challenged."

"Silence, skank! Not to be challenged? I will challenge her until she succumbs. I am well aware of the carnage she has caused," Lucifer said, throwing his goblet of blood against the wall, "and I have the numbers to defeat this upstart. I will make her life miserable."

"It's all I have to report."

"The Glory Child?"

"What?"

"What of the Glory Child?"

"The Glory Child lives. And he's closer now to achieving his goal to eradicate hunger throughout Earth."

"Unbelievable! Begone harlot, I must think. I will find a way to send that upstart angel back to scrubbing floors!"

"As you wish, Sire."

Lilith carefully backed away from the throne to the doorway. She cracked open the door and slithered out into the crusty lava tube hallway.

The two broke through the clouds and approached the pearly gates of Heaven under the golden sound of violins regaling them to enter. Blisdon stepped timidly beside Evangelina as they neared their time of judgment. To imagine spending his days without fear of being hunted by evil and live among those *committed* to fighting evil, seemed surreal.

The Rock of the Church emerged from a shimmering mist ahead, dressed in a white tunic sparkling in the sun with his long, white beard flowing freely. His arms spread open to entreat them to come forward. Evangelina approached St. Peter first; Blisdon followed close behind.

"Greetings and peace unto you, Peter."

"Peace unto you, Evangelina," bowed Peter. "Who do we have here?"

"Blisdon, the Quick," she replied.

"And who assigned you this mortal?"

"This is no mortal, St. Peter. This being is a fallen angel who has been granted forgiveness by the Almighty Father."

St. Peter looked confused. "I've never dealt with a situation such as this. I must consult with our Higher Authority. You wait here."

St. Peter dissolved into thin air. Blisdon looked at Evangelina, "I knew it was too good to be true."

He paced back and forth, anxiety etched into his face. *I was so close*, he thought. *Well, at least I have Nori back on Earth. It's much better than having nothing at all.* He looked to Evangelina for words of comfort or optimism.

"Stay composed, he'll be back soon. You'll get your wings. The Almighty does not say things he doesn't mean. So, calm yourself."

At last, St. Peter reappeared through the pool of brilliance, his eyes twinkling with good news. "Sorry it took so long, but I needed to familiarize myself with the proper procedure to allow this fellow to return to his rank of angel. I've never done this before, so please be patient."

Reaching up, he plucked a small book from thin air and, under his command, it fluttered it open. He raised his arms and sang out "Blisdon the Quick!" A feathered pen materialized and advanced to scribe the name across the top of the front page. No names preceded his and no names followed because, during the entire time of existence of the universe, it had never happened before. He recorded notes of this extraordinary occurrence under Blisdon's name. When finished, he smiled down at this returned wayward angel.

"Prostrate yourself, Blisdon the Quick!"

Blisdon immediately fell to his knees and then to the ground, face first, spreading his arms and legs wide.

Holding his staff, St. Peter circled around the sprawled demon and recited a prayer of contrition and forgiveness. He touched the demon's head three times with the crown of the staff and a halo encircling Blisdon's head appeared. St. Peter touched each of Blisdon's shoulder blades and miraculously small nubs sprouted and enlarged until beautiful white wings adorned his back.

"Arise, Angel!"

Blisdon stood, fanned his new wings and floated up. He laughed in lighthearted merriment as he circled around St. Peter and the Evangelina in a personal victory lap. To his amazement, he was still Blisdon the Quick as he began to pick up speed.

"There's no stopping me. I'm back! And as quick as ever."

"Come, Blisdon the Quick, I'll take you to the Archangel Zadkiel for your assignment here in Heaven."

The two angels held hands and glided through the gates of Heaven together. As they travelled the long heavenly way, Blisdon slowed to ponder his new position.

"I wonder if Zadkiel will give me my old job back?"

"Do you mean messenger angel?"

"Yeah, I was one of the best."

"I would not push it if I were you. There is a line of gifted angels who would love to have that position."

"Or how about a guardian angel?"

"Ah, your first day back and you want my position?"

"I think I would be good at it, ya know. I like caring for humans. I took care of Nori. And don't forget I fought to save Jonathan from Lucifer. The best part about it would be I would be back on Earth."

"I think you better downgrade your possible options, buddy."

"Whaddya mean?"

"Well, considering less than twenty-four hours ago you were a demon on the lam, waiting to be reduced to a mass of ashes and returned to Beelzebub for eternal torture. You should stop to enjoy your life here, regardless of your assigned job. It's not like you've toiled away for eons in heaven and are an exemplary minor angel."

"I suppose you're right."

"Be grateful you received your wings and are admitted to rove in heaven. Once more, let me stress: Be thankful you are not a permanent resident of Hell, suffering under the thumb of Beelzebub. Through the goodness of God, you've been offered a miracle—a second chance. Hold this thought with you at all times."

They came to the gates to the Choir of Dominions. Standing before the golden gates, Evangelina turned to Blisdon, "We're here. Now go in there and be humble and thankful for whatever assignment you are given. Do not protest. Do not complain. Take whatever he gives you with great gratitude and joy. Understand?"

"You are right. I get it. Don't worry about me. I'll do what's right. Who am I to complain.? Got it."

Blisdon touched the gate and it opened slowly. His eyes bulged and he turned to face Evangelina with an "Is it possible?" look. She smiled widely then, with an uncharacteristic burst of mirth, sang out, "Go in there and make me proud."

"Whatever you say, chief," said Blisdon, turning a summersault before trotting off down the path to his audience with the Archangel Zadkiel

Chapter 39

QUEEN'S NERD MALL

T HE PLANE TAXIED ON the tarmac and coasted to a stop at the gate. The jet's exit stairs deployed, and the family scurried down the steps to assemble on the tarmac and await their car. Jonathan, so full of joyous energy, jumped up and down in youthful exuberance at the gate. After a short period of time, a black limousine rolled to their side and the chauffeur promptly exited to open the rear door for the family to pile in.

"Where are we going?" Jonathan asked of the driver.

"The Waldorf Astoria, young squire."

"Wow, and where's the meeting tomorrow?"

"The Queen's Museum at 8 a.m. I will collect you from the lobby at 6:30 a.m."

"That's awfully early."

"Traffic, young squire, traffic."

The family sat back and oohed and aahed over the towering skyscrapers winking on to illuminate the city like blinking Christmas trees. When they approached the Queen's Midtown Tunnel, Jonathan spoke.

"Is that the Atlantic Ocean?"

"No, it's the East River. We're taking the tunnel beneath it."

"Amazing!"

The driver rolled through the E-Z Pass toll lane and sped to the entrance of the tunnel. The tight, two-lane road took them beneath the waves of the East River. Bright lights above lit their way and reflected off the cream-colored subway tile. Red taillights intermittingly flashed as the stop and go traffic slowed their progress. With the loss of the New York skyline supplanted by the drab walls of the underground passage, Jonathan grew antsy, wanting to exit the stifling air in the worst way. Resigned to his situation, he pouted in the back seat. A voice in his mind scolded, *Be patient, young man, you'll get there soon enough.*

The limo finally exited the tunnel. Once again Jonathan was enthralled with the city. He pressed his nose to his window and marveled at the stars intermingling with bright city lights across a black velvet backdrop. The driver pointed out the United Nations complex as they passed. Upon coming to 50th Street, they travelled east until they reached Park Avenue and the legendary Waldorf Astoria Hotel.

Entering the lobby, the group moved as one in awe of the luxurious appointments of the celebrated hotel. As they approached the famous lobby clock, Joe checked his watch against it, proud to find the two coincided. Jonathan circled the clock, admiring the Art Deco workmanship.

"Ya know, Nori, we're standing where common folk, movie stars, and even presidents, over the years, stood." Nori, however, ignored Jonathan, and remained frozen in awe of the hotel's elegance.

They finally checked in at the front desk, then followed the bellman escorting them to their room.

While Joe tipped the bellman, Jonathan ran to the window to survey the city. He stood with his hands on the window, wonderstruck by the city view. Everything looked like the hustle and bustle of cars, people, streets, all in miniature. It captivated the young man slowly realizing he was about to enter a new world, far from what he knew in Farmington.

Nori retired to her own room, but not before asking to help the men unpack.

"Nope, Nori, we're good," Joe responded, throwing his suitcase on the bed.

"Hey champ, time to unpack."

"Huh?"

"Yes, young man. Get your suit out of your suitcase so it won't be too wrinkled." You need to unpack and get to bed." Nori offered to steam it in the morning.

"Aw, Dad."

"Five a.m. comes mighty early, buddy. You need to be at the top of your game."

"Aw, nuts."

After settling in with everything packed away, Jonathan changed into his night clothes, brushed his teeth, jumped under the covers. Although he wanted to explore the hotel, he understood tomorrow was the big day and his performance was crucial. He could only hope the men he needed to convince were smart enough to understand the concepts and engineering he intended to present. He knew in his heart it would work, but he needed to convince them to give him money to build the prototype. As his father pointed out, he needed proof of concept and, without a working machine, it was just an idea.

After spending over an hour on the road, the limousine pulled onto the Queens Science and Cultural campus. Jonathan plastered his face against the window, oohing and aahing at the opportunities available to those engaged in solving world challenges. The New York Hall of Science and the Queen's Zoo were places he'd like to spend a day exploring. He could not believe the size of the world sculpture and fountain in the center of the complex. He thought to himself, *We're entering a nerd shopping mall.* He spotted the building with signage letters larger than him declaring THE QUEENS MUSEUM. The chauffer pulled to the front of the building and popped up to escort his passengers out. The trio thanked him, and Joe extended a healthy tip. The chauffer tipped his hat in return.

The fresh air and sun invigorated the group, sending them sprinting up the steps of the museum only to stop just inside the cavernous entry. As the museum didn't open until 9 a.m., the bodies milling about were employees. From the far end of the room, a smiling, young lady with a clipboard walked hurriedly toward the trio to introduce herself.

"Hello, my name is Meera. I am Dr. Singh's Executive Assistant. You must be the Puro's. I am so glad to meet you."

"Hi, I'm Joe and this is my son, Jonathan. Ah, we have an appointment to see him and his board members."

"I, Nori," the little Asian woman piped in.

"Oh, sorry," said Joe.

"I, hero."

"I see. . . . All right then. Please follow me to the boardroom to commence with our meeting." Linking Jonathan's arm with hers, she brought him ahead of the others and turned directly to face him. "Jonathan, the board is looking forward to your presentation."

They travelled the length of the room and ascended marble stairs to the meeting rooms. Outside the closed doors, Meera instructed them to have a seat on the bench outside the doors. "Jonathan, I will return to usher you into the meeting room when they are ready." The trio sat down and waited patiently.

"Jonathan, did you notice how she directly addressed you? It makes me proud to realize how seriously they take you."

"I guess I did." Jonathan fidgeted with the thumb drive in his pocket. His entire presentation depended on the drive. It represented the hopes and dreams of his young life. His dream is to convince the stuffed shirts inside to give him a million dollars.

As he sat contemplating his presentation, he heard a voice in his head. *Worry not. I am here with you.*

"What?" he questioned aloud.

Your presentation will be brilliant, and you will get to build your machine. Simply do your best and leave the rest to me.

He nodded his head in response to what he thought he had heard and puffed out his chest with new confidence. The heavy oak doors to the conference room opened and Meera emerged. Her broad smile comforted the three guests, and she beckoned them into the room. Dr. Singh stepped to greet the trio and introduce himself. He then escorted them to the podium to face twelve gray-haired men decked out in three-piece suits, each studying them with pleasant faces. Dr. Singh's smile reassured them.

"I'd like the board members to meet our wunderkind, Jonathan Puro." As members clapped politely, he continued, "and his father, Joseph Puro. And . . . " he trailed off, looking to Nori.

Nori stepped forward, bowed. "I, Nori. Protector of boy. Fierce tiger." Her self-introduction brought mild laughter and friendly grins.

"All right then, Master Jonathan, are you ready to present?"

When Jonathan stepped to the podium, Dr. Singh clipped a remote mic to his collar and directed him to a laptop. "Good morning, gentleman . . . as I prepare for my presentation, Nori will pass around a small sampling of our homemade Nori patties, which will be produced by the 'Nori Machine.' I think you should experience our product as I show how it is a viable solution to be made with our machine. And for your information, the Nori patty has been submitted to the FDA for approval that it meets the food code and standards we claim.

Jonathan stepped to the head of the table and Dr. Singh directed him to a laptop. Jonathan pulled the thumb drive from his pocket and inserted it into the computer. As he prepared, Nori opened her bag and proceeded around the board room table passing samples of the first homemade Nori Machine paddies. The gentlemen examined the bars with curiosity, each taking nibbles of the bar. From their expressions it was apparent that they enjoyed their little tastes. The murmurs of approval gave Jonathan confidence. After manipulating the files, he turned to see the screen behind him light up with the first page of his presentation. Turning to the board members he began with a shaky voice.

"World hunger has plague . . . ." He paused and cleared his throat.

Joe patted his shoulder and whispered, "You got this."

Envio rolled over from the pile of hay serving as his bed and rubbed his eyes. He laid dazed, staring at the rafters, wondering how long he had been asleep. As he hadn't been summoned by Andras, he had no concept of time. He feared the demon and his dog had called for him while he slept . . . Not responding would be disastrous. Possibly fatal.

In a panic, the imp rolled out of his straw bed and ran to the barn door. When he threw the doors open, the blazing sunshine blinded him. He thought, *It's midday. Oh no. I missed Shadow's breakfast? I'm doomed.* Envio ran to the wooden porch and timidly knocked on the door. *I hope Archduke Andras will understand . . . fat chance.* He knocked again and again, without an answer. Quaking, he slowly turned the doorknob and peeked in.

Tiptoeing into the doorway Envio was amazed to find everything neat and in order, so unlike the cluttered and unclean days living with Andras and Shadow. No cigar stubs, half-filled liquor bottles, paw prints on the floor. Looking down, he watched families of wolf spiders, jauntily carrying their multitude of children on their backs, parading past him through the open door and head to the barn. *Had the archduke and his beast left? Did they return to the Philippines as he said he desired time and time again?* A smile spread across his face. His arms pumped over his head as he jumped up in the air and shouted, "YES!"

The imp wandered the museum aimlessly contemplating his next move. *What do I do next? Do I return and report to Lucifer? If Andras is gone, I'm sure he has already spoken to Lucifer. I have no need to speak to the Emperor.* His eyes continued to swivel the room, looking for answers. Then they landed on a needlepoint hanging on the wall. The crafted art simply said "HOME." Envio smiled. It was time to go home.

Taking no time to reconsider, he squeezed his eyes shut and spoke the word "Home." The name triggered a flashback to his happiest days when he played pranks on birds, squirrels—anything that lived, even caterpillars. In his mind's eye, he found himself surrounded by the life he loved so much. He wandered the forest to reacquaint himself, eventually making his way down to the babbling stream running through the forest. Envio plunked down on the bank of the running water and reached for a sweet clover to chew. Leaning back, he listened as the chirping birds blended with the babbling brook to give background orchestration to the breathtaking beauty of the woodland. It felt so grand to be home, at least in his imagination.

When a gentle touch brushed his shoulder, he quickly twisted to face the imp he dreamed of for so many years. The smiling face of Freya forced tears to well up. He rose to clutch her gently in his arms. After their embrace, he stood back and said, "I've thought of you every day since I left. I hope you'll still have me."

With a shake of his head, Envio awoke from his wonderful daydream. He bit his lip and wished his trip home would be so easy. He had a long, long way to go and nothing, but nothing, would stand in his way.

Chapter 40

JANITORS AND NOMINEES

B LISDON, NOW A SOFTER, smiling version of being, lay languidly on his favored cloud before tending to his chores. It was tough being the newest angel, delegated with menial chores in the Kingdom. He imagined himself handling more challenging work. At present he'd been busy midwifing the birth of stars and coalescing dust clouds into meteors and planets. Though time consuming and boring, he was informed some-one needed to do it. He only hoped he had become so proficient at his job, in fact, so exemplary, that it showed in his performance and others were taking note.

Blisdon wanted desperately to return to Earth and interact with God's creations. Seeing so much from his previous situation on the paradise called Earth, he aspired of once again becoming a messenger angel. He watched other angels in his position move up the ladder, but when the calling came, he always seemed to be passed over. He refused to let himself get depressed about his situation and simply doubled down and continued to work at his present vocation. Anything was better than being hunted by demons with Beelzebub waiting to pour molten lead into your eye sockets.

Today's work centered on cleaning and sweeping up after a star in a far galaxy which melted down. It exploded, leaving a huge gassy mess which spanned many light-years. A task this big once took many millennia to remedy, but he adopted a trick his friend Evangelina had devised. Her method significantly reduced the work time. She called her method the Ev

Factor. Ev being short for Evangelina. At the time, she felt quite proud of her innovation, but dared not mention it to the others because it could be considered prideful and not a becoming attribute of an angel. She learned from Blisdon's previous mistakes. There was no future in being prideful. She shared the strategy with him as a tribute for helping her while they'd been on Earth together.

Blisdon prepared to set out and tend to his daily mission. The hardest part proved to be locating the wandering rogue planets roaming the universe. Once he located enough of them, he would give them a little nudge, which changed their trajectory, and send them much like a pinball machine hurtling toward the giant debris field of the nebula. Once the rogue planet found its way traveling through the fragmentation field, its gravitational force would literally suck billions of tons of refuse. Evangelina clued him in, and he found his favorites were the huge rogue gas giants. Their massiveness sucked in a hundred times the litter than your average rocky rogue planet. These little boosts, along with the inevitable black hole, pretty much cleaned the debris field.

Blisdon readied himself to go out to perform his daily chores when he witnessed a bright light drawing closer and closer. He watched it grow and position itself directly overhead, and finally evolve into the angel Evangelina.

"Peace be unto you, Blisdon."

"And peace be unto you, Evangelina. What brings you to these parts of the Kingdom?"

"I come bearing news."

"You're now a messenger angel?"

"Oh, not me. I was just here for a short ceremonial event and thought I'd pop by to see you."

"So, tell me, please, nothing interesting ever happens here."

"Ah . . . well . . . so, Archangel Zadkiel is retiring from overseeing the guardian angels. He initially determined what you were assigned to and your duty. So, the next head will determine where you fit best in heaven. At the ceremony they announced the nominees to replace him."

"Well, who are they?"

"The Archangel Michael was one, but he declined the nomination. Seems he has more important things to do. Gabriel, who once was the guardian angel of the Prophet Mohammed, declined also. So, the choice is between the Archangel Samael and . . . uh, me." She trailed off into a whisper.

"And who?"

"Who?"

"You said it has come down to Archangel Samael and WHO?"

"Ah . . . Well, um . . . me."

"YOU? How?"

"They say I've, well, defeated all the who's who in Hell and my experience would bode well to share with the current and new guardian angels."

"Really! What a wonderful thing, kiddo."

"I dunno. I don't think I have a chance against an archangel."

"Listen, word among the angels is that Samael isn't who you think. He is known as the accuser, the seducer and the destroyer. At one point, some considered him to be a fallen angel, but since he destroys sinners, they gave him a reprieve. It's his only redeeming quality. You have as good a chance as he does."

"I really do not have time to think about it. I've to get back to Earth and defend the Glory Child."

Blisdon wryly smiled, "Hey, if you get the job, do not forget your old buddy, Blisdon. I've got talent and speed!"

Evangelina laughed and swooped down the cloud lined path, rose up and dove back to the watery blue gem below. She felt happy and content knowing she, once again, defeated the demons of darkness and the Glory Child was safe to go forth building his dreams.

www.ingramcontent.com/pod-product-compliance
Lightning Source LLC
Chambersburg PA
CBHW051131020726
47501CB00005B/1456